# WAGON TRAIN BABY

## LINDA FORD

# 1

---

**Santa Fe Trail, October, 1848**

Donna Grace Clark knew from the expression on the wagon master's face that he was the bearer of more bad news. Her father had already delivered an unwelcome message, saying he wasn't prepared to join them on the trail to Santa Fe as he had previously agreed.

She stood tall and straight and put on her most commanding face, hoping it would give the man pause to deliver his announcement.

It failed to slow the man in authority even a fraction. He drew to a halt several feet away and whipped off his hat.

Donna Grace glanced around. To her left a campfire glowed, its smoke one of the more pleasant smells in this place burgeoning with people and animals. A man hunkered down beside it, nursing a cup of coffee and pretending he couldn't hear every word, not only of this conversation, but also of the recent one with her father. With wagons, animals and people all crowded together, the noise a constant din, it was impossible to expect privacy. She knew that from the trip she'd made four years ago at age sixteen with her father from Santa Fe to St Louis, Missouri. Of course, back then, she hadn't cared if everyone knew her business. She was simply happy to be traveling with her father. Now at twenty years of age, she wished she could hide the truth about many things.

She stared at the seemingly indifferent man crouched by the fire. Luke Russell. One of the freighters who would be on this wagon train along the Santa Fe Trail. She'd also met his brother and sister and learned a few things about them. Luke was twenty-four. His brother Warren was four years older and their sister, Judith, younger than her brothers. The men had been trading on the Santa Fe Trail for some time. Judith seemed to have recently joined them.

She pulled her attention back to Mr. Williams, the man in charge of directing the wagons on their journey.

"Ma'am, your father told me he's changed his mind about going to Santa Fe or even as far as Bent's Fort. I'm sorry, but without a man to accompany you, I can't let you and your sister join us."

She opened her mouth, intending to argue, to make him see that they didn't need a man. *She* didn't need a man. A man had gotten her into this horrible situation. She pressed her hand to her bulging stomach.

"My rule is any woman traveling with us must be accompanied by her father, husband or brother. I make no exceptions." He plopped his hat on his head and strode away.

Mary Mae, almost a mirror image of Donna Grace and younger by one year, poked her head out of the wagon. "We'll have to abandon our plans," she whispered, in the futile hope that no one would hear her except her sister.

"And do what?" Donna Grace moved closer, also hoping to keep their conversation private. "I can't stay around here. Not with Melvin and his wife… " The word practically burned her tongue. "… prancing around and people looking at me and whispering ugly things."

Mary Mae squeezed Donna Grace's arm. "It wasn't your fault that Melvin lied about already being married when he married you. The scoundrel. He should be drawn and quartered. I know Grandfather Ramos would have made him pay dearly."

At the mention of their maternal grandfather, Donna Grace grew momentarily quiet. "Perhaps." She didn't want to think of their grandfather and his harsh treatment of her. "But I can't stay. I know the sort of things they'll say about my baby. I'm going back to Santa Fe." She'd grown up there and it was the only place she'd ever felt accepted—at least, until Mama had died and Grandfather Ramos had taken charge of the girls. Thankfully, Papa had rescued them and brought them to St. Louis. She hoped to reach her destination before the baby was born. *Please, little one, don't come before then.*

"What will you do there?" Mary Mae asked, even though they'd had this discussion before. Donna Grace knew her sister clung to the hope of persuading her to change her mind.

"I'll rent a house and take in boarders and feed travelers." The money Melvin had paid her to disappear would fund her venture. She hadn't wanted to take his guilt money but their baby deserved that much. "Maybe I won't go to Santa Fe. There are lots of other towns where I could do the same."

"But we can't travel with this lot."

They both knew it was the last train to head out this fall.

"There has to be a way. I won't believe otherwise." Donna Grace wanted nothing more than to escape the shame of being with child, but with no husband. Through no fault of her own. Melvin had lied to her. Never again would she trust a man.

But she would take care of this wee one.

"Excuse me, ma'am."

She turned at the sound of a deep male voice behind her. It was Luke Russell.

"I couldn't help but overhear your conversation."

She fixed him with a hard look. Not unlike the one her grandfather often used, she suspected. "You might have had the courtesy to pretend otherwise."

He grinned crookedly. "Might have done so, except I think I have a solution to your problem."

She resisted the urge to cradle her hands about her stomach. Her baby was not a problem and she refused to let anyone think otherwise. "And what would that be?"

"You could get married."

"Never." She covered the baby bump with her palms.

The crooked grin widened. "All you need is a husband in name only to get you to your destination."

Her eyes widened and then narrowed as she comprehended his meaning. "A pretend marriage?"

"Or you could call it a marriage of convenience."

"I don't expect it would be very convenient for either party."

He laughed at that. "It never hurts to have someone on your side, helping with chores and things."

She wondered what things he meant. Nevertheless, she couldn't stop herself from asking, "Are you volunteering?"

"Yes, ma'am. I am."

"Why would you do that?"

"Donna Grace, you wouldn't." Mary Mae looked about ready to swoon.

Donna Grace held up her hand to signal her sister to be quiet. "Let's hear what the man has to say."

∾

LUKE RUSSELL STOOD before the Clark ladies waiting for the shock of his offer to disappear from their faces. He knew the moment it did so with the elder sister—Donna Grace. And he knew it was time to press his case.

"Miss Clark, would you walk with me so we can talk?"

She gave her sister a look he couldn't interpret and then nodded. "I'd like to hear what you have in mind." She fell in at his side.

They edged past the wagons crowded together and sidestepped two mule skinners, their wide shoulders forcing Luke and Donna Grace to press against the nearby wagon wheel. He had long ago grown used to the sound of animals bleating and men yelling. With everyone occupied with their own affairs he and Miss Clark could hope to talk without being overheard and misjudged.

He got in the first word. "It's impossible for me to stand back and not help someone when it's in my power to do so. So when I overheard you ladies wondering how you were going to get to Santa Fe I knew there was something I could do." He didn't add that there had been a time when he put his own affairs first and because of that, blamed himself for the murder of Ellen, his betrothed. He should have been beside her, protecting her. Instead, he had left her on her own to follow his own interests.

They resumed their journey, dust rising from each step.

"But marriage? That's rather a big way of helping."

He heard the reservation in her voice and perhaps a bit of curiosity.

She continued. "Perhaps you should explain exactly what you have in mind."

"I'm proposing we get married and honor our agreement until we reach Santa Fe. After that, we will both be free to go our own way." Would she note the hesitation in his voice? And if so, what would she think it meant? She had no way of knowing about Ellen and how he'd failed her. He wouldn't admit that he hoped by helping Miss Clark, he might in some small way atone for his failure. "It would give your baby a father and a name."

They reached a quiet area close to the river and drew to a halt. The waterway was busy with river traffic. Water would be a challenge on the trail, which is why they planned to go by way of Bent's Fort, and not the Cimarron cut-off across the dry route.

Miss Clark stared at the stream for a moment, then sucked in a deep breath. "I know what it looks like." Her hands cradled her stomach to make sure he understood her meaning. "But it's not as awful as it might appear." She shifted to look directly at him, her dark eyes boring into his. "It's worse."

He'd overheard enough to guess she'd been treated poorly. All the more reason to offer his help.

She held his gaze as she continued. "I thought I was married to a fine, upstanding man. Instead, it turns out he was a scoundrel of the worst sort. He was already married, so our marriage is null and void, and my baby is … is … " She shook her head. Fire filled her eyes. "I don't care what anyone says about my baby. He or she is a precious gift to me."

"And so it should be." He'd once dreamed of a home and family. Little ones to fill his heart with joy. That dream no longer existed. "Let me help you. After you are safely to your destination and settled, we will dissolve the marriage."

Her snort was filled with derision. "Seems I am only good for mock marriages."

Her comment gave him pause. "I'm sure that isn't the case. My only reason for offering to do this is so you can get where you want to go." Perhaps it wasn't the only reason, but she didn't need to know about his guilt.

"Let me get this straight. You are suggesting a marriage in name only. A temporary one." One shoulder came up. "Not unlike the one I just left. Except for one thing." She leaned close and spoke in a low voice, every word clear and distinct. "This marriage will not include the right to my bed."

He let his gaze go to her stomach letting her know her condition made that unlikely. Or at least unappealing. "Agreed. This is solely so wagon master Buck Williams will allow you and your sister to make the journey,"

She turned her gaze from him and stared across the river, though he doubted she saw the fading leaves on the trees, nor took note of the children playing on the opposite bank.

Realizing she had a lot to think about before she agreed, he let her take her time considering his offer.

Finally, she sagged as if the starch had left her backbone. "I can't stay here. I won't. And I can't go where I want to go on my own." She faced him. "Seems I have little choice if I am to reach my destination before my baby arrives."

He had to force himself not to stare at her baby bulge, but it looked to him like she couldn't possibly carry that burden two more months. But surely she knew when to expect the baby and he, admittedly, knew nothing whatsoever about the process except having viewed it secondhand when his brother, Warren, and his wife had a baby. Although he refrained from voicing his concerns, she correctly read them.

"I want this little one born into a world where it will be accepted as a worthy individual. Where it will begin a life of security and safety and most of all, love. I will give it enough love for two parents."

"Good for you, but don't be afraid to accept help to reach your goal."

She nodded. "I see the wisdom of your words. So I will marry you in order to get where I need to be. And thank you for your generous offer."

"I'm pleased if I can have a hand in getting your child to the place you have in mind." Seeing her and the infant to a safe place would go a long way toward easing his guilt over Ellen's murder and—he realized with a jolt—help ease the pain of losing Warren's wife and baby. He would, at the best, be a temporary father to the unborn baby, but he would gladly give it his name and prevent the cruel words that it might otherwise encounter.

Did bestowing his name on the child give him any rights? Like being involved in daily activities and decisions?

He knew their agreement allowed for no such thing and he pushed aside a fleeting regret.

"If you're still certain this is what you want to do?" The doubt in her voice made him wonder if he had somehow given away his thoughts.

"I'm a man of my word."

"What do we do next?"

"You know, I have no idea." He laughed at his unpreparedness.

Her fine black eyebrows went toward her hairline. Beautiful black hair that seemed to catch the flash of silver from the water. "I suggest we decide what to do soon." Her words contained a hint of humor. "Mr. Williams wants to leave in the morning."

"You're right, of course. We'd best tell our families and then find someone to marry us." He crooked his elbow toward her and was pleased when, with only a slight hesitation, she took his arm.

"Are we going to tell them it's only a pretend marriage?" he asked, drawing to a halt to look into her face.

She lifted her chin. "I don't see that anyone needs to know, but seeing as this is your idea, I suppose I will have to go along with what you decide."

"It's no one's business, but ours. I think it's best if we're the only ones who know about our agreement."

"I concur." Relief flickered across her face.

Pleased that he had given the right answer, he drew her back to the path. "Then let's do it."

They returned to the dusty area between their two wagons. Luke saw his brother sitting in front of the fire, "Warren is back. Good. We can tell them all at once."

Donna Grace's sister stood nearby watching them cautiously.

Luke called to his siblings. "Judith, Warren, I have an announcement to make."

Donna Grace signaled her sister to join them.

Judith climbed down from the wagon where she had been arranging things. Warren rose from contemplating the live coals of the fire. He took in Donna Grace's hand on Luke's arm and did his best to hide a scowl. Not that Luke could blame him for wondering at this intimacy.

As soon as everyone gathered around, Luke spoke. "Miss Clark and I have agreed to get married." He smiled.

Silence greeted his words. Mary Mae looked ready to cry.

Judith stared. She was nursing a broken heart, and

likely found his announcement a painful reminder of her broken engagement.

Warren recovered first. "Why would you contemplate such a thing?" He yanked his hat from his head and threw it on the ground. "Are you both crazy?"

His brother's anger triggered an unexpected response in Luke. He shifted to his right so he and Donna Grace stood shoulder to shoulder. His role was to protect this woman. "Neither of us is the least bit addled. We've discussed the matter, and agreed it is what we want to do."

Donna Grace stiffened and her chin lifted. "I am perfectly capable of making sound decisions, thank you very much." She lowered her head and added, "Usually," in a whisper Luke knew no one but himself would hear.

He understood she meant her marriage to the man who had left her with child, and her regret filled him with a fierceness that took him by surprise. He would do his best to prove to her that not all men were scoundrels.

Warren had the grace to look uneasy at her response. "Likely so, but marriage is a big commitment. One not to be taken lightly."

Luke felt Donna Grace shudder. "I'm very aware of that," she said.

He understood, she'd learned not everyone took the state of marriage seriously.

"It does seem rather sudden," Judith said.

Neither Luke nor Donna Grace seemed inclined to argue about that. It *was* sudden.

Mary Mae edged closer to her sister. "Does this mean your baby will have a nice home?"

Donna Grace pulled her sister to her side. "If it depends on me, then yes. And—" She hesitated, then drew herself tall and straight. "And a name." The words were firm but with a hint of teariness. She gave each of those facing them a look that Luke could only describe as a combination of determination and entreaty.

Judith nodded. "So be it. I trust you both know what you're doing."

Mary Mae gave her sister a sideways hug. "I like the idea."

Warren wouldn't meet Luke's gaze. The darkness in his brother's eyes made Luke understand how painful his memories of his dead wife and child were. It must hurt to see his younger brother acquiring a wife and soon, a child.

He went to Warren's side. "I'm sorry this reminds you of your loss."

Warren sucked in air. His smile went no further than his mouth. "I won't let it stand in the way of your happiness. You have my blessing, if that's what you want."

"Thanks. That means a lot." He looked around at the others. "So let's go find us a preacher to marry us."

"Now? Today?" Judith's mouth opened and closed

as she tried in vain to find words to express her surprise.

"Yes, today. Did you think we would make the journey to Santa Fe without tying the knot?"

"Really, Luke, you've hardly given us time to think one way or another."

"We can't delay. We'll be leaving in the morning. There's a church just beyond the center of town. The preacher lives next door. Let's go see him." He waved his arm. "All of you."

Judith glanced down. "Why, here I am in an old dress. I can't attend a wedding like this. You'll have to give me time to freshen up."

"Us too," Mary Mae said. "Come on, Donna Grace, you need to get ready for your wedding." She led her sister to their wagon and they climbed aboard. They could be heard whispering and laughing, followed by Donna Grace's murmured protests.

Warren and Luke looked at each other and then down at their clothes.

"I suppose we're expected to get fancied up, too," Luke said. He had one good shirt that he saved for special occasions and what could be more special than getting married?

Warren caught Luke's arm. "You are about to become the husband of a woman carrying another man's child."

Again that unfamiliar burst of fierceness. "Would you love a child any less because of who the father is?"

Warren considered his answer. "No, I suppose not.

But it's not to say I would plan to raise such a child as if it were my own."

Luke gave a tight smile. "I guess you and I differ in our opinion."

Warren studied Luke a moment. "I can't help but worry you're making a mistake, but it's plain you aren't going to change your mind. So let's get ready for your wedding."

They announced their presence to Judith, then retrieved clean shirts from the wagon.

Warren chuckled. "If I'd known I was going to my brother's wedding, I would have bought a new shirt."

Luke nodded. "And I would have bought a ring."

Judith poked her head out of the wagon and held out her hand. "Mother gave me this when she thought I was to be married. Said she wanted someone in the family to have it. It was our grandmother's. You can have it." A plain gold band lay in the palm of her hand.

Luke stared at it. He was about to take vows before God, vows of fidelity and forever. The ring symbolized an unbroken promise and the idea stabbed him because of his insincerity. He felt the accusing eyes of his parents and grandparents on him.

God would understand that he was doing this to help a woman and child.

He took the ring, and thanked Judith.

This was the right thing to do, and he didn't intend to let doubts crowd into his mind.

## 2

Mary Mae opened her trunk and pulled out a black dress. "You'll wear this."

Donna Grace shook her head. The traditional black symbolized a bride's devotion until death. She couldn't bring herself to portray such dishonesty.

*Yet you'll swear before God and man to love, honor, and obey this man until death do you part?*

She'd sworn it once before, and meant it with her whole heart. That promise would surely cancel out this one she'd be making without intent to fulfill.

"I'd never fit into it." She pulled a steel gray dress from her trunk. Knowing how dusty the trail would be, she'd brought only dark clothing.

Mary Mae folded the dress with a look of regret. Then she brightened. "But you will wear this." She lifted out Mama's mantilla wedding veil.

Donna Grace stared. "I threw it out." In a fit of

anger after learning of Melvin's deceit, she'd tossed the mantilla aside.

"I retrieved it. I thought I might get a chance to wear it."

Remembering her sister's own romantic disappointment, Donna Grace was stung that she hadn't considered that the mantilla belonged to both of them. "I'm glad you did."

Mary Mae fingered the lace. "It's so beautiful. Just like Mama was." She handed it to Donna Grace. "She would want you to wear it today."

*Oh, if only Mama was alive.* Donna Grace wouldn't have been so eager to rush into marriage with a man who proved to be a fraud. All Donna Grace wanted was to be the most important person in someone's life. Something she hadn't had since their mother died. But, she silently vowed, she would be that in her baby's life.

"Let's get ready." They hurriedly dressed and helped each other with their hair. Donna Grace tucked the mantilla into a reticule that had been their mother's. Mary Mae climbed from the wagon first and turned to assist Donna Grace, but Luke took her place and held out his hand.

Donna Grace hesitated. She'd gladly accept her sister's help, but this man? This man, she reminded herself, was soon to be her husband and it would look strange if she didn't allow him to assist her. Nor did she care to risk climbing down on her own. If she fell, the baby could be hurt. She would do anything for the child she carried, so she took Luke's steadying hand, finding his strength provided much more assurance than Mary Mae did.

"You look nice," he said.

She eyed him. He'd scrubbed his face and brushed back his dark blond hair. He wore no hat and had donned a clean shirt. The same color as her dress. Perhaps that was a good sign. "You look nice, too."

He leaned close to murmur for her ears only. "I know it's unusual for the groom to see the bride before the wedding, but nothing about our union can be considered usual. I have to ask, are you okay with this?"

Surprised that he should know or care about such details, she smiled at him. "We'll have to get used to doing things our way, won't we?" They were so close she could see the sun-bronzed color of his face, and the patience in his eyes—eyes the color of rich chocolate.

His smile sent fan lines from his eyes. He had a generous mouth.

She pulled her attention from him. He meant nothing to her except as a means of getting to Santa Fe. And a name for her baby.

His family joined them, as they headed toward the center of Independence, Missouri. Mary Mae clung to her on one side as they walked, and Luke was on her other side. She welcomed their support as her nerves began to tremble at what she was about to do.

They reached the church and went to the manse.

The preacher opened the door. "Yes, what can I do for you?" he asked.

Donna Grace's mouth had gone dry as autumn grass. She couldn't have spoken to save her life.

Thankfully, Luke answered. "We'd like to get married."

The preacher's gaze dropped to Donna Grace's absent waist line. "I think you better come in and attend to a long-overdue matter."

They followed him into the parlor. Donna Grace wondered if she should correct the man's assumption that it was Luke's fault they hadn't married before making a baby.

Luke caught her gaze and gave a tiny shake of his head and an encouraging smile.

She tipped her head very slightly to indicate she understood his meaning and pulled the mantilla over her hair. If only Mama could be here. Or Papa.

She'd have to let him know of her marriage. She almost asked to delay until they could find him, but she couldn't keep everyone waiting.

At the preacher's direction, she stood before him with Luke at her side. Their family members gathered behind them.

Luke pulled her arm through his. He must have felt her quivering, for he placed his hand on top of hers and squeezed.

"Is there anything to hinder this marriage?"

She curled her fingers. If only Melvin had

answered that question truthfully, she wouldn't be in this awkward position.

"No sir," Luke said with conviction.

Donna Grace realized the preacher waited for her answer. "None."

He directed his gaze to those behind her and received their answers. "Very well. Let's proceed."

She heard the words and responded appropriately, all the while telling herself God would forgive her for this.

Luke slipped a ring on her finger. She hadn't expected a ring. Didn't that make it more real, more binding? She curled her fingers into her palm.

"I now pronounce you man and wife. You may kiss your bride."

She jolted out of her half stupor and turned to Luke, wondering if her eyes were as large as they felt.

He pushed the veil back from her face. "You are now my wife," he whispered.

She shuddered. Was he going to demand things they hadn't agreed to? Things he had a right to as a husband?

Had she made another huge mistake?

His smile reassured her as he leaned close and brushed her lips in a kiss so gentle and quick she didn't have time to react.

They signed the necessary papers. Their family ushered them out the door.

Out in the street, Luke signaled them to stop. "We are going to celebrate this event by eating at the hotel."

"My father should be here," Donna Grace said.

"By all means. Where can we find him?"

"I don't know." She'd been so shocked and dismayed at her father changing his mind about taking them to Santa Fe that she hadn't heard his entire explanation.

Mary Mae answered. "He'll likely be with his cronies in the barber shop."

"Then we'll go that direction." The five of them marched down the street, turned left, and drew to a halt.

"I'll go in," Donna Grace said. "Perhaps it's better if I go alone."

"No," Luke said. "We'll do this together."

Again, she wasn't sure if his offer was because he meant to be in charge, or if he wanted to protect her. Either way, it sent tremors up and down her spine. She wasn't about to be subservient to a man she'd married simply to get passage on the wagon train, nor was she in any need of his help.

But as she climbed the steps to the shop, he stayed at her side.

She spied Papa sitting forward on a chair, likely telling the other men of some of his exploits. "Papa?"

He looked up. "Donna Grace, what are you doing here?"

"I've come to tell you Mary Mae and I are leaving for Santa Fe tomorrow."

"How did you persuade Buck Williams to let you go?"

She stood back and indicated Luke. "I'd like you to meet my husband."

Papa came to his feet suddenly enough to send his chair skidding back. "Your what?"

Luke stepped forward and held out his hand.

Papa ignored Luke's outstretched arm and pulled Donna Grace aside. "What do you mean, you're married?"

"It's not hard to understand. We visited the preacher and tied the knot." She gave him a hard look to match his own and held out her hand to show him the ring.

"Where did you meet this fellow, and more importantly, when?"

"He's one of the traders on the Santa Fe Trail. I thought you might have met him. He and his brother have been back and forth a few times."

Luke had edged closer. "Of course we've met."

"That's of no importance." He turned back to Donna Grace. "Why have you done this?"

"I mean to get to Santa Fe and start a new life there."

Papa studied her a moment then faced Luke. "You better be a more upright man than the last one."

"I can assure you I am. I have nothing in mind but doing what is right for Donna Grace and her baby."

The men eyed each other for a moment. Papa's friends all leaned forward, anxious not to miss a word of this drama.

Donna Grace could well imagine it would fuel much speculation and storytelling for several months.

"What's done is done," Papa said, his tone indicating he didn't like it.

"We are on our way to the hotel to celebrate the wedding," Luke said. "We'd like for you to join us."

"Of course I will." He draped his arm about Donna Grace's shoulders. "The least I can do is wish you well and give you a proper send off."

Donna Grace wanted to say how she would rather be traveling with him, but that conversation was over, and there would be no point in him changing his mind now.

They joined the others and continued to the Sharps Hotel across the street from the majestic courthouse. Mary Mae paused to admire the structure.

"I'm going to miss seeing this," she murmured, but then Mary Mae always placed a good deal of store in proper places.

Donna Grace didn't care where she lived so long as she could provide for her baby. It could be a tent or the back of a wagon, for all it mattered to her.

For the next two or three months, it would be one of those places.

And she'd have a husband.

What would that mean on a daily basis? She clamped her jaw tight. So far as she was concerned, it would mean nothing different than if they'd been traveling with Papa.

LUKE LOOKED AROUND THE TABLE. Donna Grace sat on his right, and on her other side, her father. Seeing the older man's concern about his daughter made Luke realize what an enormous step they had just taken. They both knew it was temporary, but even so, it carried responsibilities and expectations. Mr. Clark had made him see that.

He would live up to those responsibilities to the best of his ability.

He lifted his glass. "I'd like to make a toast to my beautiful wife and the journey we are about to embark on." He'd been struck by her beauty as she faced him before the preacher, her face framed with the lacy veil. Her eyes full of determination.

He turned to her now. "To Donna Grace."

"To Donna Grace," they others said, and the tinkle of china followed.

Mr. Clark got to his feet. "My daughter is a special woman. She has been all of her life. I hope you all realize that. And you, Luke Russell, I ask that you allow her to be the strong woman she is, while treating her as kindly as she deserves to be treated. I wish you both happiness in the future." He lifted his cup. "To Mr. and Mrs. Russell."

More clinking of glasses and then the meal was brought to them and conversation died as they concentrated on the thick slices of roast beef, mounds of mashed potatoes and gravy, and buttery baked squash. A delicious meal, and knowing he would not enjoy this kind of cooking for several months, Luke dug in with pleasure.

Half way through the meal, he noticed Donna Grace was mostly moving her food about on the plate. He slowed his own eating and leaned closer to her.

"Eat up. Last meal like this for some time."

She nodded and lifted a forkful to her mouth, but she didn't take another bite.

"Are you okay?"

"I'm fine." She met his gaze, her eyes filled with an emotion he couldn't identify. Was she afraid? Ill? Tired?

Ah, it was likely the latter. He knew mothers-to-be tired easily. He'd seen it with Warren's wife. Donna Grace needed to be back at camp, resting. Though if this little bit of activity wore her out, how was she going to manage to walk all day and tend to camp chores? Yes, she had her sister to help, but right then and there, Luke promised himself he would do everything he could to make life as easy for her as possible.

Satisfied that he could handle the challenge, and still carry his share of the work keeping the Russell freight wagons going, he settled back to enjoy his food and the conversation around the table. They finished and no one seemed inclined to linger, least of all, Luke. He had much to take care of before they departed in the morning. One of them was to assure Donna Grace that he would help her.

Mr. Clark bid them goodbye, hugged each of his

daughters, shook hands with Warren then faced Luke. "If I hear you've done her wrong in any way, I will find you and exact justice."

Luke hung back. "I hear you. I won't be found wanting, but it seems to me if you are so all-fired concerned about either of them, you would be escorting them yourself."

The man looked flustered. "They could just as easily stay here. Would save a long trek with winter coming off the mountains soon."

"You know why she doesn't want to stay."

"It's not her fault."

Luke's mouth tightened until he could hardly speak. "Explain that to the gossips."

Donna Grace hung back waiting for him, likely wondering why he was in such an intense conversation with her father.

"She'd get used to it after a bit, and learn it didn't matter."

Luke's insides soured. It did matter and she shouldn't have to get used to it. He lowered his voice so she wouldn't hear. "What you're saying to me is *she* isn't worth the effort to leave your cronies and escort her and her sister to Santa Fe."

Mr. Clark blustered a response, but he didn't deny it. "You just see you do what's right for her." He strode away before Luke could respond. Not that there was anything more to be said. The man had made his decision and was prepared to justify it no matter what.

Donna Grace waited, her eyes full of darkness.

Luke went to her side. "Tell me you didn't hear what was said."

She shrugged, a weary gesture if he'd ever seen one. "It's nothing I haven't heard before."

He wasn't sure what she meant, but he could well imagine her father's words and actions hurt. Seems this young woman was the brunt of more than one man's neglect. He had to make her understand he would be different. "You can count on me to take care of you and keep my word."

She ground about to face him. They had fallen behind the others. Strangers rushed past without paying them any heed, allowing them to speak freely. "How can you even say that? We just vowed before God to be together until death do us part, with no intention of keeping that vow. I fear God will punish us for that."

He pulled them out of the hurry and scurry of the street into a quiet alcove. "Is that what's been bothering you?"

She nodded.

"I'm sure God understands the circumstances. After all, they weren't of our making."

She rocked her head back and forth. "Dare we venture down the trail without God's protection?" A shudder crossed her shoulders.

"I give God little mind most days, but my parents raised me right, taught me scriptures and took me to church. I believe in His love and forgiveness. I think God watches over us even when we don't think of

Him."

"He sees and judges."

"You've had a harsh teacher in your life that you think to fear God's judgment. Who was it?"

She lifted her troubled gaze to him. "That would be my Grandfather Ramos in Santa Fe."

He jerked back. "Then why are you wanting to go back there?"

She snorted. "Not to see him. But when Mama was alive, it was a happy place for me. I plan to buy a little home and take in boarders and feed travelers and create a place of safety and love for my baby." By the time she finished, her voice filled with resolve.

"Then you did what you had to do to accomplish that. God will understand."

The fire in her eyes died. "Will He?"

"I think He understands how frail we are. Reminds me of a song I learned recently." He cleared his throat then sang softly, for her ears only, "'Frail children of dust, and feeble as frail, In thee do we trust, nor find thee to fail. Your mercies, how tender, how firm to the end—" He stopped as she shook her head. "What? You don't like my singing?" He brought a wounded note to his voice hoping to lighten the atmosphere.

"You have a very nice voice." A weak smile accompanied her words. "But I can't help wondering where God was when Melvin married me. Why didn't He stop it? Why didn't Melvin's wife return before I wasted nine months thinking I was married to him?"

Luke did not intend to open his heart, risking more

pain and loss, but her distress cut through his defenses. She did not deserve to be in this awkward position—with child by a man who had lied to her, and now desperate enough to marry a stranger.

He opened his arms and pulled her to him, feeling the tension in her body. Her arms remained over her chest, a firm barrier between them. "Donna Grace, whatever may come, whatever lies before us on the trail, you have my word that I will not forsake you. I will be there beside you every step of the way. We will trust God to show us His favor despite the falseness of our vows. How does that sound?"

She straightened, and took a deep breath. "I will do what I need to for the sake of my child. I have no need of help from anyone. Only Mr. Williams's silly rules forced me into this situation." She put two steps between them. "Now we need to get back to camp and make sure everything is in order for our departure in the morning."

He fell in beside her as they continued on their way. Her answer left him slightly unsettled, but what more could he expect? He had agreed to this arrangement. He, as much as she, had willingly given false vows before God.

Did that mean they would venture into the wilderness without God's protection? He shuddered at such a prospect.

D onna Grace, in her unsettled state, would have walked faster, but her present condition made it impossible. Her hurry could best be described as a waddle. Papa had as much said it was too much trouble to take her to Santa Fe. His unconcern for her hurt like a knife stab, echoing as it did, Grandfather Ramos's similar and oft-repeated phrase, "Child, you are too much trouble."

Seems she was too much trouble for God as well. Too much trouble to protect her from the likes of Melvin Brunt. And the broken promise of her papa. Or even the silly rules of the wagon master. Well, she'd be no trouble to anyone in the future.

Before they got any closer to their own wagons, she would make something clear. She drew to a halt. Luke stopped, his eyes full of caution and curiosity.

She'd soon relieve him of both. "You've helped me by marrying me. Don't think I mean to take advantage of it. You go about your business and I'll go about mine. I'll be no trouble at all to you." Before he could respond, she hurried onward in her ungainly waddle.

He caught her arm. "Donna Grace, I will be your husband in name only, but that doesn't mean I won't do my best to make the journey easy for you."

They faced each other, both breathing hard. Her determination reflected in his eyes.

She broke the tense silence first. "I will need nothing from you."

He opened his mouth but before he could answer, Buck Williams saw them and jogged over.

"What's this I hear about you two getting married?" He crossed his arms and looked every bit the man in charge.

Donna Grace drew herself up tall, prepared to defend herself.

Before she uttered a word, Luke pulled her close. "You heard right. May I present my wife, Mrs. Russell."

Donna Grace heard the conviction in his voice and felt the tension in the air.

Buck rocked back on his heels and narrowed his eyes. "Fine. But I expect to see you taking care of your wife's wagon and seeing to her livestock. I'm not playing games here. You are in charge of getting both these women safely to the end of the trail. I will tolerate no delay because of them. If anything makes me think this is simply a move to counteract my rules, I'll turn you back. Now see to making sure the wheels are properly greased." He strode away without a backward look.

Donna Grace pulled away from Luke.

He adjusted his hat as if to buy himself time to deal with a wife who had just informed him she didn't need or want his help, and a wagon master who expected his rules to be obeyed to the letter. Finally, he brought his gaze to her. "You heard the man." They closed the distance to the others. He grabbed a pot of grease and hunkered down beside the nearest wheel of her wagon.

She stared at his broad back, frustration mounting within her. This was not going as she planned, but then why was she surprised? Nothing much did. Her baby kicked and she pressed her hand to the tiny foot. "Settle down, wee one. We'll be fine. I'll do whatever it takes to keep you safe."

"Good to hear." Luke's deep voice came from the side of the wagon.

She hadn't thought he would overhear her talking to herself. "I hope you aren't going to listen in on all my private conversations."

He laughed softly.

Beneath her palm, the baby turned and settled. *Don't get used to that voice*, she warned the little one.

Mary Mae poked her head out of the wagon. "Are you done out there?"

Donna Grace chuckled. Seems every word was going to be overheard from several directions. Before this journey was over, she wouldn't have a secret left to hide.

"I'll help get things organized." She began to climb in the back when a pair of hands lifted her from the ground. She gasped.

"Don't fight it," Luke growled. "I don't think either of us have any desire to see you fall and perhaps injure yourself or the baby."

She ducked inside.

"He's right, you know," Mary Mae said. "You need to be careful and accept help—and what better person to give it than your husband."

Donna Grace squinted at her sister in the waning light. Did she think this marriage was real? Maybe she did. Mary Mae was a dreamer, thinking everything would come up roses if only one believed. Donna Grace glanced about. "You've got things almost put away."

"Everything but your trunk." It stood open.

Donna Grace pulled the mantilla from her bag and handed it to Mary Mae. "I hope you get a chance to use this soon."

Mary Mae pressed it to her cheeks. "I always think of Mama when I see this." She slowly folded it and put it in her trunk.

"Help me get out of this dress." Donna Grace turned so Mary Mae could undo the buttons for her and help her slip the dress over her head. She put on her older dress and folded the good one and returned it to the trunk. Tiny baby garments were stored neatly to one side and she trailed her fingers over the soft flannel material of the little gowns and tiny little diapers.

*For you, my sweet baby, I will do whatever I must.*

"Ladies," Luke spoke from the end of the wagon. "Do you have a tent in there?"

Mary Mae threw open the back closure. "It's right here."

He lifted the canvas out and disappeared.

Donna Grace stared. "Mary Mae, we can do it ourselves." She scrambled out, not waiting for anyone to help her and hurried after Luke. "We know how to set it up."

He continued stretching out the canvas and driving in the pegs. "Have you forgotten that I'm your husband and as such, it is now my job?"

She fought for an answer. The baby kicked a protest and she pressed a hand to her stomach. A cramp grabbed her and she leaned forward holding her stomach.

Luke straightened. "Are you okay?"

She nodded. "Just a Charlie horse."

"Is that what they call it now?"

She caught the hint of irony in his tone and managed a smile. The cramp stopped and she straightened. "That's what I'm going to call it." Maybe it hadn't been a good idea to climb from the wagon in such a hurry. "Now let me set up my tent."

He came round to face her. "Don't look, but a certain Buck Williams is watching us. I don't think it would take much to convince him to refuse you on this train. What is it you really want? Is it to prove you don't need help? Don't need a man? Or is it to get to your destination and have a home for the baby?"

She ducked her head, unable to meet his gaze. She wanted only one thing—to make a home for the baby. But he hadn't said *your* baby. He'd said *the* baby. It was such a small difference and likely meant nothing to him, but it meant so much to her.

Tears threatened at how it changed her view of him. She could almost imagine—

She would not let her emotions rule her, though. They'd been erratic these last few weeks.

"All that matters is the baby, and if Mr. Buck Williams is looking for a reason to send me back, he won't find it. Go ahead and set up the tent."

"People might expect us to spend our first night as a married couple together."

She gasped. "Are you already changing our agreement?"

"Not at all. But Buck is only too anxious to cut you out."

"Show him the wedding certificate we signed, along with Mary Mae and Warren as witnesses."

"Do you think it will cause him to change his

mind?" He held up a hand to silence her protests. "If we sleep in the same quarters, he'll have nothing to question. You notice I said sleep. Nothing more."

Two lying side by side in the wagon box would be pressed together. The tent allowed slightly more room. She turned to stare into the darkness past the fires. She had left beans baking and the aroma made her remember all the things she needed to do before the morning.

"For appearances we must," Luke whispered.

She shuddered. "Very well. We'll sleep in the tent. But only for appearances."

"I'm a man of my word."

She clenched her teeth together and hurried to the fire. Using a heavy towel, she lifted the lid and stirred the mixture. Enough to last her and Mary Mae several days. Along with biscuits, they would do okay.

Was she expected to feed Luke? Her panic died as quickly as it came. They had brought provisions expecting Papa to be with them. So it didn't matter if it was Luke instead.

Judith joined her at the fire. "It seems to me we could cut our work in half by joining forces. One fire, one meal. What do you think?"

"I like the idea." Donna Grace turned to Mary Mae. "What do you think?"

"It's a great idea." For a few minutes the women discussed how they would divide the chores. But Donna Grace was distracted by watching Luke set up the tent and carry his bedroll inside.

Mary Mae watched as well. "I'll sleep in the wagon tonight."

Heat rushed up Donna Grace's neck. Thankfully, it was too dark for anyone to see the color come to her cheeks. Suddenly a number of chores called for her attention. She scurried about heating water to wash in, and checking the water barrels to make sure they were full. Back and forth she went.

"You're soon going to find yourself coming as you're going." Luke's quiet voice came from the shadow of the wagon. "Everyone else has gone to bed."

A glance revealed she was alone with Luke. Her heart stalled. The baby kicked a protest. She sucked in a deep breath, which did nothing to calm the kicking.

The time had come to face the consequences of her choice.

⌇

LUKE FELT Donna Grace's tension as she passed him and entered the tent. He was as anxious and confused as she, but he knew they must give every indication of being a happily married couple if Buck was to allow Donna Grace and Mary Mae to travel with them.

He gave her a few minutes to get settled, then pulled off his boots, left them under the wagon, and slipped into the tent.

She lay on her side, facing the tent wall, the quilt pulled up to her chin. If rain came, it would wick through every place she touched the canvas, but the sky had been clear with no threat of precipitation.

He grabbed his bedroll and unfurled it beside her, staying as close to the opposite side of the tent as he could, his back to her. Every breath brought some part of them in contact. Tension made it impossible for him to relax.

"You didn't have to give me a ring," she murmured.

"It seemed the right thing to do."

A moment of silence before she spoke again. "I can't help wonder how you came to have a ring with you." She stiffened. "You're not married and running away from a wife are you?"

He chuckled. "Shouldn't you have asked that question a few hours ago?"

Her sigh pressed her back to his. "I'm a great one for running headlong into trouble."

"I consider myself duly warned."

"There is no prior wife, is there?"

He shifted to his back so he could talk to her more easily. "I have never been married, though I was once betrothed to a woman."

"Is this the ring you bought her?"

"No. It was my grandmother's ring and Judith had it."

"Oh." She shifted to her back and lifted her hand.

It was too dark for him to know for sure, but she seemed to study the ring.

"Is your grandmother still alive?"

"No, both she and grandfather died before I was

born." He waited as she continued to twist and turn her hand.

"Are your parents alive?"

"Yes, they live on a farm near Crestheight, Missouri." His one regret in leaving the area was having to leave his parents to manage on their own.

She pulled the quilt tighter to her chin. Her elbow jabbed into his arm and he tried to make himself smaller.

"Where's your intended? What happened to her?"

"She's dead." He didn't want to discuss it further and turned his back to her. "Go to sleep. Tomorrow will come soon enough."

She grunted as she eased herself over to her side away from him.

Sleep did not come easily to Luke as he tried to keep his distance from Donna Grace. Did she know she groaned and grunted in her sleep? Perhaps she wasn't comfortable. How would she make the trip, if already she was finding the conditions unpalatable?

He woke slowly, aware of something warm pressed to his side. Donna Grace. His wife. He let the information settle in his thoughts and then smiled. A wife, and soon a child. Not for keeps, but he might enjoy it well enough until it was over. Perhaps it would help in some small way to make up for his dreams that died along with Ellen.

Careful not to disturb her, he slipped from the tent, pulled on his boots and hurried to start the fire. Warren crawled from under the wagon and joined him. Neither spoke. They worked together with the ease of experience and with little need for conversation. As soon as the fire was going and the coffee set to boil, they headed for the livestock.

"Do you know which animals belong to the Clark wagon?" Warren asked.

"Can't say as I do."

Mr. Clark stepped from the shadows. "I'll give you a hand. I came to bid my daughters goodbye."

The older man pointed out the mules he'd purchased for the journey, and together, he and Luke led them back. Warren followed with the mules for the wagon Judith would ride in.

As they returned, Donna Grace crawled from the tent, her hair flying away in every direction. "Hello, Papa." She wiped her hands over her hair. "I can't believe I overslept." She straightened and shook her skirts. "It won't happen again."

Mary Mae hunched over the fire, stirring a pot of simmering oats. "It's impossible to sleep with everyone yelling, and the animals snorting and bellowing. And the language some of those teamsters use." She shuddered.

Judith tested the biscuits baking in the big black skillet and removed them, adding them to a pile already done. "Breakfast is ready."

"You'll join us?" Luke asked Mr. Clark.

"My pleasure."

Activity around them increased as everyone dished up hurriedly, anxious to be on the go. Mr. Clark stood.

"May I ask the blessing?" He looked to Warren, Luke and Judith for their approval.

"Go ahead," Warren said.

Donna Grace's father bowed his head. "God in heaven, we thank You for Your blessings of food and provisions. I ask that You go with these people each mile of the way and bring them safely to their place. Amen." He sat and began eating.

Luke, seated on the ground next to Donna Grace, felt her silent sigh. He quirked an eyebrow at her, but she only shook her head.

And then Buck rode by. "Let's get this journey underway. The lighter wagons can go first." That meant the Russell wagon, the Clark wagon and a third one that drove toward them.

The driver called out a greeting. "I'm Reverend Shepton and this is my good wife. We're on our way to New Mexico."

Introductions were made all around.

The reverend noted Donna Grace's condition without staring. "My wife is a midwife. Looks like she'll be needed soon."

Donna Grace shook her head. "Not until we reach Santa Fe. That's where my baby will be born."

Mrs. Shepton leaned forward to pat Donna Grace's shoulder. "Babies make their own schedule. But never fear, we'll be ready whenever the little one is."

Buck rode by again. "Folks, let's go." He waited as Mr. Clark hugged his daughters goodbye. Warren got up beside Judith. Luke had in mind to check on their freight wagons, even though they had experienced teamsters that they had used in the past, but Buck nodded toward the Clark wagon. "Guess you'll be driving your wife's wagon."

Luke recognized the words for what they were—an order. "Yup. Come on, Mrs. Russell." He helped Donna Grace to the hard seat and climbed up beside her. Mary Mae got in the back. Soon enough the women would weary of the constant jolting and swaying and get down to walk, but for now, riding would get them out of the melee of wagons trying to get in line with the resisting oxen and mules who preferred the life of ease here. Warren led the way, Reverend Shepton followed in his wagon and Luke trailed in his dust. Behind them the uproar increased. Inside the wagon, pots and items hanging from the hoops rattled and banged.

Donna Grace sat back and chuckled. "Some people think this journey is quiet and peaceful. It's nothing of the sort."

He glanced at her. "After a bit you don't hear the noise."

"I don't mind. It's music to my ears. It means I am on my way." She lifted her hands toward the sky and laughed. "Santa Fe, here we come." She patted her baby bulge. "Baby, we are on our way to our new home."

Luke leaned down a bit to speak to the baby. "Just make sure you wait until we get there to put in your appearance." He lifted his head and met Donna Grace's dark, sober eyes. Their gazes held even as he straightened. If only he knew her well enough to read the message there.

She gave a nod. "I will not be any trouble to you. I can drive the wagon and you can look after your own things."

"Who said you were going to be any trouble?" Hadn't she already mention the idea a couple of times? Said her grandfather told her she was too much trouble. Even her father had insinuated taking care of his daughters was an inconvenience.

She turned her eyes forward and lifted one shoulder.

"Donna Grace, look at me." She brought her gaze back to him. "Whatever happens to either you or me we are in this together."

"For better or worse. Good times and bad. Just not forever."

She repeated that condition a little too often for Luke's peace of mind. "It's what we agreed upon, but if you're wanting to renegotiate the terms of our agreement…"

She shot him a look full of so many things—disbelief, protest, followed by defeat, and acceptance. And then she laughed, the sound so unexpected that he looked about to see if he'd missed the antics of a man or animal.

"Something amuses you?" he asked, when he saw no explanation for her merriment.

"You do." She sat back, a smile playing about her mouth and her attention on the road ahead.

He didn't ask why. Didn't care. Because it felt good to be the one to make her laugh.

They reached the last of the oaks and before them lay the wide-spreading plains. Nothing ahead as far as the eye could see but dry, dusty grass and wind.

"We are on our way," she announced, her voice filled with awe and joy.

Mary Mae moved forward and knelt behind them. "There's not much to see, is there?" She sounded small and afraid.

Donna Grace took one of her sister's hands. "I see a future of hope and love." Her gaze met Luke's. "For all of us." Her words blessed him, even though he had no expectation of love. He'd learned the folly of inviting such pain into his life. Never again.

The other wagons followed and the slow journey began. After an hour, Judith left their wagon and started walking to the side.

"I'd like to walk too," Mary Mae said. Luke let her scramble off.

"Do you want to join them?" he asked Donna Grace.

"In a bit. I'm a little tired."

"You didn't sleep well?"

She slanted him a look. "It was a little awkward."

"Not to mention how hard the ground was. Perhaps you'd be more comfortable in the wagon."

"We'll see." The wheels made a few more turns, then she shifted to look at him. "Luke, I meant it when

I said I could drive the wagon. Papa taught me on our trip here."

"Uh huh."

"If you want to go check on your wagons, I can manage just fine." She reached for the reins.

He held them firmly. "If I wanted to I could, I suppose."

"Well?" she prodded.

"Well what?" He guessed his lazy tone bothered her, for she let out an impatient gust of air.

"I don't recall saying I wanted to," he added, in a tone that he hoped indicated it was the last thing on his mind.

She rumbled her lips. "Luke Russell, I think you might be a stubborn, mule-headed man."

A grin started deep inside. "Guess the good Lord knew what He was doing when he sent a stubborn man into your life."

She scowled at him. "Why would you say that?"

The grin reached his mouth. "Because you are a stubborn woman."

"I am not." She flounced about. Then with a little toss of her head, added, "I'm just determined to do what needs to be done."

He roared with laughter. Judith and Mary Mae came closer to demand to share the joke.

Donna Grace shifted about to give him nothing but a view of her back. Did her shoulders tremble? Had he offended her? Hurt her feelings?

"Donna Grace, I am sorry. I meant no—"

She waved him away and pressed a hand to her mouth to muffle the sound.

He narrowed his eyes. "Are you laughing?"

She turned so she could answer him with a nod. Her eyes brimmed with humor and her face lit with it.

The two other women jammed fists to their hips. "What's so funny?" Judith asked, sounded as peeved as curious.

"He called me stubborn," Donna Grace managed in fits and starts.

"And rightly so," Mary Mae agreed. "But why is that so funny?"

"Because—" She lifted her hands in a sign of I-don't-know. "I guess you had to be there." When she looked at Luke they both grinned.

*Yup, you had to be there,* he silently agreed and decided being married to Donna Grace, even if only for the length of this trip, might prove pleasant enough.

The two ladies wandered off to the side to avoid the dust and Luke settled down to the rhythm of the wagon. There was little to do but keep the mules following the trail.

Donna Grace's head bumped his shoulder. He glanced down at her. Her eyes were closed and her head lolled against him. Poor little mama was tired. He angled his body toward her so she could lean into him.

How was she going to make this long, tiresome trip?

He smiled. By sheer stubborn determination and with his help.

Buck Williams rode by and gave Luke and Donna Grace a hard look. His gaze lingered on Donna Grace as she slept against Luke.

Luke could almost read the wagon master's mind. He'd allow no delay for the sake of Donna Grace's condition. It was up to Luke to see that Donna Grace and her sister made the trip safely and without inconveniencing the traders.

Inconveniencing. Cause of trouble. Seems they were words Donna Grace heard applied to her more than once in just the few hours he'd known her. How many times throughout her life had she heard them? No wonder she had grown into a determined woman.

Buck rode to the front wagon and called a halt for the noon meal.

Luke pulled the mules to a stop.

Donna Grace jerked awake. "Oh my, did I sleep? I surely didn't intend to. You shouldn't have let me. I have to do my—"

He didn't let her finish. "I think your share of the chores is to take care of that baby, and that means taking care of yourself." He jumped down and helped her to the ground. "Move around a bit and get the circulation going good while I tend the animals." They needed to be unhitched and left to find grass and water.

"I can do it." She went to the lead pair and reached for the halter. With a groan, she bent over.

He rushed to her side.

She waved him away.

If she told him she could do anything more without help, he would be sorely tempted to make her spend the rest of the trip in the back of the wagon. Even the thought of trying to do so brought a smile to his lips. A smile that was gone as quickly as it came.

"Are you okay?"

"Just another Charlie horse." She straightened slowly and gave a weak smile that did not erase the tension from her face.

"I'm getting so I don't much like this Charlie fella and his horse."

The smile made its way to her eyes. "I don't much either. Guess I sat too long."

"I'll take care of the mules. You move about and get those kinks worked out."

The fact that she nodded and walked away without one word of argument, made him watch her with more than a little concern.

Judith joined him. "She's trying to make everyone believe she's tough."

"I know." And he'd let her do so as long as possible. But should there come a time—He would never stand back and let ill befall her.

He'd learned that lesson and wouldn't repeat it.

Judith must have read his mind. "You can't make sure nothing bad happens to everyone in your life."

"Not everyone. Just her."

"I fear you will be hurt again."

"Some hurts are more bearable than others." He led the animals away. The worst hurt was doing nothing when he should have done something.

He would not do so again.

Not even if Donna Grace resented his help.

Would she understand that it was for her good?

## 4
---

P lease stop. *Please stop.* Over and over Donna Grace ordered the cramps in her stomach to end. She shouldn't have stayed sitting on the wagon seat so long. She closed her eyes as heat rushed up her neck and pooled in her cheeks. How had she fallen asleep against Luke? It was the man's fault she was so tired. She hadn't been able to sleep with him taking up so much room in the tent. Every time she moved, she bumped into him.

Buck Williams rode by, checking on the freighters and their wagons.

They had surely convinced the man that she and Luke were well and truly married.

She looked the direction Luke had gone with the mules. He strode back, a short dark-haired man at his side. She'd seen the man before and recognized him as one of Luke and Warren's teamsters. They were in deep conversation, with the driver pointing toward a wagon.

Luke nodded and accompanied him to the spot. They examined one of the wheels.

Guilt assailed her and started the cramps again. Because of her, Luke hadn't been able to check his wagons this morning. She would never forgive herself if she was responsible for him losing some of his goods.

She'd tell him again that she could drive the wagon. Her back ached, and the thought of riding several more hours on the jostling hard seat wearied her clear through. Determined to make this trip with little fuss, and without causing trouble for anyone, she pushed aside every pain and discomfort, and hurried to help prepare the noon meal.

They wouldn't take time to build a fire, but beans were already cooked and ready. There were cold biscuits and bacon from this morning.

Warren and Luke joined them, ate hurriedly and then left together. Donna Grace watched them as they went from wagon to wagon. She counted five wagons. Knew they could carry up to two thousand pounds each of goods for trade in Bents Fort or Santa Fe. Would he normally be keeping a closer watch on the needs of his wagons, his oxen and his teamsters?

Judith observed Donna Grace's interest. "This is the first trip they've made with women to accompany them. At least women that were their traveling companions." She laughed softly. "I don't think it will take long for them to find it to their liking."

"How so?"

"They'll have their meals made and I dare say, far better meals than they would make for themselves. Or even shared with the teamsters, which, I suppose, is what they've done in the past. Not to mention, our pleasant company to amuse them."

A dog wandered by the men and Luke reached down to rub his head. The animal dropped to its haunches and sat by Luke's leg.

For some reason, that little scene brought a sting of tears to Donna Grace's eyes. How silly. She jerked away and grabbed the only item not yet put away—the cast iron pot that held the cold biscuits. Only a few remained.

"Seems we'll be kept busy baking and cooking to feed them," she murmured, showing Judith the container.

Judith laughed. "Like I said, they're going to appreciate having some women with them on this trip."

The idea lifted a weight of guilt and worry Donna Grace had carried for almost twenty-four hours. Was it only that long since she and Luke had struck their agreement?

Up and down the line of wagons, the weary men stretched out on the ground and rested. From the snores nearby, Donna Grace knew many of them slept. A short time later, as if on a given signal, they scrambled to their feet, went to get the oxen and mules and hitched up the wagons again.

She watched Luke, torn between appreciating his help and wanting to refuse it.

He turned to her. "Do you want to ride or walk?"

"I'll walk with the others." She joined Judith and Mary Mae.

Mrs. Shepton called to them. "May I join you?"

They waited for her, then walked far enough away from the wagons to avoid the dust.

Donna Grace found the pace suited her and she relaxed and looked about her. "It looks different than when we came with Papa."

Mary Mae looked around. "We were young and eager back then."

"True. But it was also early summer. The grass was greener and spattered liberally with wild flowers. Now the grass is dull and dusty and there are no flowers." The fact troubled her.

They marched onward, mile after mile. Needing to think and plan for the future of herself and her baby, Donna Grace fell behind the others. The wagons rumbled onward, accompanied by the shouts of the teamsters and the crack of whips.

The absence of flowers made her consider how late in the year it was. October. It would be late November before they arrived. Later, if they ran into problems.

She couldn't think of being delayed and pressed her hands to her stomach, the baby kicking against her palm in response. "You stay right there until we get to Santa Fe."

The morning had started out cool, but the heat intensified throughout the afternoon. If only she could feel a cool breeze. She waved her hands at her face. So hot. She took huge gasps, seeking relief from the stifling air.

Her boot caught on a tangle of grass and she went to her knees, struggling for a moment to catch her breath.

There before her, hidden among the blades of dusty grass, waved a cluster of blue harebells. So cheerful. She sat back on her heels and stared at the blossoms. Even though she hadn't expected to see flowers at this time of year, she couldn't help wishing for them, longing for the bright encouragement they would provide. To find this almost-hidden bunch brought a tear to her eyes. What was wrong with her that she cried at the least thing?

～

LUKE KEPT HALF his attention on the women walking —or more correctly, on Donna Grace—and the other half on guiding the mules. Donna Grace moved slowly, her gait that of a woman heavy with child. And yet, there was a grace to her movements. Perhaps inherited, in part, from her Spanish side of the family. But also born of overcoming challenges and using them to fuel her determination.

She fell behind the others.

He watched her more carefully. Had she tired herself? But it didn't appear so. She plodded onward, looking as if her thoughts required solitude.

He brushed the back of his hand over his brow to wipe away the sweat, and smiled as Donna Grace waved her hands before her face. She was hot, too.

He gasped as she fell, and held his breath waiting for her to get up. She remained on the ground. Had she injured herself?

With a flick of the reins, he turned the wagon off the trail and set the brake, then leapt to the ground, breaking into a run. He reached her side and knelt beside her.

"Are you okay? I saw you fall, and when you didn't get up—" He didn't finish. He expected her to scold him and remind him she could take care of herself.

Instead, she lifted her face to him. Tears had left a trail down her dusty face.

"You're hurt. I should never have let you walk."

She shook her head. "I found these flowers." She pointed to a bunch of harebells.

"Flowers?" She wasn't making any sense.

"It's too late in the season for them, but here they are."

"Yes?" Still not making sense.

"Like a gift."

"Okay."

"To remind me of—" She shrugged.

He got it. "A gift from God to remind you that He is here with us, each step of the way."

She nodded.

"'Consider the lilies of the field, how they grow; they toil not, neither do they spin. And yet I say unto you, that even Solomon in all his glory was not arrayed like one of these.'" Silently, he thanked his parents for the many memory verses they'd had him learn.

"They are so beautiful. So pure." She smiled at him, easing his mind of its worry. "What is that song you sang?"

"Do you want to hear it?"

"Please." Her eyes held his in a grasp so firm he couldn't look away.

"'Oh, worship the King, all glorious above. Oh gratefully sing his power and his love.'" He sang the hymn from start to finish. He'd always loved singing, but to do so for Donna Grace caused his voice to tremble. He finished and still they continued to look deeply into each other's eyes.

She broke the spell. "Thank you." She looked around to see their wagon to one side, the others moving away and scrambled to her feet. "You shouldn't have stopped. I'm fine. There's no need to worry about me."

He grasped her shoulders. "Donna Grace, you are my wife. I will take care of you."

"Wife in name only."

Always it came back to that. "Do you care to tell Buck that?"

She looked past him to the wagon train that continued its steady journey. "No, I do not. But—"

He touched her lips to silence her. Her gaze returned to his.

"When I married you, I promised myself I would take care of you as you deserved. I also promised your father I would. So please, no more arguing about this." He watched her mental struggle to accept his request.

Her eyelids flicked. "Very well. I suppose we must keep up appearances." She dashed toward the wagon.

He caught her arm. "Slow down unless you want to fall again."

"I just want to catch up." But her pace slowed considerably.

They reached the wagon. "Do you want to ride on the seat or in the back?"

He guessed it was a measure of her fatigue or the heat, or a combination of both, that she said she'd ride in the back and he helped her in.

It didn't take long for the mules to catch up to the slow moving freight wagons and they were soon back in their place.

Mary Mae hurried over to speak to him. "Is she okay?"

"I'm fine," Donna Grace's voice answered from the back.

"Glad to hear it." Mary Mae rejoined the other ladies.

A short time later, Luke glanced to the back. Donna Grace was sound asleep. He smiled. He'd never suggest she should take it easy, but it seems her body demanded it.

As they traveled onward, he hummed the song he's sung for Donna Grace.

Buck rode by. "Stopping at Lone Elm."

Luke nodded. He knew the spot and had expected it would be their destination.

Donna Grace poked her head from behind. "You shouldn't have let me sleep." She sounded peevish.

He hid his smile. "Why, did you have something important to do?"

"I'm not usually this lazy."

"I'm sure you're not, but perhaps it will take a few days to get used to being on the go all day."

"I suppose."

He pulled his wagon in behind Reverend Shepton's and soon the entire train circled. Besides the Russell freight wagons, there were four other traders with wagons, bringing the total, including the smaller wagons, to thirty. A smallish train, but less people would hopefully mean fewer problems and a quicker journey.

He jumped down to take care of the mules, but first helped Donna Grace from the wagon. She glanced around.

"I remember this place and the little lone soldier-elm keeping watch on that mound. Somehow I thought it would have changed more."

"You can tell me about your earlier trip, but first I have to take care of the animals." He wanted to check the oxen and the freight wagons as well.

"I need to help with supper."

They went their separate ways. He returned some time later to find the ladies had boiled a ham and potatoes.

Warren brought his friend, Sam Braddock, to the campfire. "I told Sam he could join us. It's better for his little girl if he eats with us."

"Fine by me." Luke knew he answered for the others as well.

Warren introduced Sam and his ten-year-old niece, Polly, to everyone.

"You're welcome to share our meals," Judith said.

Polly and Donna Grace eyed each other with interest.

Finally the child spoke. "You're going to have a baby, aren't you?"

Donna Grace nodded. "Yes, I am."

"My mama was going to have a baby."

Sam took a step toward his niece and then stopped, waiting to see what the child had in mind.

Luke also watched with interest. Perhaps Donna Grace would reveal something to Polly that she hadn't told him.

"And did she?" Donna Grace asked.

Polly shook her head. "She died before she did. Her and papa died in an as'kedent."

Warren and Luke knew the circumstances of her

parents, but the others didn't and the news shocked them into silence.

Donna Grace recovered first. "I'm so sorry to hear that. You must be very sad."

Polly hung her head to one side. "I am when I think of them." She brightened. "But it's fun being with Uncle Sammy."

Sam chuckled, perhaps more relieved than the others to see her smile. He held out his arms and Polly threw herself into them and was tossed into the air.

Sam set her down again.

"I'm really too big for that." Polly did her best to sound grown up.

Her uncle laughed. "Perhaps I should stop doing it."

"Oh no. I wouldn't like that."

Donna Grace chuckled. She turned to Luke and as their eyes connected, her smile faltered.

What was she thinking to grow so sober?

"I have something to add to the meal." Sam hurried back to his wagon and returned with a pie.

All four ladies looked at his offering.

"You bake pies?" Donna Grace asked. The look she gave Luke seemed to say she might have chosen the wrong man to marry, when there was one who could bake pies.

Sam laughed. "Wouldn't know how. I bought a half a dozen at the restaurant in Independence. Figured they might add a bit of variety to the beans, bacon and biscuits we usually eat on the trail." He sniffed appreciatively. "Didn't know we'd be so fortunate as to have so many ladies along to cook a decent meal."

Donna Grace gave a tight smile. "Not that you've tasted our food to know if it's any better."

Luke, Warren and Sam all laughed. "No need to taste it," Luke assured her.

Their plates full, they all sat on the ground around the fire. Luke made sure he sat next to Donna Grace. Polly chose to sit on Donna Grace's other side and continually glanced her direction. Luke wondered if it was the expected baby that held her attention.

"The pie is delicious," Luke said. "Apple pie is my favorite."

"I thought it was peach," Judith said.

Her innocent voice didn't fool Luke. He knew she teased him.

"I thought it was rhubarb," Warren added.

"Nope. We're both wrong. It's raisin. No wait, its lemon." Judith lifted her hands in a gesture of surrender. "I give up. Truth is, Luke loves pie in every flavor."

Luke wasn't about to be bettered by his siblings. "Tonight's pie is apple. So today, apple is my favorite."

Donna Grace nudged him in the side. "I just learned something new about you."

He caught her elbow and pressed it closer. He leaned over to whisper. "I have lots more secrets for you to discover." He chuckled as she ducked her head, suddenly shy.

Warren cleaned his plate and pushed to his feet. "Time to check on the animals."

He waited for Sam and Luke to join him.

First, Luke again whispered to Donna Grace. "I'll be back soon. Don't go away." Then feeling just a tad pleased with himself, he fell in beside his brother.

They walked around the wagons, checked axles, spoke to the freighters. But only half Luke's attention dwelled on the tasks. He couldn't wait to get back to Donna Grace.

"Are we done?" he asked, after a bit.

Warren gave him a little shove. "Go see your wife. We can manage without you."

Luke didn't argue. He sauntered back to the wagon. The ladies had cleaned up the dishes and Donna Grace was baking more biscuits for the morrow. She watched him approach, part curious, part guarded.

He'd like to change that to all welcoming. "Judith, can you watch the biscuits? I want to take Donna Grace for a walk."

"Of course. Mary Mae and Polly have gone for a walk, too. You might see them."

"I don't—" Donna Grace began to protest.

"There are things we need to discuss."

"Judith?" His sister seemed lost in thought and Luke followed the direction of her gaze. She stared at the fire of Reverend Shepton and his wife. Buck hunkered down, visiting with them and another man.

"Who is that?" Judith asked.

"That's Gil Trapper. He's the scout for the wagon. An old friend of Buck's."

"I see." She blinked, and turned toward the fire. "I'll watch the biscuits."

Luke shook his head in confusion over his sister then dismissed it, knowing she was going through a rough time of her own.

Donna Grace looked from one to the other. Opened her mouth as if to protest, then seemed to think better of it.

Good. He preferred her to come without argument. He took her hand and led her to the area beyond the wagons. Pete, one of the freighters, played his harmonica. Flickering light from the campfires gave them some guidance on their walk, but he pulled her hand around his elbow and held her close. "Wouldn't want you to stumble and fall again."

"How nice of you to think about me."

He couldn't tell if she spoke with gratitude or resignation, or perhaps a bit of both, and then she quickly changed the subject. "What goods are your wagons carrying?"

"Mostly manufactured items from the east."

"Such as?"

Her father was a trader. Surely she knew the things they carried, but still, it pleased him to have her show this bit of interest in what he did.

"I have bolts and bolts of fabric—ginghams, linens, muslins, percales, silk—sewing materials such as needles, threads, buttons. Stockings, shoes, ready-made items of clothing. There are hats, axes, jewelry, inkwells, glass bottles, tobacco and trade beads."

"Enough to fill five freight wagons?"

"How do you know how many wagons we have?"

"I saw you and Warren checking them." She watched him.

He grinned in the gathering darkness.

"And you bring back gold, silver and furs?"

"Mostly we do."

She slowed. "How long have you been doing this?"

"Three years and a bit." He found it hard to believe it was that long. The days and months and years had slipped away, consumed with the challenges of everyday living.

"Since the woman you loved was murdered?"

"Yes, but how did you know that?"

"Judith mentioned it. You must have loved her very much for her loss to still hurt so much."

He contemplated her remark a moment. "I did, but I see now that it was the way she died that hurt the most."

"Murder is so senseless."

They had stopped walking and she faced him. He could make out her features in the half dark but not read her eyes.

"Tell me what happened."

He held her shoulders, finding a strange kind of strength in doing so. He'd never spoken of Ellen's death since the day it happened, but now the words came easily. "We were to be married. I'd saved up enough money to buy a little farm. I always wanted to raise horses and train them." He smiled. It had been years since he'd admitted his dream to anyone. Thought it was dead, but surprisingly, it still tugged at his thoughts. "I had taken Ellen—that was my girl—to see our place. Three men rode up. I recognized them as ne'er-do-wells that hung around town. They said the farm was theirs and we'd have to leave. I told them I had bought it from the bank and had the papers to prove it. The oldest spat on the ground. Said the bank had cheated them out of it. I told them to take it up with the bank and if it truly belonged to them, we would move out. I knew it didn't. They'd lost it by mortgaging it and then not paying what they owed.

"They fussed about a bit until I said they should go speak to the banker. Finally they informed me it wasn't over and rode away. I thought I'd seen the last of them." He filled his lungs with the warm evening air and held it for several seconds, then let it out. "Turns out I was wrong. Ellen wanted to explore the house and see what needed to be done. I wanted to look at the barn and corrals and outbuildings so I left her. I don't know how long I was gone, but the sound of a gunshot jerked me from my planning and I raced to the house, my heart in my mouth. I saw three men ride away as I rushed inside. I found Ellen on the kitchen floor in a pool of blood. She died in my arms." He swallowed hard and couldn't go on.

"You poor man. How dreadful." Donna Grace pressed her head to his shoulder and made comforting noises.

He rested his cheek against her hair and let her

soothe away the horror of that day. "That wasn't the worst of it," he murmured, surprised that he wanted to tell the rest. "I took her to her parents. Her father took her from me and said, 'She deserved better than you. You let your plans take precedence over caring for her.' He was right. I shouldn't have challenged those men. I should have known better than to leave her there alone, knowing they were in the area. I didn't pull the trigger that ended her life, but I was responsible nonetheless. It's a burden I will carry to my grave."

Donna Grace turned her face upward. "You can't blame yourself for the actions of evil men. It's too great a load for any man."

"Your words are easy to say. But I learned a lesson I won't ever repeat. I will never again put my interests above someone else's safety and well-being."

She nodded. "Now I understand why you insisted on marrying me."

"I learned another lesson." He eased away from her. "I will never again care deeply for anyone. It can hurt too much."

"On that we are agreed."

Why did he want to try and persuade her to change her mind about allowing love into her life when he would not do so himself?

## 5

Donna Grace walked away from Luke. His story made her insides ache, but even worse was his assertion he would never again allow love into his life. What a waste. He was a young man with so much to offer. A gentle, kind, caring man. She would try and convince him to change his mind, but how could she offer advice in love, when she had vowed to never trust a man again? It wasn't quite the same, but without trust, there couldn't be love, so they were effectively living the same life.

The baby kicked as if in protest. The kicks were so hard, they started a cramp and she fell to her knees, groaning.

Luke was by her side instantly. "Are you hurt?"

She gasped against the pain and ground out the words, "Another Charlie horse."

He knelt beside her and rubbed her back.

Slowly the pain eased and she sat back on her heels and drew in a long breath.

The nearest campfire flared, lighting Luke's features. His brows scuttled together. His mouth drew in, a hard line in his face.

She had to reassure him. "Don't look so worried. It's nothing."

He took her by the shoulders and looked her squarely in the face. "Donna Grace, when is this baby due?"

She held his gaze, proud of herself for not blinking before his demanding stare. She swallowed once, twice.

He gave her a tiny shake. "You keep saying not until we get to Santa Fe, but I wonder if that's really the case."

"The truth is, I simply don't know."

"You must have some idea."

She gave a sound of derision. "One would think so, but I have never had regular monthlies." Her cheeks burned at the intimate details they were discussing. "And then I began to worry because Melvin grew more and more distant, and so I didn't pay it much mind. Turns out his wife had located him and started writing him. I suppose he found it difficult to be living a double life."

Luke snorted. "The man should have been locked up in jail for what he did to you."

"It wouldn't have changed anything. By the time I realized I had a baby inside me, I was too confused to think about dates. And then three months ago, the real Mrs. Brunt showed up and shooed me from the house." Her voice caught and as she had a few minutes earlier offered him comfort, he did the same for her, sitting on the ground and pulling her close.

She nestled into his embrace, clinging to his arm, feeling the strength and security it offered.

He held her for a moment then spoke against her hair. "Donna Grace, how big were you when you left that house?"

She didn't want to tell him that she'd already begun to show. She knew she was too far along to hope to make it to Santa Fe unless the baby decided to wait. Hadn't Mrs. Shepton said babies come in their own time? "I want the baby born in Santa Fe."

He rubbed her back again, the touch so soothing, she leaned into his chest. "I think we might have to consider the possibility that your little one could be born before we get there."

"You mean on the trail?"

"Other women have done it."

"Oh, I can do it. Not a problem. But what kind of home is that for a baby? A covered wagon, full of dust and insects. I want my baby to have a safe, secure home."

He took her arms and formed them into a cradle. "Donna Grace, this is where you will give the baby safety, security, love and everything he needs."

She hugged her arms close to her chest. "You make it sound like I can be enough."

"You are enough."

"How can you be so sure?"

He chuckled a little. "How can you doubt it? You are a strong, independent, stubborn-as-a-mule woman. Any baby of yours will be well take care of."

She leaned her head against his shoulder. "You are a very nice man."

"How can you be so sure?" He perfectly imitated her tone as he repeated her question.

She eased back so she could look into his face. She carefully repeated his words. "How can you doubt it? You are protective, strong, and encouraging. Any woman would be—" She broke off. She did not have the right to say any woman would be safe and secure in his care. Instead, she tried to rise.

He caught her and pulled her back to his arms. "Donna Grace, will you go see Mrs. Shepton and talk to her about your Charlie horses?"

It seemed a little thing to do for a man who had done so much for her. "I'll talk to her tomorrow."

"Thank you." He scrambled to his feet and pulled her up beside him, holding her arm in his as they made their way back to the camp.

He went immediately to the back of their wagon, pulled out the tent and quickly set it up. Warren set up Judith's tent at the same time.

Done, Luke asked, "Do you want to sleep in the tent or the back of the wagon? I'll be nearby sleeping under the wagon."

His assurance of being close should have brought a

protest to her lips. Where were the words that she didn't need him, nor want him? But there were no words. She put it down to being too weary to argue. "I tried the wagon. It wasn't all that comfortable." It rocked and banged over ruts. She knocked her elbow into the trunks several times. Even standing still, it would be too crowded for comfort. "Mary Mae and I will sleep in the tent." She took her blankets from the wagon.

"Wait." Luke went to the back of the Russell wagon and lifted out a buffalo fur. "This will cushion you." He ducked inside the tent with it.

She wanted to protest. There was no point in her getting used to having him help. But to say anything would surely arouse curiosity in those around them so she kept still. "Thank you," she murmured, when he backed out.

He paused close to her side to whisper. "Doesn't hurt a bit to accept help, does it?" He strode away before she could answer, grabbed his bedroll and settled under the wagon.

"Donna Grace, go to bed," he said.

She scurried into the tent and lay beside her sister.

"Did you have a nice walk?" Mary Mae asked in such an innocent voice that Donna Grace wasn't sure if she was truly interested or wanting to tease.

"Yes, I did."

Mary Mae giggled. "You both looked like a cat who'd been in the cream."

"We did not."

"Yes, you did. But that's okay. After all, you are married. Newly married. Of course, you want time alone to do… well, what married people do."

Donna Grace would not ask her sister to elaborate. "You have a very vivid imagination. Plus you always see things through wishful eyes." She found Mary Mae's hand and squeezed it. "Someday you will find the love you so desire. I know it."

"How can you be so sure?" Mary Mae asked the same question Donna Grace and Luke had asked each other.

Donna Grace smiled. "How can you doubt it?"

THE NEXT MORNING, she sought out Mrs. Shepton after breakfast. The two women walked side by side as the wagons began moving.

"How can I help you, my dear?"

Donna Grace explained her frequent cramps. "I call them Charlie horses." She smiled as she recalled Luke saying he didn't like Charlie and his horses.

Mrs. Shepton asked several questions as to when they occurred, and how severe they were. "They could be something as simple as your muscles complaining about the load you're carrying and the amount of walking you're doing." She chuckled. "Even when you're riding in the wagon, the constant jarring puts a strain on your muscles." Her expression sobered. "Or it could be false labor." She stopped and held her hands out toward Donna Grace's stomach. "May I feel the baby?"

Donna Grace nodded.

Mrs. Shepton's hands were firm, yet gentle. The baby kicked hard. Mrs. Shepton chuckled. "He's strong. I could tell more if you were lying down, but your baby is big. I think you are closer to your delivery time than you think."

Donna Grace blinked back tears. "I want my baby born in a real home."

"Child, your baby isn't going to know the difference."

Donna Grace realized she cradled her arms the way Luke had shown her. Her gaze found him. He watched them, though the distance was too great for either of them to see the other's eyes clearly. She nodded. He was right. Her baby would find what it needed right here in her arms.

Even so, she still hoped to make it to Santa Fe. She recalled words from the hymn Luke sang for her. *Frail children of dust and feeble as frail. In thee do we trust, nor find thee to fail.*

She had given up trusting God some time ago. Perhaps around the time Grandfather Ramos tried to make her go to his church and renounce the things her father and mother had taught her. Maybe it was time, for the sake of her unborn baby, to start trusting God again.

She thanked Mrs. Shepton and hurried toward the

wagon. Luke stopped long enough to help her up to the hard bench.

He noticed the way she eyed the plank of wood and reached back and got a cushion. "Try this."

She sat on it.

"Better?"

"Much. Where did you find that?"

He waggled his eyebrows. "I have my way of getting things done for my wife."

She should protest the claiming way he said that, but she didn't. Nor would she admit she rather liked the way it made her feel.

"What did Mrs. Shepton have to say?" he asked.

She told him.

"Are you ready if the baby should come before you get to Santa Fe?"

"I believe so. And Mrs. Shepton assured me she has everything needed." She lifted one shoulder. "I'm not the first person to birth a baby."

He laughed. "Nor the last I would hope."

She laughed and then turned to him.

"What is it?"

His quick assessment of her need surprised and pleased her.

"That song you sing?"

He sang the first line to indicate he understood what she meant.

"Could you sing it for me again?"

He did so, holding her gaze throughout the entire time.

"'In thee do we trust, nor find thee to fail.' I want to have that kind of faith." Her voice caught with longing.

"Then I believe you do."

She blinked. "Just like that?"

"What else is necessary? You trust or you don't, and by saying you want to, aren't you?"

"Luke, is everything so simple and plain for you?"

He considered her question for several minutes. "Right now it is." His look informed her she had something to do with his answer.

She couldn't think how that could be. Much of her life, she had heard how she complicated things for others. How could it be different with Luke?

～

LUKE HAD to remind himself more and more frequently that his role in this relationship was temporary and mainly for show. But how could he pretend his heart didn't slam into his chest when he saw Donna Grace fall to her knees, groaning? How could he ignore her pain and distress? Not offer her comfort? He couldn't, and in doing so, he wavered on the brink of a line he didn't want to cross. He wanted to protect her, but not open his heart to the pain that caring would surely bring.

Besides, caring was not part of the agreement between them.

He watched as she considered his words that trust was as simple as saying she wanted it.

She pressed her hand to her stomach and looking into the distance, smiled as if anticipating a new home at their destination.

Her serenity pulled at some deep longing in him. It took a moment to recognize it as his long-ago dream of home and family. He thought of the letter in his saddlebag in the Russell wagon. It was from an acquaintance who had headed to California some time ago. *There is land here aplenty. Great for cattle. You couldn't find a better place to start ranching if you're still interested.* But going back to the land meant going back to his dream. His dream was dead.

"Luke?"

Donna Grace's voice brought him from his troubled thoughts.

"Would you be embarrassed if I let you feel the baby?" She patted her stomach to indicate what she meant.

He'd watched Mrs. Shepton pressing her hands to Donna Grace's tummy and wondered what she felt. "Not if you aren't."

"I want you to feel this." She took his hand and placed it palm-down on her belly.

The firmness of it surprised him. He'd expected it to be soft.

"Do you feel that?"

"Is that the baby kicking?"

She nodded, her eyes glowing. "He's strong, isn't he?"

"Maybe it's a girl."

"It doesn't matter to me either way."

He couldn't look away from the intensity of her gaze, full of love and promise. It sucked at him, making him want to be a part of what she felt.

"You want to feel more?" At his nod, she added. "Sing again."

He did so and what he could only think were little feet, fluttered against his palm. He laughed. "What's he doing?"

"Maybe it's a girl."

He laughed again at the way she imitated him, her face alive with teasing and something more... something he couldn't name. It made him think she had opened her heart and invited him in. He knew he should think twice about that idea, but she answered his question at that moment, distracting him.

"The baby likes to hear you sing."

Their gazes went on and on, the mules proceeding down the trail without any guidance from Luke. It was as if her heart was wide open.

His wasn't and he withdrew his hand and turned his attention back to the task of driving the wagon. "It's nice the baby likes my singing. But perhaps you are only imagining it."

"I'm not."

He didn't want to argue with her any more than he wanted to be pleased that she thought the baby responded positively to his singing.

She settled back, seemingly content.

He did not feel calm and stared hard at the trail

ahead. They were in the lead today and he suddenly pulled back on the reins and stared at a muddy draw.

Buck sat on horseback eyeing the spot. "It's not deep." The mud on his horse's legs came to its knees.

Plenty deep in Luke's estimation. And he said so.

Buck shook his head. "Sorry. There's no way around it for miles. We'll have to cross it but by the time the last of the wagons crosses, it will likely be a sinkhole." He waved Luke forward.

Mud spattered up from the heels of the mules and the turning of the wheels. With a final slurp they reached the other side and climbed up the slope. He continued onward a hundred yards, then stopped. "I'll have to see to the other wagons."

Warren pulled up beside him with the Russell wagon, and jumped to the ground. The two of them hurried back to the mud hole.

The first ten wagons made it across easily enough, the teamsters driving the oxen with whips.

Each succeeding wagon struggled more, the wheels sinking deeper and deeper.

"Three wagons left to go." Luke hadn't realized the women stood nearby watching, until Donna Grace spoke.

"Will they make it?"

"They'll make it." They would not abandon three heavily-laden wagons.

The first stuck in the mud. The teamster drove the animals mercilessly, the air as foul with curses as the mud beneath the hooves of the oxen.

Slowly, with a slurping sound, the wagon inched forward. Everyone cheered as it climbed to dry ground.

The second wagon likewise inched through the quagmire.

The third one settled into the mud hole and refused to move despite every effort.

"What are they going to do?" Donna Grace asked.

Luke answered her question. "They'll use a second team." Already, rested oxen were being unhitched. It took time to get the second team in place, but eventually the animals strained together. At first, it looked impossible; then the wheels turned. Inch by inch the wagon crept forward to the grassy bank.

All the wagons were safely across. Men and animals were mud-crusted.

"Let's get on the trail," Buck called. Luke and Donna Grace hurried back to their wagon. He helped Donna Grace up, then paused to brush off the mud that had mostly dried.

They traveled onward until Buck called out, "We'll noon here."

The weary animals needed the rest, and were turned out to graze and drink from the nearby stream. Most of the men cleaned up in the stream as well. Then, as soon as they'd eaten, they stretched out for a rest.

Luke and Warren did the same. Luke pulled his hat low over his eyes and turned his head so he could watch Donna Grace. She rubbed her back often when she thought no one was looking. But she conscientiously did her share of the chores. The three women talked softly as they worked. He wished he could hear what they said. His eyelids drooped and he blinked them open to see Donna Grace watching him, unaware that he saw her.

A tiny smile curved her lips as she pressed her palm to her belly.

That claiming motion and her insistence that the baby responded to his voice, brought an answering smile to his mouth.

THEY SETTLED into a routine over the next few days as the prairie rolled on mile after endless mile. Donna Grace alternately rode in the wagon or walked with the others.

He hadn't seen her bend over with a Charlie horse the last two days. "No more cramps?" he asked.

"Mrs. Shepton was right. My muscles were simply getting used to all the walking."

"That's a relief." Though how she could move with that heavy stomach, beat him. Of course it was more of a waddle than a walk, but he refrained from saying so to her.

They traveled beside a creek, with steep banks covered with trees and undergrowth.

Donna Grace looked that direction. "Might there be berries?"

"In the summer the bushes are laden with raspberries and gooseberries. There could still be some, I suppose."

"Let me off."

She would have jumped down as soon as he stopped, but he told her to wait and went round to help. She called out for Mrs. Shepton and Judith to join her. Mary Mae and little Polly heard and hurried toward them.

"Be careful," Luke called, but she and the others didn't hear him as they scurried toward the banks. He held his breath as he watched her descend, clinging to bushes to keep from sliding down the steep slope. And then she was out of sight.

"Be careful," he said, for his own benefit. He would have slowed the wagon, stopped even, but Buck rode by and gave him a hard look. *Please God, take care of her and the others.*

He sat up straight as he realized it was the first time he had prayed for a woman since Ellen's death. Not that it meant anything. Except, a tiny voice insisted, it did.

Well, of course it did. He had vowed to take care of her until they reached Santa Fe and he didn't intend to fail.

It was nothing more than that.

Gil Trapper, the scout, rode toward the caravan. He spoke to Buck then fell in beside Luke. "Riders coming."

"Indians?" Luke glanced to his right where the women had disappeared.

"Worse. Half a dozen, hard-looking men. Have your guns ready."

Luke lifted his rifle from his feet and stuck his sidearm into his waistband. He wanted to rush after the women, but they were out of sight. So long as the approaching men didn't see them, they were safe.

A cloud of dust announced the men's approach before the riders came into view heading straight toward them on the trail.

*Come on. Face a bunch of armed men. We're ready. Just don't go after innocent women and a child.*

The leader reined in and pointed toward the creek.

Had they spotted the women?

Luke couldn't breathe as he waited for them to make the first move.

They turned to his right.

"They've seen the women," Luke shouted. Buck and Gil headed that direction.

Oh, for a horse! But it would take too long to catch one. He jumped to the ground and broke into a run. He heard pounding feet behind him and guessed Warren followed, and maybe even the reverend, but he didn't take the time to glance back.

A flash of blue caught his eyes. Little Polly. The women would not be far away. He slid down the slope, jamming his boots against bushes in order to slow his descent. The intruders picked their way down the hillside, slowed by the necessity of guiding their horses.

Luke reached the bottom. He couldn't see the

women anywhere. "Donna Grace," he called, as he raced toward where he'd last seen Polly.

He saw a movement ahead in the bushes. The riders had reached the bottom and rode his direction. Unaware of the approaching danger, Polly bent to examine something at her feet. Luke stumbled on the rocky bank, righted himself and hurried onward. So far the men's attention was on Polly, but any minute now they would notice him.

He pulled his pistol out, and had it ready to use. He wanted to call to the child but didn't want to alert the men any sooner than necessary.

Then Donna Grace stepped from the bushes, calling Polly's name.

The men reined in. They saw him at the same time and pulled out guns.

"Drop your firearm," the leader called.

Luke considered his options. With Donna Grace and Polly in the line of fire, there was little he could do. He lowered his arm, but kept hold of the gun and eased forward.

"Drop the gun." The shout left little doubt that the man meant business. Then he gave a mirthless laugh. "Sure wouldn't want to see either of these fine females hurt."

Luke lowered the gun to the ground. If he kept it close...

"Kick it away."

Polly stood frozen, staring at the six men leering at her.

Donna Grace looked ready to fly at them and scratch their eyes out.

He spoke softly. "Stay calm. Don't do anything." He took stock of the situation. Mary Mae, Judith and Mrs. Shepton had pulled out of sight. There came no sound of Warren or Gil or Buck. Wait, a twig snapped somewhere. The intruders didn't notice and Luke eased his breath out. He needed to distract the men so the others could sneak closer.

"Polly," he called. "Don't move. Don't be afraid. These men aren't going to hurt you."

That elicited raucous laughing. "Brave talk. This your woman and kid?" The man who sat in the front of the riders sneered. "Whatcha gonna do to protect them?"

A shot rang out.

Polly sucked back a sob and rushed to Donna Grace.

Luke leapt forward, pushed them to the ground and threw himself over the pair.

He would die before he'd let Donna Grace suffer the same fate as Ellen.

## 6

Donna Grace could barely breathe. She'd heard the shot. Expected to feel the searing jolt as a bullet hit her. Mentally, she checked all her body parts and could detect no injury. How was that possible?

More shots rang out.

She bit her bottom lip and tears stung her eyes. Would someone have to push Luke's lifeless body off her? Tears clogged her throat. *Please God, save us.* She silently repeated the words over and over.

The thundering of racing horses reached her. The gunshots became sporadic and then ended all together.

Luke rolled off her.

She would not move, would not look toward him for fear she would see the life seeping from him.

"Are you in one piece?"

At the sound of his voice, she sucked in a steadying breath.

He helped her sit up then ran his hands over her shoulders and arms.

The tears she'd been holding back broke free, and she wrapped her arms about Luke, clinging to his strength.

He rubbed her back and made soothing noises.

Warren stood beside them. "Is everyone okay?"

Luke nodded. "Thanks for showing up when you did. There was nothing I could do." His arms tightened around Donna Grace.

"Is Polly safe?" she managed to gulp.

"She's with the ladies getting hugged and kissed," Warren said, with a touch of humor.

Not unlike herself, Donna Grace thought. She should leave the shelter of Luke's arms. She should get to her feet. She should return to the safety of the caravan. But she didn't move.

Warren strode away. Murmured voices reached her. Mary Mae said something about wanting to go back. The voices faded. She knew by the sounds that they climbed the hill to where the wagons waited.

"I was so frightened," she murmured against the front of Luke's shirt.

"Me too. I thought I'd be part of another woman being murdered."

"Oh Luke, I never thought of how it would be for you." She looked into his face. "You poor man." She pressed a palm to his cheek.

He closed his eyes and leaned into her hand. "Thank God, you and Polly are okay. I thought the men were shooting at you, but it was Warren and the others shooting at them."

"Yes, thank God." She was more than willing to acknowledge divine intervention and protection. "And thank you for protecting me. You were prepared to give your life." Her throat thickened and her words came out in broken syllables. "I would not forgive myself if something happened to you because of me."

He looked deep into her eyes. "Don't suggest you aren't worth it."

"I wasn't going to." Though the thought hovered at the back of her mind. "I have a baby to think of."

He got up and pulled her to her feet. "I better get you both back to the wagons. Buck won't be happy about the delay." He took her hand and assisted her up the steep slope.

She was out of breath when they reached the top and had to stop a moment. The baby turned over and gave her a hard kick against her ribs. She pressed a hand to the spot. "At least the baby is okay."

Buck had called for the noon break and they joined the others. Mrs. Shepton reached for Donna Grace's hand.

"I'm glad to see you are safe."

"And you, too." Donna Grace reached for Judith's hands. "You, too." She smiled at Mary Mae who was busy with food.

There was no sign of Gil or Buck. She wanted to

thank them for coming to their rescue. Perhaps they had followed the nasty gang of men to make sure they truly left.

Mary Mae served cold biscuits and ham. She squatted before Donna Grace. "I was so scared when I saw you out there." She shuddered.

She squeezed her sister's hands. "I'm fine."

Mary Mae nodded. "I have never prayed so hard in all my life. Thank God for taking care of us all."

Reverend Shepton got to his feet. "I feel a prayer of gratitude is in order." He held his hat before his chest and lifted his face toward heaven. "God, I know You are always our help and shield and defender, but today we saw it so clearly. We humbly thank You." He was silent a moment before he said, "Amen."

Donna Grace murmured her own, "Amen."

She sought out Polly who sat on her uncle's lap, clinging to him.

"You were very brave," Donna Grace said.

"I was scared." The child sobbed into her uncle's shirt front.

"Fear and courage go hand in hand," Donna Grace said.

Polly looked at her. "That doesn't sound right."

"Yes. You see courage is simply being afraid and doing the right thing anyway."

Polly gave a shy smile. "I wanted to scream and run, but I didn't."

Donna Grace nodded. "You did really well."

Buck rode up, ending the conversation. "They were

still riding away when I turned back. I hope we've seen the last of them. We won't rest long here."

"Thank you for coming to our rescue," Donna Grace said.

He touched the brim of his hat in acknowledgment and rode down the line of wagons, letting the teamsters know.

Donna Grace saw that many of them were stretched out. They'd had the good sense to take a nap while they waited for the women to rejoin the caravan.

Her conscience stung. Had she been responsible for delaying everyone? She struggled to her feet and began to put away the supplies and discovered a number of bruises on her body. One in particular, on her hip, slowed her steps.

Mrs. Shepton came to her, supposedly helping with the chores. "I saw you go down. You hit the ground hard. Are you feeling it anywhere?"

Without thinking Donna Grace touched her hip. "A bruise or two. Nothing serious. Especially when I think what might have happened."

Mrs. Shepton caught Donna Grace's hands and pulled her round to face her. "Is the baby still moving?"

"He's let me know he's okay."

"Good. Good. But I suggest you take it easy today. Ride, instead of walking."

"I think I might." Her gaze went toward the wagon where Luke hitched the mules into their harness. He turned, and slowly straightened. The distance between them vanished as did the voices and presence of the others. Only the two of them existed and the tenuous feeling between them. He had willingly thrown himself over her to protect her. Most certainly it was because of his remorse over the murder of his intended. Somehow she must assure him that he had more than made up for whatever lack he thought he was guilty of.

He held out a hand and she went to him and allowed him to help her to the wagon seat. She discovered another bruise on her ribs and remembered his elbow pressed to her side, enclosing her so she wasn't exposed to the intruders.

They jolted along the trail. "I feel I should apologize," he said.

Here she sat wanting to reassure him and he wanted to apologize? "For what?"

"I was rough when I threw you to the ground. I worry I might have hurt you. Did I?"

She pressed her hand to his arm. "Luke, you were willing to die for me. You acted with the best of interests and I can only thank you for being such a noble man."

He looked at her hand resting on his arm. Patted it and stared at the mules. But the smile teasing at the corner of his eyes informed her that her words had meant a lot to him.

After a bit, her head started falling forward.

"Go in the back and rest," he said, and she did so

without arguing. Within moments she fell asleep.

A jolt jarred her from her slumbers and she hurried to the seat and looked over Luke's shoulder.

He turned back to smile at her. "Feeling better?"

She rested her cheek against his shoulder, liking the way his muscles corded as he moved the reins. He was such a good man. He deserved—

She drew back. She could not let his actions, born out of remorse over his betrothed, affect how she felt or acted. They had agreed to a temporary marriage. Each for their own reasons. Neither of them cared to have it otherwise. He didn't need a woman with a baby by another man. And she wasn't ready to trust a man. Besides, if he ever married, he should marry someone nobler than her, someone who would be less responsibility. But for now, they were man and wife, and he'd risked his own life to protect her. "You're a good man, Luke," she murmured. Her frankness brought embarrassed heat to her cheeks. Thankfully he couldn't see her face.

He chuckled. "Good for what?"

She heard the teasing note in his voice but also a longing to know that it was so. "For rescuing maidens in distress. That's twice you've done so for me."

He didn't turn his head but she could see he smiled. "I believe God put me in the right place at the right time. He gets all the credit."

"I prayed very hard when those shots were ringing out and I have no doubt God protected all of us, but I don't think He picked you up and threw you over me."

He shifted then to look at her. "I could not stand to see another woman I'm responsible for murdered."

That was the second time he'd said it. She must make him see he had been absolved by his actions. "You have more than made up for any guilt you think is yours in that matter." She pressed her cheek against him. "Thank you."

He rested his head against hers. "You're welcome."

Reminding herself that physical familiarity was not part of their agreement, she sat up.

They rode without speaking for a few moments. The sun hung low in the western sky. "Will we be stopping soon?"

"We'll stop at Rock Creek. In fact, we're almost there."

A few minutes later, Buck waved them aside. Soon the wagons were circled together.

Luke helped her down, and then tended to the animals. She knew it would be an hour or so before he returned, as he would also check on the Russell's freight wagons. In the meantime, she and the other women would prepare supper.

The Sheptons had joined their group. Buck sometimes shared their meal or, more often, joined one of the freighters' groups.

Gil rode in, and saw them preparing meat and potatoes. He dismounted and stepped closer. "Did anyone suffer because of those scoundrels?" He spoke to Judith more than to the others and Donna Grace watched the pair. Were they attracted to each other?

Judith turned away. "Everyone is fine. Thank you for coming to our rescue." The stiffness of her words denied any attraction on her behalf.

"I thank you, too," Donna Grace said. "Would you care to join us for supper?"

He hesitated. Seemed to wait for Judith to say something.

"Yes, please do. It's the least we can offer after you helped rescue us." Judith did not look at him as she spoke.

"Thank you. It would be a pleasure." Gil tied his horse to a wagon and sauntered to the fire.

It was a merry little group. Sam's pies had all been consumed, but Donna Grace had made an apple pudding from the store of dried apples, and everyone seemed to enjoy it. She looked to Luke for his opinion. As if it was the only one that mattered, she thought with some disgust at herself.

He smiled and his eyes warmed as if he meant his remarks for her alone. "The dessert was very good. Thank you, Donna Grace."

A round of thanks for all the cooks was given.

But all that Donna Grace heard was Luke's approval.

It wasn't until she had crawled into the tent next to Mary Mae and tried to sleep that she took the time to examine her reaction. Why did she so dearly want his approval?

The truth was plain.

Because he so freely gave it. She'd tried so hard to

please Grandfather Ramos and never could, so she stopped trying. She'd tried to please Melvin, always wondering why she failed, and then had learned nothing she could do would be enough because he had a real wife to deal with. Papa used to be pleased with her, when he was around, which was seldom. But then she'd come home with a baby in her belly, and no husband. She'd disappointed him, too.

She twisted about on the buffalo robe, trying to find a comfortable position, but the bruise on one hip and on the ribs of her other side made it impossible to get settled.

Coyotes sang from a distant hill. Somewhere along the creek, an owl hooted. The oxen lowed and the mules stomped their feet. The sounds of the evening called to her.

She slipped from the tent, pulling a shawl about her shoulders, and tiptoed beyond the wagons to stare at the water of the creek and the silvery slate walls of the creek bank.

A rustling behind alerted her to the presence of someone and she glanced toward the wagons. She should not be out here alone. What if one of those intruders had slipped back?

She gathered up her skirt and prepared to dash back to safety.

"It's just me."

Her breath whooshed out as she recognized Luke's voice. "I shouldn't have come out here, but I couldn't sleep."

"Nor could I." They walked side by side along the edge of the creek, their steps slow. The gray night surrounding them.

They reached a fallen tree. "Let's sit for a bit," Luke said.

Their shoulders pressed together. Warmth came from him and comforted her in a way that lying on the buffalo robe had not.

"Tell me about your family," Luke said. "Are you and Mary Mae the only children?"

"Yes, though we have many cousins on the Ramos side. Most of them live in Mexico City. Grandfather considers himself part of Spanish nobility. He was always disappointed with us—me, especially—because I cared more about life in the west than what life would be like in Spain or even Mexico City." She gave a mirthless chuckle. "After Mama died, he wanted to send us back to Mexico City to learn how to be proper Spanish ladies. Thankfully, Papa arrived in time to stop that."

"It sounds like you didn't much care for the life your grandfather wished for you."

"I didn't. Nor was I raised to value it. Mama adored her father, but she loved our papa and chose to do things his way. She allowed us to play with the children of the town, even though Grandfather considered them poor company for us. She let Papa take us in his wagons and follow him about his business."

"You're smiling, aren't you?"

Her smile widened. "I am indeed. Those were the

happiest days of my life. To be free of censure and judgement. I suppose that's why I want to return, even though I fear encountering Grandfather Ramos. He has a way of making me feel like I do everything wrong, and worse, cause everyone trouble." Her smile flattened. "I guess I've done it again. Made trouble for everyone."

~

LUKE HEARD the sorrow in her voice and guessed she referred to this afternoon's events. "If anyone is to blame for what happened, I think I can fairly say it was those men on horseback." He shuddered. "When I think how differently things might have turned out…"

She found his hand in the dark and rested her head on his shoulder. It was a gesture she had repeated often. He didn't know if it came naturally, or if it meant she felt safe with him. He liked to believe there was a certain amount of the latter involved.

"Things turned out the way they were meant to," she said.

"Does that mean when bad things happen, they were meant to be?"

She rubbed her head against his shoulder. "You said the blame for today's unfortunate events lay with those intruders. I think it's the same with Ellen. The evil intent of the intruders is to blame."

"How did you know I was thinking of Ellen?"

"Because her death seems to motivate much of what you do."

He thought of that a moment. "Perhaps it did at first."

She shifted to look in his face. Enough light came from the moon and reflected off the rock face of the creek banks that he could make out her features and knew she would be able to do the same. "Luke, what motivates you now?"

He studied her, wishing he could read the expression in her eyes, but it was too dark and because of that he felt safe speaking frankly. "The desire to do what is right and to protect others as much as possible."

"And when it's not possible?"

"Then I can console myself with the knowledge that I did the best I could."

She sat up. "The best you could. I like that."

They sat side by side, content in each other's company. She shifted as if trying to get more comfortable and he thought of how hard she'd gone to the ground.

"How badly are you bruised?"

"Nothing serious."

She caught his hand. "Feel this." She brought his hand to her stomach and he felt the baby kicking. "The baby is okay and that is all that matters."

He laughed. "I think he's trying to kick his way out."

"Not yet, baby. Not yet." She stretched. "I don't feel

a bit sleepy. Maybe I slept too long this afternoon, but you have to work tomorrow. You don't get the luxury of riding in the back of the wagon unless you will let me drive it."

He chuckled. "I think I can manage to stay awake."

She jabbed her elbow into his ribs. "You don't think I can drive it, do you? Well, I'll have you know Papa taught me how when we came to St. Louis. That seems a long time ago. It was such fun traveling with Papa. He encouraged me to be independent." Her voice deepened. "And now I've disappointed him by carrying a child but having no husband."

"That's hardly your fault." Just the mention of the man who had treated her so poorly made his fists clench.

"I know, but it doesn't change the circumstances. Nor how people view me and my child."

He caught her hand and held it tight. "Not now. You have a husband and your baby has a father, Mrs. Russell."

She turned her palm to his and squeezed hard. "It's a generous thing you do for me."

"But?" He'd heard the hesitation in her voice.

"Don't get me wrong. I appreciate that you are willing to give my child a name, but he will grow up without a father."

"Do you want to renegotiate our agreement?" He did his best to keep his tone neutral but wasn't sure he succeeded. He shouldn't have spoken those words. He wasn't ready to open his heart to pain. Though they might be able to maintain this marriage on the basis of mutual convenience and allow him to keep his heart safely sheltered.

"I know you're not serious." She got to her feet. "I think I might be able to sleep now."

That was her answer. A wise one.

They returned to the camp. He waited until she settled in the tent before he stretched out under the wagon. He didn't expect to sleep, but the exertions of the day caught up to him and he didn't waken until Warren kicked his booted foot. "Time to get up, lazy bones."

He was instantly awake and scrambled from under the wagon. He glanced about and didn't see Donna Grace. Mary Mae eased out of the tent and held her finger to her lips. "She's still asleep. I thought I'd leave her until breakfast is ready."

The men slipped away. Nearby, Reverend Shepton spoke to Buck. "It's Sunday. Are we going to rest as the Lord commanded?"

Buck shook his head. "Not unless you want to risk encountering snow before we get to Santa Fe."

Luke acknowledged something he hadn't even admitted to himself. This late in the season, crossing the mountains would be a real challenge and the risk of snow was almost certain. Was it possible he could persuade Donna Grace and Mary Mae to spend the winter at Bent's Fort?

"Reverend, you're welcome to have a service this evening. If people want to attend that's their choice.

But I won't have our departure delayed this morning."
Buck strode away to make sure all the wagons were
ready to leave as soon as breakfast was over.

Warren and Luke checked their freight wagons and
spoke to the teamsters. The load had shifted in one
wagon and it took some time to rearrange it. One of
the drivers complained he had drunk bad water and
was feeling weak. Warren and Luke always hired on an
extra driver or two to cover for illness and injury and
even death. So the ailing driver was told to spend the
day resting in a wagon and another driver took his
place.

By the time they returned to camp, breakfast was
ready and waiting. And Luke was more than ready to
partake. Donna Grace was up and looking just fine.
Yes indeed, just fine, with her black hair brushed back
into some sort of roll, encircling her head like a
crown. She had alabaster skin with a hint of rose.

"Good to see you're no worse for yesterday's
activities."

"I'm alive and well. The baby is kicking up a storm.
He just gave an extra hard kick when he heard you.
The sun is shining. All is right with the world."

"I think we might be in for a hot day."

"Be that as it may, I don't intend to complain about
one single thing."

He grinned. "Not even the mosquitoes or the dust?"

"Nope. Not even them." She swatted at a pesky fly.

The others laughed at her good humor. Although
Reverend Shepton wasn't happy about traveling on

the Lord's Day, he couldn't resist Donna Grace's determination to enjoy the day.

"We can sing as we walk," she said.

And so the reverend led them in song after song as they followed the never-ending trail.

Luke's prediction about the heat had been correct, and by mid-afternoon, he convinced Donna Grace to ride under the shelter of the canvas of the wagon, though the heat inside would be dreadful as well.

He glanced skyward. Buck rode by. He studied the sky as well. "I don't like it." They both knew heat like this, even in October, often led to thunderstorms.

"Push on," Buck said. "I'd like to make camp before the weather turns."

Luke was the lead wagon and he sent the mules into a trot.

Donna Grace groaned and came to join him at the front. "What's the hurry?"

"Storm coming and we want to make camp before it hits."

She poked her head out to look. "How can you predict a storm when there isn't even a cloud in the sky?"

"I've traveled these prairies before and know what to expect." Wind buffeted them. "See the wind has already picked up."

"I love storms."

He chuckled. "You might not think they're so much fun if this turns out to be a vicious one."

"I'll still enjoy it."

He laughed. "What's gotten into you today? From the first, you want only to enjoy every minute, now you're set to appreciate a storm."

Her smile widened. "So long as we are all safe, why not delight in the power of nature?"

He shook his head. The wind increased with every turn of the wheels. The mules were pulling as fast as they could. He glanced back and saw the others were doing their best to keep up.

The spot where they would camp lay ahead and he turned his wagon. Warren and the reverend quickly pulled into place and the freighters caught up and formed a tight circle. The teamsters knew what to expect and staked the wagons into place. They scrambled to secure any loose objects. He and Warren did the same, calling out to the others. "Make sure everything is tied down."

Donna Grace hurried about doing what she could to help. She stopped and stared at the sky. "It's turned cold."

"Listen to the thunder rolling over the plain." At this point it was distant but that would soon change.

Mary Mae caught a towel that blew out of the Russell wagon and took it to Judith who was arranging things in the wagon.

And then the first cold drops of rain stung. "Head for cover," Luke called.

Some of the freighters had hunkered down beneath the wagons, seeking protection under sheets of canvas. Others climbed into crowded wagons and tied the flaps shut. He didn't see where Buck, Warren or Gil went but they had sense enough to seek shelter somewhere.

The reverend and his wife hastened into their wagon. Judith grabbed Mary Mae's hands and pulled her inside the Russell wagon.

Luke helped Donna Grace into her wagon and glanced about. The Russell wagon would be crowded. Could he make it to cover with one of the teamsters? He knew he couldn't. And he didn't want to leave Donna Grace on her own.

Without waiting for an invite, he climbed into the back and closed the flap.

The wind rocked the wagon and roared like a crazed animal.

He settled down on the wagon floor. Donna Grace faced him in the narrow space. Both had their legs stretched out. He couldn't help but press his against hers.

The heavens opened and the rain descended, driven by gale force winds.

Donna Grace's eyes widened and she hugged her arms about her.

"Still think storms are enjoyable?" he asked, with a chuckle.

"Will it get worse?" She didn't sound as certain as she had a short time ago about enjoying the power of nature.

He didn't want to frighten her, but he'd seen winds lift a wagon clear off its axles. He'd seen hailstones the size of walnuts shred the canvas of the wagons and leave the occupants and belongings exposed to the vicious elements.

"I hope not, but all we can do is sit it out."

"I might get hungry if this lasts too long," she grumbled.

"I'm a little hungry myself. Do you have anything in here, or is all the food in the locker on the outside?"

She gave him a teasing look. "I might have something." She eased past him to a crate at the back of the wagon and pulled out a sack. Just then a flash of lightning lit up the inside of wagon. Deafening thunder followed immediately. His scalp tingled with the electricity in the air.

With a little squeal, she dropped to his side and buried her face in his chest.

He laughed as he cradled her head. "Still like storms?"

"Not this one." She shivered. "Did we get hit?"

"I don't think so."

She sat up. "I hope everyone else is safe."

"I'll check."

She caught him. "Don't go out there."

With a pleased chuckle, he pulled her close. "I meant when the storm lets up." If not for the dangers to man and beast, he could almost wish it would last several hours. There was something cozy and intimate about the two of them being shut up together.

He wondered if she felt the same, but he wouldn't ask for fear of spoiling the moment.

## 7

Donna Grace shivered. Not that she was cold, pressed to Luke's warm chest, but the strobes of flashing light and answering thunder shook her. She'd never seen or heard anything like it. They'd had rain and thunder storms on the trip to St. Louis with Papa, but she couldn't recall them sounding so furious.

"Did you find some food?" he asked, his words a comforting rumble against her ear.

A flood of heat raced up her throat as she realized how shamelessly she clung to the poor man. She eased as far away as possible which meant their shoulders still touched, and she allowed herself to steal courage from this physical contact.

She found the sack of biscuits where she had dropped them and handed him one. She took one as well, and bit into it as rain pelted the canvas and the storm thundered on. Water dripped from the ropes at the front closure, but she ignored it. There was nothing to do but wait for the rain to quit, and then put the wet things out to dry.

Another clap of thunder almost deafened her and the baby kicked a protest. She pressed her palm to her tummy. "Settle down, little one. You're safe in there."

"Does the noise frighten him?"

"I suppose it does." She smiled. "He settled when he heard your voice."

"Then I shall keep on talking." A silent moment. "What should I talk about?"

"Tell me about what it was like growing up."

"Okay. I can do that. There were the three of us. We were always good friends and played together."

"Sounds nice."

"It was. I remember a time when I was maybe eight, so Judith would have been four or five and Warren almost twelve. It was a special day, though I can't remember the occasion." He paused. "Wait. I do remember. It was the day Pa paid the last bank payment on the farm. Anyway, Pa was so happy. He said the next day was to be a special day. It started as soon as we got up in the morning. He told us to get ready. We were going for an all-day picnic. It didn't take us long to gather up blankets and help Ma with the food. And then we got in the wagon and went to the river. We found a place with a wide, grassy bank and Ma and Pa laughed together and played with us all that day. After lunch they said they needed to rest and lay down on a blanket, Pa holding Ma close. We all lay down beside them crowded together on the blanket. I will never forget that feeling. I don't even know how to describe it—the sun was warm overhead, but I was just as warm, in a place deep inside, behind my heart."

She waited for the roll of thunder to fade so she could be heard. "Luke, that's beautiful."

"I wanted that with a wife and family of my own, but it was not to be." His voice broke and she found his hand and squeezed it.

"You're young yet. There's still time to fulfill your dreams."

"I think that time has passed."

"How can you say that? It's like you have given up on yourself." She propped herself up on one elbow to study him. She saw something in his eyes he would most certainly deny if she mentioned it, so she kept the information to herself. But in that man who had shut his heart to the future, she saw the remnant of a dream. It flickered, as if hidden by a breeze-fluttering curtain, so that she couldn't tell what shape the dream took.

"You want another biscuit?" she asked.

"Please."

They lounged side by side, slowly eating. While she chewed, she tried to find a way to get him to tell more about himself.

"Did you always want to be a farmer?" she asked.

"I was always a farm boy. From the time I was four, I helped my Pa do chores. Pa gave me my first calf when I was six. I sold that calf and bought my first horse. I had dreams of raising a fine line of horses. By the time I was sixteen, I had six mares and a stallion with good blood lines."

"Where are your horses now?"

"I left them. Walked away after Ellen's death and never looked back."

"But surely someone is taking care of them."

"Maybe Pa is."

"You aren't the least bit curious about their welfare?"

"That part of my life is over and done with."

The baby kicked a protest. She had to agree with the little one. Luke sounded more defeated than determined.

She finished her biscuit. "Luke, how long do you plan to trade back and forth on the Santa Fe Trail?"

He stiffened and that little movement convinced her that it was a question he avoided.

"There's good money in trading," he said.

She knew that. Her papa had made lots of money the same way, but she wondered if Luke realized how defensive he sounded. As if he had to convince himself. "I don't see you as the sort of man who wants to simply accumulate wealth. You must have something you want to do with your money."

He stared up at the sodden canvas of the wagon. "Hadn't really thought of it."

She knew he was avoiding the truth, but decided to let it go. "Melvin gave me a sum of money. Guilt money, I call it, but I took it. I knew I would need help to start over again."

"What is your dream for your money?"

"Buy a house, take in boarders and feed travelers so I can provide for myself and my baby. But if I was a man, I would go west and buy land. I'd build a house and start a ranch. I'd raise cows and feed all those people who are going west to look for gold." She sighed. "I once said something like that to Grandfather Ramos and he punished me for talking so foolishly." Her laugh was half sigh. "Guess that's why I've never told anyone else. Only you."

He nudged his shoulder to hers. "I guess we both have to live with second best dreams."

"You don't. And all that matters to me now is making a safe and secure home for my baby. For him, I will do whatever it takes."

"Like marrying a stranger."

"Yes, like that. I would do it again if I had to."

He chuckled. "I sure hope I'm not going to have to drive away another man offering to marry you."

She jabbed his ribs. "You suit my purposes very well."

"You don't think you deserve better?"

"Let me think about that. Better than a man willing to marry me simply so I can travel on this wagon train. A man willing to let my baby have his name and even willing to protect me with his own life. Nope. I think I did good when I chose you."

"When you chose me?" He sputtered. "I don't

remember it that way at all."

"Really? How do you remember it?"

Their faces were mere inches apart. "Donna Grace, the way I remember it is I saw a lady in distress and knew I could help. I'm glad I did."

"Me too."

His gaze deepened, searched hers. She considered throwing open the doors of her heart. But instead, stared at the canvas overhead noting the darkening lines where the water had thoroughly soaked the material. She wasn't ready to risk her heart and happiness to a man. It was enough that he enabled her to get to Santa Fe. And although she was grateful he might have saved her life, that didn't mean anything. It wasn't because he valued her. Only that he was trying to atone for Ellen's death.

Nor did he seem inclined to look at their relationship any differently, apart from his offhand remark about renegotiating their agreement. As if they were discussing the rental of a piece of property.

Why was she even thinking this? They were both happy with the arrangement, and if she felt weepy and vulnerable it was only because she had a baby to think about.

～

"THE STORM HAS PASSED," Luke said. The space inside the wagon had grown damp and close. Donna Grace's questions had uncovered fragments of his dreams that he thought were long dead. He didn't care what became of that farm he'd bought. Whether or not Pa sold it, Luke would never return to the place of so much pain. But Donna Grace's questions about his horses sent his mind into a gallop. The mares might well have had a foal or two since he left. Unless Pa had sold them.

But life couldn't be lived hankering after the past, or wishing for things that might have been.

"I'll see how the others fared." He scrambled from the wagon hoping to outdistance the useless thoughts. But his mind simply changed direction and went to the note he'd shoved into the bottom of his bag. *There is land here a plenty. Great for cattle.* Wouldn't that be exactly what Donna Grace would want? However, her life had taken her a different direction. Just as his had.

He stopped at the closest wagon. "Judith, Mary Mae, are you both okay?"

Two heads poked out.

"Wasn't that something?" Judith said.

"I was scared half out of my wits," Mary Mae added. "Were you with Donna Grace?"

He nodded.

"I hoped that was the case. I didn't want to think of her alone. Is she okay?"

Donna Grace stuck her head out of her wagon. "I'm fine."

Luke moved on to the Shepton wagon. They, too, had weathered the storm well. He moved down the line and was joined by Warren, Gil and Buck. The canvas had torn on one wagon and soaked the contents. It would have to be repaired before they moved on. Apart from that, damage was minimal.

He and Warren headed back to the muddy camp where the women were doing their best to prepare a meal in the growing darkness. They all had a store of dry wood under their wagons, so soon a fire had them warmed up, and a big pot of tea ready for their enjoyment. The rest of the meal took longer to prepare. It was fully dark by the time they filled their plates. The ground was too muddy to sit on, so they stood by the warmth of the fire.

"I had wished we could gather and worship together," the reverend said. "But it's getting late and I know you're all anxious to get your rest."

"Maybe God has already spoken to us," Donna Grace said. "In the power of the storm and in His protection."

"Amen." Reverend Shepton lifted his arms to signal for attention.

Luke hoped they weren't going to be required to listen to an hour-long sermon. He had nothing against preaching, but the night was lengthening and everyone needed to get some sleep.

The reverend pulled a Bible from his breast pocket and leaned close to the fire for light to read by. "Let me share this one verse: Psalm 107, verses 29 and 30. 'He maketh the storm a calm, so that the waves thereof are still. Then are they glad because they be quiet; so he bringeth them unto their desired haven.'" He closed the Good Book. "May God bring us all to our desired haven. God bless each one of us and grant us sleep."

It took a moment for Luke to realize the man was done. It was the shortest sermon he'd ever heard and likely the most appropriate.

Luke knew it would be a miserable night for all of them, with no dry place to set up a tent and the insides of the wagons damp from water leaking through the canvas. He wanted to suggest that Donna Grace should get the best selection, but guessed she would resent his interference on the matter, so he held his peace.

Donna Grace and Mary Mae climbed into their wagon. Judith into the Russell's.

Luke chose to sleep under the Clark wagon, even though it had a puddle under one wheel. He wanted to be close to Donna Grace. He knew he was being overly concerned, but the events of the last couple days had left him on edge.

He wrapped in a slicker and prepared for a long, uncomfortable night.

The wagon rocked as one of the girls shifted.

"You're taking up too much room," Mary Mae complained.

"Tell that to your niece or nephew."

Luke grinned. "Ladies, go to sleep."

"There you go, listening in on my conversation again." If Donna Grace meant to sound annoyed she failed.

He heard giggling. "Good night, Donna Grace.

Good night, Mary Mae."

"Good night, Luke," they said in unison.

More rustling around and then quiet.

Luke lay on the cold ground, waiting for morning. He crossed his arms under his head. Donna Grace's words spoken during the storm came to him. *I did good when I chose you.* She'd only been teasing, but her words were at such odds with what Ellen's father had said. *She deserved better than you.* Which one did he believe? Or were both wrong, and he simply had to continue on his way alone, and bereft of dreams?

THE MUD LINGERED the next morning as Luke and Warren hurried away to catch the animals and get them into their harnesses. By then breakfast was prepared. Polly and Sam joined them. Everyone but Polly seemed unusually quiet and inclined to be irritable.

"I slept in the wagon," Polly said, bouncing on the balls of her feet. "Uncle slept under the wagon. I wish I had a cat or dog to sleep with." She eyed the old hound that followed the wagon train. Far as Luke knew, he belonged to no one but simply made himself at home. He kept the wolves away, and barked a warning when he thought things weren't right.

"He's no pet," Luke said before Polly could suggest she would like the hound to be one.

"How do you know?" Polly demanded.

"Polly, your manners," Sam reminded quietly.

"I'm sorry." But she continued to study Luke. He wondered what the child was thinking, but she soon let him know. "I expect he would like to be someone's special friend." She ducked her head and concentrated on her breakfast before anyone could argue.

Luke looked toward Donna Grace hoping she would be cheerful, but she dragged about with her face full of weariness. He caught her arm as she passed. "Didn't you sleep well?"

"No. I kept jerking awake thinking I heard thunder." She slanted him a narrow-eyed look. "It might have been someone snoring."

He held his palms toward her. "Not me. I don't snore. It must have been Warren."

Warren grunted. "I heard the same sound, so you can't blame me. Dreadful, wasn't it?"

Gil strode by in time to hear the conversation. He stopped and leaned back on his mud-crusted boots. "I came running with my rifle, certain some wild animal was tearing at a hunk of meat. Took me a moment to realize it came from that direction." He pointed under the Clark wagon.

Luke groaned. "Seems a man can't sleep in peace around here."

Laughing, Donna Grace refilled his coffee cup. "Quite the opposite. A man can sleep, but his traveling companions cannot."

The others joined in laughter.

"Buck is anxious to get traveling," Gil said, before he hurried away.

"I won't mind leaving this muddy place behind," Donna Grace said as he helped her to the wagon seat.

He could have warned her they might see more mud and rain, but what was the point? She would have to cope with whatever the weather might bring, just as they all would.

The ground steamed as they returned to the trail. By noon, the heat sucked away the moisture of the previous night's rain, and left both man and beast sweltering under the sun.

Donna Grace asked to get down and walk, but soon the heat proved too much and she asked to ride.

"Would you like to get in the back?" He thought she might sleep.

"No. It's like an oven back there." She scanned the sky from horizon to horizon. "Is this likely to bring up another storm like we had yesterday?"

"It's hard to say. The animals would welcome rain. This heat is hard on them."

She pulled a handkerchief from her pocket and wiped her brow. "I can't decide which is worse—lightning, thunder and mud, or this searing heat." She slumped into lethargy, her hand pressed to her stomach.

She groaned softly.

"What is it?" he asked.

"Nothing to be concerned about."

He watched her out of the corner of his eye. Was she merely uncomfortable, or was her time approaching?

## 8

Donna Grace would not complain. But the heat
sucked the energy from her. Her hip hurt from
being thrown to the ground. And she hadn't slept well.
On top of that, the constant roughness of the trail
bounced her around and exhausted her. What she
wouldn't give for a chair that didn't move, and a soft
bed to lay upon.

She tried walking again, but her back hurt and the
heat left her feeling ill. The poor oxen. Their tongues
hung out and they looked about ready to collapse.
Noon provided no relief, except she could sit down
and not be jostled for a few minutes.

Late in the afternoon, Buck called a halt even
though they could have traveled longer. "Don't circle
the wagons," he said.

Luke explained what Buck meant to do. "The

animals can't continue. We'll stop here and have supper, then go on after dark."

She bit her bottom lip to keep from crying.

Luke helped her down from the wagon and kept his hands on her shoulders until she lifted her head to meet his gaze. He touched his fingers to the corner of her eyes and trapped a tear. "What's wrong?"

She tried to smile, but knew it was more a grimace. "Besides the heat and the constant jolting of the wagon, nothing." She blinked her eyes clear and straightened. "I'm just a little tired."

He led her to the shady side of the wagon. "Wait here." He disappeared from view.

She leaned against the wheel, too weary to think or move.

He returned with the buffalo robe and spread it at her feet. "Have a rest while you can."

"I need to help with supper." Did he not understand she had responsibilities?

He crossed his arms and gave her a hard look. "I explained the situation and the women all insisted you should rest."

She remained standing even though the idea of stretching out on that soft fur bed beckoned. "I should be doing my share."

"Donna Grace, stop resisting."

"I hate being so much trouble," she murmured.

"I am not your Grandfather Ramos."

She jerked her attention to him. Saw an expression

she couldn't interpret. "I didn't ever think you were. That would be an unkind assessment."

"Then don't expect me to have the same opinion as him."

To do anything now, but accept his offer—or was it an order?—would make him think she put him in the same category as her grandfather. "Very well." She paused and touched his arm. "Thank you. You are a kind man."

Was it hope she saw in his eyes? If so, she would offer him more. "I am not like the man who was to be your father-in-law. I do not see you as not good enough." Before she could further embarrass herself, she sank to the buffalo robe.

He hurried away. Poor man. She had made him uncomfortable. What a strange pair they were. He was running from a painful past and words that hurt him deeply. She was determined to be all her baby needed, despite how often she'd been told she was nothing but a nuisance.

She pressed her hand to her belly as the baby turned. "Shh. Shh," she murmured, hoping to persuade the little one to settle and let its mama rest.

The aroma of food wakened her and she stretched. Her stomach rumbled. It had been too hot at the noon break to eat and she was starving. She scrambled to her feet and went past the Shepton's wagon to join the others at the Russell wagon where they all hovered in the meager shade and avoided getting too close to the fire.

Mary Mae sprang up at her approach. "Are you feeling better? Did you sleep? Luke said you weren't feeling well."

"I'm fine. The rest did me good." Even as she reassured her sister, her gaze went to Luke.

He watched her with hooded eyes. What did he see? A woman heavy with child who had caused him considerable inconvenience from the first day?

Or—?

She shook her head. She would not pine for someone to cherish her the way she already cherished her child. Loving her child would provide the only love she needed or wanted.

They ate at a leisurely pace and remained against the wagon as the shadows lengthened. The setting of the sun provided marginal relief from the heat.

Buck rode by. "Let's move."

Donna Grace couldn't have said whether she preferred the rough wagon ride to walking, but Luke pointed out it was too dark for her to walk safely. "You might stumble and fall."

So she pressed her hand to her lower back and gritted her teeth, hoping no one would notice, and with Luke's help climbed aboard for more jolting. But she soon discovered it was rather pleasant riding at night. The moon cast silvery shadows across the path. The rattle of wagon and harness seemed muted. In the distance came a series of howls and barks that she knew from her previous trip were wolves in the distance.

The dog growled low in his throat and dashed into the darkness. From one of the freighters rang out a warning call. "Dog, get back here before they eat you up."

"Wolves." She shivered. "When we came this way with Papa, an old trapper told a gruesome story about wolves catching his mules and eating them. I insisted on sleeping by our mules for days."

"You weren't afraid the wolves would get you?" Luke asked with amusement.

"I was prepared to defend the mules from any wolves." She laughed softly. "Of course it helped that Papa slept beside me with his rifle right handy."

He laughed at her admission. "It's easy to be brave with a papa and gun to protect you."

"I never thought he would leave me to manage on my own." It hurt that he'd abandoned them.

"You aren't alone. Have you forgotten I'm here?"

For now, she silently added.

"When I get to Santa Fe, I will have my baby and Mary Mae."

"What about your grandfather Ramos? Don't you think he would help you?"

She grunted. "I hope he doesn't hear I'm there. Though he will probably ignore me as a shame and a disgrace to his name."

"I'm sorry he's so unfair to you."

Luke's acknowledgement of the situation went a long way toward erasing the hurt of it.

He wrapped an arm about her shoulders. "I'm sorry

your papa has disappointed you. I'm sorry that man pretended he could be your husband. I fear you have every reason to think men are not to be trusted."

She knew she should say she trusted him, but she couldn't bring herself to utter the words. Trust required she let go of all the fences she had built around her heart and she wasn't prepared to do that.

"I hope you can see me as an exception," he murmured.

Still she did not answer. She couldn't. She daren't. To trust a man, meant letting him control her future. Her baby's future mattered more than anything a man could promise her.

On the pretense that she needed to adjust her boot, she eased away from his embrace. She knew her lack of response hurt him. Likely made him believe she didn't think him good enough. But that wasn't the case. He was a good man. He deserved a good woman.

Sometime later her head fell forward and she jerked awake. "How long before we stop?"

"I don't know. Gil and Buck must have a place in mind they want us to reach. Rest your head on my shoulder if you want."

She couldn't. She shouldn't. But she was too tired to argue with her body and put her head on his shoulder. He wrapped an arm about her, and held her tight.

Safe in his arms, she slept until Buck rode by. "We'll spend the night here."

She jerked awake.

Somehow, in the faint light of a gibbous moon, the

men managed to get the wagons into a circle. The animals were taken to the nearby creek to water.

Luke put up a tent and Donna Grace and Mary Mae crawled inside and fell into an exhausted sleep.

THEY WERE UP BEFORE DAWN, eating a hurried breakfast. Luke and Warren barely paused to eat, too busy getting animals hitched up.

The sun had barely broken over the western horizon when they began the day's journey. It promised to be another hot day. Mary Mae and Judith walked, saying it was cooler a distance from the animals and dust, but Donna Grace couldn't think of putting one foot in front of the other, weary mile after weary mile. She rode in the wagon until it grew too warm, then she joined Luke on the seat. She would not complain. She would not indicate how uncomfortable she was. Everyone else faced the same unrelenting heat and dust and movement.

But oh, she was grateful when it was time for the noon break and Luke again spread the buffalo robe in the shade for her.

She awoke when Mary Mae nudged her. "You better eat something before we move on."

Donna Grace shook herself awake. "How long did I sleep?"

"Not long."

"I am so sorry. I've been shirking my share of the chores."

Mary Mae handed her some biscuits and cold beans. "We talked about it, and all of the women agree you should be free of any duties until you feel better."

Donna Grace struggled to her feet, her food forgotten. "I can't allow that. I have to do my share."

Mary Mae pushed her back. Judith and Mrs. Shepton overheard them and came forward. "There are plenty of us to do the work," Judith assured her.

"You must take care of yourself in order to give your baby the best birthing." Mrs. Shepton's counsel caused Donna Grace to sink back to the fur.

"I am such a nuisance to everyone."

"Nonsense," Mrs. Shepton spoke with firm conviction. "You are doing the most important job of any of us."

Mary Mae remained at Donna Grace's side as the others moved away. "Now eat up. You need your strength." She waited until Donna Grace started eating. "I know Grandfather said unkind things to you when we had to live with him, but why do you still believe him? Why did you ever believe him?"

Donna Grace kept her attention on her food for a moment. "Am I really so obvious?"

"Only to me."

*And to Luke,* but she didn't say it aloud. "I sound like a pathetic whining woman, don't I?"

Mary Mae burst out laughing. When she could finally speak, she turned to Donna Grace, her words overflowing with amusement. "I think pathetic and whining would be the last words that come to mind when people think of you."

"Really? So what would the first be?"

"Strong, independent, responsible, kind... oh and did I almost forget?—determined." Mary Mae hugged her, then took away her empty dish, laughing as she went back to the other women.

The camp dog sat down a few feet away and watched her.

"What's your opinion, dog?"

The animal tilted his head to one side and looked at her hand.

She chuckled. "Only one thing matters to you... food." She tossed him the bit of biscuit she held.

Polly trotted over and sat close to the dog.

Remembering Luke's warning that the dog would not make a pet, she thought to warn the child to move away, but Polly simply watched the animal.

"No one knows his name," she said. "He needs an important name, so I'm going to call him Mister King. How do you like your name, Mister King?"

The dog rose and walked away without so much as a backward look.

"I think he likes it," Polly said and skipped after him.

Donna Grace chuckled.

"Good to see you feeling better." Luke spoke from the front of the wagon.

"I shouldn't be letting people spoil me like this."

He came round to squat in front of her. "What

makes you think you don't deserve it?"

"I didn't say—"

"You didn't have to." Not waiting for her to respond, he held out his hand. "It's time to move."

～

IF LUKE ever met this Mr. Ramos who had said such critical things to Donna Grace, he wasn't sure what he'd do, but somehow he would make the man understand just how unfair and wrong he was.

He helped Donna Grace to the wagon seat and put away the buffalo robe. Not that informing the man would undo the damage his words had done. If she would give him a chance, he would help by giving her all she needed and deserved.

At least until they reached their destination and then they would go their separate ways. She to raise a child on her own, he to continue making the journey back and forth along the Santa Fe Trail. Not many days ago, he had been content with that future, but thanks to Donna Grace's probing, he wondered how long he would be interested in making the trip.

He had enough money saved up and stored in a safe place to buy some of that land in California. And cows like Donna Grace wanted. Horses that he wanted.

He stopped at the side of the wagon and pressed a fist to his forehead. What was he thinking? Foolishness and empty dreams. That's what.

Warning himself to remember how much it hurt to care strongly about anyone, he held his silence for the first hour of the trip until several antelope raced alongside them and stopped to watch. "See them?"

Donna Grace sat up to peer past him. "They are such graceful creatures. I love to watch them run."

"Did you know they are the fastest animal in North America?"

"I'm not surprised. But how do you know?"

"We had a naturalist on one of our trips and he told us all sorts of things about the plants and animals around us."

"Such as?"

For the better part of the afternoon he told her the things he'd learned and she listened in fascination until Buck rode up.

"Looks like a storm coming, but thanks to our travel last night, we're going to make it to Council Grove." He rode on by to inform the others.

"Council Grove! Why we've only begun our journey," Donna Grace said. "Yet I feel like we've been on the road forever. I feel like I've known our traveling companions almost as long."

He wondered if she included him in the feeling. In a normal marriage he could say they would be together for always. For the first time, he let himself think how he'd miss her company when they went their separate ways.

They set up camp near the cluster of trees at Council Grove. Earlier in the season the place would be a gathering place for wagon trains headed on other trails. However, they were the only ones there. Seems everyone had the good sense not to head to Oregon this late in the year. Going toward New Mexico took them through safer climates.

Again, the thought of crossing the Sangre De Cristo Mountains in November, or even December, with Donna Grace and Mary Mae troubled Luke. Could he persuade them to spend the winter at Bent's Fort?

The storm held off as they made camp and the women prepared food. Remembering the challenge of trying to cook in the rain and mud of a couple of nights ago, they set about making enough food to last a few meals.

Donna Grace seemed to feel well enough to assist the women. Or, he thought with a bit of resignation, she simply wouldn't stand by and not help, no matter how she felt.

She was unaware he watched her from beyond the wagons or she wouldn't have pressed her hand to her back. No one else noticed, but he promised himself he would make an opportunity to speak to Mrs. Shepton about Donna Grace.

They enjoyed a pleasant meal, despite the black clouds building in the west. And then knowing what to expect, the women quickly put everything away. He and Warren made sure the wagons were chained together. The teamsters were experienced and had everything battened down.

Judith called to Mary Mae. "Why don't you climb in with me like last time?" She sent Luke a look that informed him he should stay with Donna Grace. He had no objection and shrugged.

Warren had already joined his friend Sam with Polly.

"Is it alright if I share the protection of your wagon?" he asked Donna Grace.

"Seems we have no choice."

"That doesn't sound very welcoming," The first drops of rain came, soft and gentle, so unlike the previous storm. He didn't climb inside. If she didn't want him there he would shelter with one of the teamsters.

"Get in before you get wet," she said.

He scurried inside and closed the flap. The rain pattered against the canvas, almost like a lullaby. He sat with his back against the gate, his legs pulled up so he didn't crowd Donna Grace.

She moaned and rubbed at her hip.

"How badly bruised are you?"

"It's nothing." She folded her hands in her lap, but despite her attempt at a smile, her eyes revealed pain.

"Would you admit anything else?" He waited, but she didn't answer. "I saw how you pressed your hand to your back out there. I recall how Warren's wife said it got worse just before her time."

She pressed her palms to her stomach. "My baby isn't coming until Santa Fe."

He longed to point out she couldn't stop the baby

simply because she wanted to. There were so many things he wanted to say to her. How he admired her courage and determination. How he wanted to take care of her. He didn't feel he had the right to say any of those things, but one thing he did want to talk about— the dangers of trying to cross the mountains this late in the year. He knew better than to come at it directly.

"I'm having a hard time understanding why you want to go to Santa Fe when you know you will undoubtedly encounter your grandfather."

"I already told you that I don't expect he will bother me." She relaxed and smiled. "The happiest I've ever been was in Santa Fe." Her smile disappeared. "Until Grandfather Ramos interfered." A beat of silence and then she smiled. "I had a best friend there. Rosa Garcia. The best friend I ever had. I could tell her anything. We made plans to start a ranch together." She chuckled. "We figured we would never marry. Guess I should have kept that promise." She fell silent.

"What happened to your friend?"

"Grandfather Ramos." The bitter tone of her voice made Luke shudder.

"What did he do?"

She pulled in a long breath and released it slowly before she answered. "Mama let me play with Rosa. We often played in the plaza along with the other children. One day Rosa and I were there when Grandfather rode up on his big black stallion. He saw me. 'No Ramos plays in the plaza with street urchins.' He used a Spanish word but I knew exactly what he meant. I grabbed Rosa's hand and told him she was my friend. He rode his horse toward us. Real close. I held tight to Rosa and backed away but he kept coming and forced us to step apart and then he herded me home like a wayward mule." Tears glistened in her eyes.

Luke pulled her into his arms. "That was very unkind."

She nodded against his chest. "I was so angry. He told Mama I was not allowed to run free like a wild animal. When he left, I told Mama I hated him. 'You must never hate your grandfather,' she said. 'God would not want you to.' 'Maybe I don't care,' I said back."

Donna Grace found Luke's hand and clung to it. "Mama said that made her very sad. She said knowing and trusting God had enabled her to live the life she chose and still honor her father. 'He clings to the old ways and cannot see that they will not last.'" Donna Grace sighed. "I try not to hate my grandfather, but it's hard."

"Where is Rosa now?"

Donna Grace stared straight ahead. "I don't know. I never saw her again after that day."

"How is that possible?"

"Her family moved away the next day. I think Grandfather somehow made them leave."

"I'm sorry you lost your friend." Señor Ramos seemed more and more a harsh, unfeeling man who had taught Donna Grace to mistrust men. "No wonder you have a hard time believing any man would see you for who you truly are." He knew the moment the words were out he should not have spoken them. He wasn't prepared to put into words what he thought. Wasn't even sure he could. To stop her from responding to his comment, he asked another question.

"I'm going to guess that was the worst day of your life. What was the best?"

She tipped her head back against his shoulder. "The day Mama died and Grandfather made us go home with him was equally bad. As to my best day… " After a long pause she spoke again. "I don't think I've had it yet."

"Maybe it will come while we are on this trip."

"Maybe." She sounded less than convinced. "I think I know what your worst day was."

"If you refer to Ellen's murder, you're right." He couldn't even talk of it without his voice cracking.

"What's your happiest day?"

He had to think about it. "At one time I would have said when I bought that farm, but now it seems mean-ingless. Or when Ellen agreed to marry me, but we'd grown up together, and we just knew we belonged together. I told you about the day Ma and Pa took us on a picnic. That, I guess, is the happiest day so far."

She chuckled. "Maybe you'll have a happy moment on our trip. Something that will shine in your memory so when you're asked in the future what was the best moment of your life, you'll know it for sure."

He liked the idea of something so special it would

shine in his thoughts. But looking for that sort of occasion would only lead to disappointment. "I'm happy just doing what I need to do each day."

They fell into silence broken by the pat-pat-splash of rain on canvas. He shifted to peer out the opening. The sky had darkened to gunmetal grey. "It shows no sign of letting up." The best they could do was stay right where they were. What would Donna Grace think of him spending the night in the wagon with her?

"It's dark already." Was it doubt he heard in her voice, or caution?

"Do you want me to leave?"

She sat up and stared at him in the grey light. "If you go out, you'll get soaked to the skin. Besides, where would you go?"

"I'm sure I could find room in one of the freight wagons."

She laughed, though it seemed full of disbelief. "You think anyone is going to welcome you all dripping wet?"

"Are you saying I can stay here until the rain lets up? You're comfortable with that?"

"We are married, after all. As to comfort, I haven't enjoyed that since we started our journey."

He understood she referred to her physical discomfort, but he couldn't help wondering if she might also mean the discomfort of their unusual marriage. At this point there wasn't anything either of them could do.

# 9

Donna Grace shifted to one side and tried to get comfortable. Luke had gone to the back of the wagon and stretched out, now snoring softly. His feet butted into her. She tried not to disturb him as she sought for a position that would allow her to sleep, but the ache in her back would not let up. And the baby turned and kicked, as if it, too, sought a comfortable position.

Accepting she would not sleep, she listened to the continuing rain. The cooler weather made the journey easier for the animals, but she could almost cry at the thought of contending with more mud.

The words of the song Luke liked to sing came to her. One stanza in particular played over and over in her head. *Your bountiful care what tongue can recite?* God did care for her. She no longer doubted it. Nor could she say when she came to that conclusion. Perhaps when she realized she had a child, but no husband, and knew she would have to be father and mother for her baby. Or perhaps it was when Papa had so disappointed her. She smiled into the dark. Part of it might have been when Luke offered to marry her. Had God put him there in the right place at the right time? Somehow it was a comforting thought and she fell asleep.

She wakened as Luke got up. "Has it stopped raining?" she asked.

"I believe it has. Come and see."

She joined him at the end of the wagon. Sun glistened off drops of water on every blade of grass, on every leaf clinging to the trees and on the spokes of every wheel. "It's beautiful," she whispered. "Like God has kissed the world."

He draped an arm about her shoulders and sang softly. "'Your bountiful care what tongue can recite? It breathes in the air, it shines in the light.'"

She caught his hand as it lay on her shoulder. The world was fresh and clean and she felt invigorated and ready to face whatever it brought. "This might be one of those moments."

"What do you mean?"

She turned to look into his face. "I'll always remember this special morning when God's love and care shines in the light."

His brown eyes darkened and his smile widened. "Me too."

Mary Mae and Judith climbed down from the

Russell wagon and started breakfast preparations, while Luke jumped down and reached up to help Donna Grace.

The ground was wet from the rain but the grass underfoot kept it from being muddy. Besides, even mud wouldn't dampen her spirits this morning, and she eagerly joined the other women as they gathered about the fire. She made coffee while Mary Mae set a pot of cornmeal to cook and Judith fried bacon. Mrs. Shepton tended potatoes in a fry pan.

Warren and Luke came for breakfast, Polly and Sam on their heels.

Donna Grace studied them. "Why so downcast?"

Warren answered her question. "The river has risen twenty-five feet overnight. We won't be able to cross until the level falls."

"We'll be here a day or two," Luke added, taking the cup of coffee Donna Grace offered him.

"That gives us time to do some laundry," she said. "I'll not let anything spoil this beautiful morning."

Luke brightened at her encouraging words. "We'll make good use of the time, too. We'll cut some timbers from the hardwood trees and lash them to the bottom of the wagons so we'll have them handy for repairs."

"And we'll chop wood," Warren added. "There won't be much ahead of us."

"What am I to do?" Polly demanded, feeling very left out.

Mary Mae reached for the little girl's hands. "You

can help me make enough biscuits to last us a few days."

"Will you teach me how to do it so I can make them for my uncle?"

No one laughed at the child's seriousness. Truth was, she would likely be carrying adult responsibilities long before she should, simply because of her circumstances—an orphan being raised by a trader.

Reverend Shepton asked the blessing on the food. "And thank You, our Heavenly Father, for cooler weather and safety."

Eager as everyone was to get started on the work, breakfast was hurried. Donna Grace and the others grabbed buckets and headed to the river for water. As soon as Luke saw their intention he jogged to Donna Grace's side and took her buckets.

"I'll bring water for you."

She thought to protest for about two seconds then thanked him and accompanied him.

They drew close to the river. The banks were short and steep and the water a wild torrent.

Donna Grace stared in fascination and fear. "I don't recall it being like this when we came before. In fact, Papa and I fished here. I enjoyed that." She was beginning to wonder if she had spent that journey in a cloud of blind optimism, seeing only the adventure and the way her papa faced each challenge without so much as a quiver of fear.

"We'll have to wait until the levels drop." Luke eyed the sky. "It won't take long if it doesn't rain."

Donna Grace studied the sky as well. "It's deceiving. It can be as clear as glass and then suddenly, a storm is upon us."

"Pray no more storms for a couple of days."

She heard a tone she hadn't noted before. "You're worried at the delay?"

"The rest and a chance to graze will do the animals well."

"I know what you're not saying. It's late in the year and delays make it possible we might run into snow."

"There will be snow in the mountains."

His voice said it wasn't a maybe. Donna Grace shivered. "I shall pray this delay is short. Just long enough to get caught up on chores." She turned at the sound of voices to her left. "Are there other people here?"

"Yes. We greeted them earlier. Half a dozen trappers. They're heading north. I don't think they'll pose any problem, but it doesn't hurt to be cautious."

He filled her buckets, and filled buckets for Mary Mae and Judith; then they began their return journey.

Donna Grace stayed close to Luke. She'd had quite enough of encountering strangers and had no desire to test these men and see if they were good or not.

The women put water over the fire to heat, and then gathered the items that needed washing. Working together made the job pleasant.

Mrs. Shepton stood elbow to elbow with Donna Grace as they hung the wet garments on lines between the wagons. "Your husband asked me to check on you."

Donna Grace paused with a wet towel suspended from her fingers. Her husband? Their agreement did not give him the right to use his position that way. "Really?" She kept her tone neutral. "About what?"

"About the baby, of course. Tell me about the ache in your back."

"It's nothing."

But Mrs. Shepton asked probing questions and again desired to feel Donna Grace's stomach. "The baby has dropped. It won't be long now before you deliver."

Donna Grace resisted the urge to argue. She didn't want the baby born on the trail. Never mind that others had done it. Her dream was for the baby to be born into a warm home where he would know nothing but love and security. She would never tell her child he was too much bother or didn't live up to expectations.

But what if the baby came before Santa Fe? She would do what she must do and provide her baby with the security of her love. The security of a home might have to wait a few days or weeks.

She finished the laundry, letting the others carry on the conversation. As she moved about, she noticed it helped relieve her back pain. "I'm going for a walk to explore."

"Wait, I'll go with you." Mary Mae looked at the Dutch oven where she had biscuits browning. Polly stood at Mary Mae's side intently watching every move.

"You have your hands full. I'll be fine. I won't go far."

"Be careful." Mary Mae tilted her head in the direction of the trapper's camp.

Donna Grace headed the opposite way. Her travels took her past the wagons. Men sawed and chopped in the woods. She went on, seeking some quiet. The camp grew distant. Now she could enjoy the birds singing. She paused to take in the golden leaves, the silvery grass and fuzzy tops of flowers and grasses gone to seed.

"It's so beautiful and peaceful," she murmured. She was about to turn back when she saw a cluster of red leaves. If she gathered them and pressed them into a book, she would have a permanent reminder of this day… one she felt sure she would always remember as special.

With hurried steps she went toward the bright spot of color. Without warning, her feet went from under her and she fell to her backside, grabbing for a hand hold as she slid down a slippery slope. The grass she caught at pulled from her hands. The bumpy ground hit her bottom and jarred her teeth. She came to a sudden stop and hunched over her knees sucking desperately for a satisfying breath. Finally one came and then another. Her head cleared and she looked about her. She had fallen down a narrow gully that was almost invisible. She hadn't seen it because her attention was on the red leaves up the hill to her left. To her right lay a scattering of rocks. "That would have hurt," she mused and lifted her face to the sky. "Thank you, God, for stopping me before I bashed into those."

She pulled herself to her feet. Ouch. She hurt all over. It took several seconds for her to be able to straighten then using hands and feet like a four-legged animal, she scrambled up the slope. Again she stopped, and waited for pain to pass.

"It's just from falling," she assured herself. Had she hurt herself or her baby?

The red leaves still beckoned, and she gathered a bouquet, then set her feet on the path back to camp.

More pain. Sharp. Clawing at her stomach. She must stop and wait for it to pass. No. She must get back to the camp. Where was it? She clutched the leaves to her chest and straightened. The wagons couldn't have disappeared, but where were they? She stumbled onward. The pain returned and she stopped. Surely, this wasn't right. The fall had injured her. She prayed for the spasm to end and let out a huge sigh when it did.

She needed to find the wagons and she blinked to clear her vision. There they were over the slight hill before her. And there was Luke striding toward her. His gait recognizable before she could make out his features.

As soon as she could see his face, she knew he was both worried and annoyed. "You should not be out here by yourself."

"I found these. Aren't they beautiful?" She held out the bunch of bright leaves.

He grabbed her hand and opened the fingers. "How did you skin yourself? And your skirt is torn."

"I wasn't paying attention and I stepped in a hole." Let him think it was nothing more.

He turned her around until she stood face to face with him again. He brushed his knuckles over her cheek. "What am I going to do with you?"

The question echoed similar questions from her grandfather and burned her insides. "You have done all you need to do. You've made it possible for me to come on this journey. I want no more."

His fingers stilled. "I didn't mean to sound like I thought you were too much trouble. I think nothing of the sort." He trailed his fingers to her chin. "You say you want no more but I think you do. I know I do."

She would not be distracted by the way his touch reached deep into her heart. Nor would she let him be distracted by having to worry about her. "Do you? I seem to remember you wanting to continue being a trader on this trail. And don't I recall that you have vowed to never care about anyone again for fear of being hurt?" If he hadn't said those exact words, she knew he meant them. Just as she meant to be all her child needed.

He dropped his hands and stepped back. "You're right, but until this marriage is legally ended, I take my responsibilities seriously. And that includes protecting you and the baby."

She pressed her hands to her stomach. "He's kicking, so he's okay." She'd had no more pains, which meant they had just been from her fall. Almost overcome with gratitude, she grabbed Luke's arm. "I'll try not to cause you any troub-" At his warning look, she changed her mind and said, "Worry."

They returned to the wagons without her experiencing any more pains. It made her almost giddy with relief.

Mary Mae rushed to greet her. "You were gone so long."

"I saw these leaves and wanted to bring them back."

"Pretty," Polly said. "What are you going to do with them?"

"I'm going to press them so I've have something to always remind me of this day." Luke hovered nearby and she sent him a look that she hoped spoke how she felt. "It's been a good day from the start."

His expression softened. His eyes filled with warmth, and she knew he recalled the special moment they had shared that morning. He touched his fingers to the brim of his hat and strode away.

"I learned something today," Polly said. She showed Donna Grace the biscuits she'd made. They were oddly shaped but nicely browned.

"They look delicious."

"They are. Mary Mae let me have one with syrup on it." The child skipped away. Mister King, the dog, ran after her.

When Mrs. Shepton had alerted Luke to Donna Grace's absence, the bottom fell out of his heart as he imagined a number of disasters from being accosted by one of the trappers to her delivering the baby on her own. Seeing her coming toward him with an armload of red leaves had flooded him with relief. He hadn't meant to blurt out those words. *What am I going to do with you?* He would never tell her she was too much trouble.

And then he'd said he wanted more. He shook his head. It was simply a reaction to the worry and relief that overlapped each other and left him momentarily unable to think.

He smiled as he returned to his work. She had sent him a private message when she said it was a good day, reminding him of that sweet moment when they had greeted the crystal-draped world.

She saw this day as special.

He meant to see that it ended well. As he worked, he tried to think how he could do that. It was hard to do anything within the constraints of their circumstances, but by supper time he had a plan. It was nothing exceptional, but he recalled how much she had enjoyed spending time with her papa. Maybe she would like this.

As soon as the meal was over, he went to the Russell wagon and pulled out fishing gear. "Donna Grace, would you like to go fishing with me?"

Every pair of eyes looked his direction. He pretended he didn't notice. "I thought you might enjoy it."

"Okay." She seemed guarded, but fell in at his side.

"The water has already gone down a lot," she commented as they reached the river.

"We should be able to cross tomorrow." He didn't look to the sky, didn't mention the possibility of rain. This evening was for enjoyment, not worry. "That looks a likely place." He didn't know about fish, but it offered a grassy spot where they could sit side by side.

He prepared the lines and handed one to Donna Grace and they waited for a bite. He hoped there wouldn't be one. Fresh fish would be nice for breakfast, but not as nice as quiet time with Donna Grace.

"It's been a good day," he said. Why was it he couldn't think of anything better than that to say?

"One to remember," she agreed.

Had she forgiven him for his harsh words?

They sat side by side without speaking. He didn't find it uncomfortable, but still, he wished they had something to say to each other.

"Did you get the leaves pressed?"

"I did. Did you get all the wood cut you hoped to?"

"Yes." His heart stirred with things he wanted to say, but could not find words. "How's the baby?"

She pressed her hand to her stomach. "He's quiet right now." She rubbed her stomach. "Why isn't he moving? Did I hurt him when I fell?" Her voice grew thin with worry.

Without asking for permission, he put his hand by hers to feel for movement. "Hey, little one, are you sleeping?"

A tiny foot kicked his hand.

Luke laughed. "I think he's saying he doesn't want to be disturbed."

"Well, I hope he doesn't sleep now and then kick all night."

"Does he do that a lot?"

"Define what you mean by a lot?"

He laughed at her dry tone. "I never realized how much work it is to be a mama."

She turned her face to him, her eyes dark with feeling.

Was she asking for support? Understanding? Suddenly, he knew what she needed. "You are going to be the best mama this baby could ask for." He put an arm about her shoulders and drew her close, pressing his forehead to hers.

She nodded. "I will be like my mama. She was a good parent."

"As was my mama." His throat tightened as he thought of his parents and their pain at how their children had suffered.

"Tell me about your mama," Donna Grace said, still leaning into him.

"Judith looks like her. In fact, Judith is like her. Calm, matter-of-fact. But has deep feelings. Did you know Judith's betrothed took his own life?"

Donna Grace jerked back. "How awful. She never said anything."

"She won't. Please don't let on I told you."

"Of course not." She rocked her head back and forth. "Your family has suffered a lot of tragedy. Your soon-to-be wife murdered. Warren's wife and child dead. And Judith's—" She shuddered.

"I sometimes forget that all of this happened to my parents' children. They must feel it deeply."

Donna Grace pressed her hand to her stomach. "And then for all of you to leave. How do they bear it?"

"They always appeared so strong to me."

"I suppose they want to support you as much as they can."

"I am going to write them a letter the first chance I get and let them know we are all doing reasonably well."

She grinned at him. "Are you going to tell them you are married?"

The question left him wordless for at least two seconds. "If I don't Judith or Warren might. I don't know what I should say. Maybe I shouldn't write them."

"Oh Luke. They surely want to hear from you. You could tell them the truth: that you saw a woman in need and offered this solution, but neither of us meant it to be permanent."

"I don't know that they would understand."

She shrugged. "I'm sure you'll think of something."

"Nice of you to have so much faith in me." He

slumped over his knees and stared at the water. "This was supposed to be a special moment for you, to add to all the enjoyable moments of this day."

With a little chuckle, she gave a playful punch to his ribs. "So make it enjoyable."

"What do you suggest?" He studied her full, inviting mouth. Her lips like rubies. Whoa. Was he talking like the Song of Solomon? A bride and her lover? No way. They didn't fit that picture at all.

"You could start by pointing out the beautiful sunset."

He looked at the western sky. "I almost missed it." The colors deepened and grew more vibrant.

"I don't think you could have." The color spread across the sky, like a runaway blaze. Her voice deepened with awe and she reached for his hand and clung to him as she drank in the sunset.

He alternated between admiring the sky and admiring the look of pleasure on her face. One thing he could say for certainty about this young woman: she didn't let the sad things of this life keep her from enjoying the good things.

She almost made him believe he could put the past behind him and find joy in what the future offered.

## 10

D onna Grace could not take her eyes off the banners of orange and gold. "God has certainly filled this day with color." She spared a quick look at Luke, and smiled at the bemusement on his face as he watched the sunset. The light reflected on his features, making them all sharp planes. Somewhere in the distance an owl hooted, "Who. Who." The sound became a question in Donna Grace's mind that circled, catching at the corners of doubt in her thoughts. Who could she trust besides God? Did she want to trust anyone else?

"A day to remember?" Luke's question stopped her thoughts before she could answer them, and turned her attention back to the colorful sky and the events of the day.

"I do believe so." She hovered on the brink of something that both drew her forward and at the same time caused her to hold back. Was she letting the shifting, dancing music of the sunset mesmerize her to the point she lost sight of who she was and what she wanted?

A rock dislodged to their right, rattling down the slope. They turned toward the sound. A man she didn't recognize, clattered down the hill and stopped by the river. A thin, tallish man with a wide-brimmed hat pulled low over his face. Donna Grace could see only his chin and it seemed tinted with red from the sunset reflecting off the water.

"It's one of the trappers," Luke said. "We should go back." He got to his feet and held out his hand to assist her.

"We've caught nothing."

"It will soon be dark. No fish will bite." He darted a glance to the man by the river then gathered up the fishing poles.

"Why does he make you nervous?" They would surely encounter many strangers on their journey.

"He asked questions about the wagon train and who traveled with us when we met the trappers earlier. I didn't like his inquisitiveness."

She clung to Luke's arm as they began the climb up the bank. "Why would he want so much information?" Until Luke had expressed his concern, Donna Grace would not have given the man more than a passing thought. Now she wondered if he posed a risk. Hadn't she already learned the dangers of encountering strangers? She shuddered.

"I don't know, but I don't intend to provide him a chance to make further inquiries."

Donna Grace glanced back as they made their way up the hill. She stared at the man. He looked at them, the tilt of his head giving her an opportunity to see more of his features. Swarthy skinned, dark eyebrows, a hard set to his mouth.

Seeing her interest, he turned away. "He looks familiar."

"You know him?"

"He reminds me of someone, but I can't think who." She hurried onward. "I suppose it's simply that he looks like many of the men I saw in Santa Fe."

They returned to the others.

Buck and Gil sat around the campfire telling about the wolves they had encountered as they explored the river, looking for an alternate crossing.

"We didn't find anything better than this place," Buck said. "We'll cross tomorrow."

"One wolf was pure white," Gil spoke as if the conversation was still about the wolves. "I've heard tales about a white wolf who is larger than normal and very aggressive, but I thought they were exaggerated."

Polly clung to her uncle and Mary Mae crowded to Donna Grace's side. "I don't like talk about big wolves," she whispered to Donna Grace.

Gil heard her. "They won't bother us while there is plenty of wildlife for them to eat."

Polly gave a wail. "You mean deer and those cute antelope. That's dreadful." She sobbed.

Sam picked her up. "I think it's time for us to go to our wagon." As he left, he spoke to Polly. "I'll read you a nice story."

"The one about the mama hen who took care of her baby chicks in a bad wind?"

"If you like."

Gil rubbed his chin. "It appears I misspoke to mention the wild beasts with a little one around. My apologies. I am used to being surrounded by men." He rose, emptied his cup and handed it to Judith.

"No need to rush away," she murmured.

"Thank you, but I need to check on things." He planted his hat on his head as he left.

Buck joined him.

Warren stood. "It will be a long day tomorrow. Good night."

Judith headed for the wagon.

Luke went to get the tent for Donna Grace and Mary Mae. He set it up and insisted on spreading the buffalo robe for Donna Grace.

"Thank you." He took his role of husband seriously, even if it was temporary, and only for show. If it helped cleanse his guilt over his betrothed's death, then it went a long way, in Donna Grace's mind, to justifying their deception about their marriage.

They were soon bedded down for the night. With Luke sleeping nearby, Donna Grace decided she didn't need to fear white wolves or strange men who asked too many questions.

She tried not to disturb her sister by moving too

much, but found it impossible to find a comfortable position. She'd bruised herself in some new places. In an attempt to relax, she buried her face in the buffalo robe, breathing in the scent of leather and wildness. She drifted close to sleep. A dream of a large white wolf jerked her from any hope of slumber. A pain speared through her and she sucked back a moan, determined no one should guess at her state. The pain ended. She should have been more careful out walking.

Mary Mae turned toward her. "Are you okay?"

"I'm fine except for some bruises." She told how she had fallen. "I should have been watching where I went."

Her sister murmured, "I'm glad you didn't hurt yourself seriously. Now go to sleep. You heard Warren say tomorrow will be long."

Donna Grace made a disbelieving sound in her throat. "Seems to me every day has the same number of hours in it, so I don't see how it will be any longer than today or yesterday."

Luke's deep-throated chuckle made her realize that she had spoken above a whisper.

"Go to sleep, Donna Grace," he said.

"I would if everyone would stop talking to me." She flipped to her side and willed sleep to come.

Darkness still surrounded them when she woke with another stabbing pain. She bit back a groan. This could not be anything more than the after-effects of her fall. The pain grabbed at her back and spread across her middle. All she could do was breathe deeply, waiting for it to pass. It lasted long enough for Donna Grace to wish for morning so she could move around.

Faint dawning light brought on another pain. She shifted to ease the pressure on her back. As soon as she could move, she hurried from the tent to join breakfast preparations.

Buck rode up, stopping only long enough to call out orders. "Get the animals hitched. It looks like more rain coming. We need to get across before that happens."

The men hurried to bring in the mules. Around camp, the teamsters brought in the oxen. Shouts rang out as they yoked the big animals.

Breakfast was hurried, eaten mostly on the run.

They lined up the wagons in preparation for crossing. Luke and Gil stood at the bank, guiding the wagons forward.

Warren's was first, Judith clutching the wagon seat beside him as they drove down the slope and straight into the water.

Donna Grace strained forward as the wagon began to float.

Her sister grabbed her hand and squeezed so hard it was all Donna Grace could do not to protest. She felt the same surge of fear, wondering if Warren and Judith would make it. Even worse was the knowledge they would soon follow. If their wagon tipped they would be thrown into the rough water. Donna Grace was not a strong swimmer at the best of times. Would her huge belly impede efforts to swim? Or would it make her more buoyant?

She didn't want to find out.

"Will they make it?" Mary Mae asked as the current caught the wagon and it swayed perilously.

"I hope so. I pray so." *Dear God, help them cross safely.* Each second stretched out slowly enough to make her head pound. She realized she had forgotten to breathe, and sucked in air.

Then the mules reached solid footing and pulled the wagon to the far bank.

Reverend and Mrs. Shepton were next in line. The reverend stood, his hat held to his chest and prayed for safety for each and every one. For a moment, the cavalcade was quiet and then the reverend's wagon drove down the bank and into the water. The wagon twisted.

Mrs. Shepton squealed. The reverend prayed loudly.

Mary Mae and Donna Grace clung to each other. Luke charged into the water, ready to aid the Shepton's. Fear stirred hotly inside her. If the wagon tipped over on top of him, he could drown. If he caught the mules to guide them, one of them could—

Her grip on her sister's hand grew so fierce Mary Mae protested and tried to free herself.

The mules reached solid ground and pulled the wagon to the far bank.

Donna Grace relaxed her hand and Mary Mae

curled and uncurled her fingers. "You almost crushed them." She eyed her sister. "Are you okay?"

"I'm fine." Would Mary Mae hear the tremor in Donna Grace's voice?

"I understand why you're frightened, but we can't stay here. We must cross."

Donna Grace nodded. Let Mary Mae think her only source of worry was crossing the river. She'd never guess seeing Luke in danger frightened her more.

And no amount of telling herself she didn't worry any more about him than Warren or Gil or Buck, settled her thoughts.

"It's our turn." Luke climbed up to the bench. "Hang on tight." Donna Grace doubted anyone could pry her hands from the wooden seat.

He turned to Mary Mae in the back of the wagon. "Hold on."

Luke flicked the reins. They tipped forward, the wagon pushing the mules as they descended the slope. Donna Grace caught her breath and closed her eyes as they entered the water. The mules were soon up to their heads. The wagon floated. It twisted to the side and then jerked. Donna Grace was thrown forward. Luke caught her and pulled her back. "Hold on." He let her go, his hands busy controlling the mules.

Donna Grace hung on and prayed. The wagon surged forward, carried along by the faithful mules. She promised herself she would personally thank them when they were safely on solid ground again.

The jostling started another spasm but thankfully Luke's attention was not on her. After what seemed an eternity, they reached dry ground. The pain ended.

Luke studied Donna Grace. She wondered if he saw tension lines about her mouth and eyes.

"We're safely across. You can be breathe again." He rubbed her shoulder.

He'd taken the strain in her face as fear over the crossing.

She took in a refreshing gulp of air.

He withdrew his hand making it hard for her to let her breath out. He looked back. "I have to see to getting the freight wagons across."

"Of course."

"You'll be okay?"

"Why would you think otherwise?" She would not interfere with his work.

"Would you admit it if you weren't?"

She had told him too much and now he saw her every reaction as evidence that she heard an echo of her grandfather's words. So she'd let him believe he was right. "Not likely."

He laughed. "You think you need no one. Maybe someday, you'll be willing to admit you do."

"About the same time you stop trying to outrun your dreams."

Their gazes burned with acknowledgement that they had reminded each other of the reason this marriage and their time together was based on hurtful things in their past.

Warren had unhitched two mules as Donna Grace and Luke talked and he led one to Luke.

"If you and Donna Grace are done fighting, let's go."

Donna Grace and Luke spoke at the same time. "We aren't—" They stopped in unison.

Behind Donna Grace, Mary Mae giggled. "Sounded like an argument to me too." She and Warren grinned at each other.

Luke met Donna Grace's eyes. "I don't intend to defend myself to my brother."

"Nor I to my sister," Mary Mae said.

The flash of amusement in Luke's eyes and the way they warmed make Donna Grace duck her head.

Luke swung to the back of the mule. He and Warren rode across the river.

Mary Mae, Judith and Mrs. Shepton went to the bank to watch as the men doubled hitched oxen to the first wagon.

"I'll stay here." Donna Grace sat in the wagon where she could watch, but where she was out of sight.

It was noon before the crossing finished and Buck allowed them a brief time for lunch. "I'd like to make a few miles yet today," he said. The sky had clouded over, but the rain held off.

"I think I'll ride in the back," Donna Grace said, as they prepared to leave. No one asked as to her reasons, which saved her from trying to come up with an excuse. She had no intention of telling them the truth.

Mary Mae opted to ride with Judith for which Donna Grace was grateful. The pains were coming more frequently, but if she rode alone in the back, no one need know. This being her firstborn, she expected it would be some time before the baby would make an appearance.

The contractions increased in frequency and severity throughout the afternoon. She bit her lip to keep from crying out as they grew stronger. She feared if Luke heard her or guessed her condition he would insist on stopping.

She would not be responsible for causing delay.

In an attempt to divert herself from her discomfort, she focused on the canopy above her. The rain had left ugly water streaks on the canvas. She shifted her attention to the trunk. Inside were the baby items she would need in Santa Fe. *Please, baby, wait until then.* Santa Fe, she admitted in a cloud of dark defeat, was weeks away yet. This baby wasn't going to wait. Perhaps she'd known it all along, but hadn't wanted to admit it.

A tear escaped and ran into her ear. She dashed it away. All she wanted was a safe place for the baby. Maybe she thought she would find such a place for herself as well, where she would be valued, even if she was a nuisance at times.

But from now on, meeting her baby's needs was the only thing that mattered.

The next contraction took her in a grip that made her want to scream.

Luke stopped the wagon and turned around. "What's wrong?"

Had the scream left her throat? She hadn't meant for it to. "Drive on," she ground out.

He continued to watch her, and try as she might, she couldn't lay calm and still when the next one hit. She rolled her head back and forth and wished for it to stop.

"How long has this been going on?" His tone held judgment and impatience.

The pain passed and she gave him a look as full as impatience as his. "There's nothing to be gained by stopping. Drive on."

He studied her a moment. "I hope you know what you're doing." He flicked the reins and they continued.

"Obviously I don't," she muttered. "Or I wouldn't be in this situation."

He chuckled. "Nice to see you haven't lost your sense of humor."

She hadn't meant for him to hear her. "It wasn't meant to be funny." She barely managed to get the words out between her gritted teeth.

How long did this go on? How much more could she endure?

"Are you okay?" Luke asked.

She couldn't answer as one contraction transitioned into another. Her whole body consumed by it. Nothing else mattered. Nothing else existed.

Warm hands brushed her hair back.

"You'll soon have a baby." Mrs. Shepton knelt beside her. How had she gotten into the wagon?

Donna Grace concentrated. The wagon was no longer moving. Before she could protest at Luke stopping, her mind was diverted by a baby needing to be born.

She heard nothing but Mrs. Shepton's calming voice. She knew nothing outside the confines of this small space and the demands of her body.

~

LUKE'S INSIDES felt scalded as he listened to Donna Grace. She wouldn't thank him for stopping, but he couldn't go on with her in such distress. Was she having the baby or had she injured herself in her fall? He didn't know, and knew she wouldn't tell him. The woman was so afraid of being a nuisance, she would suffer alone, rather than admit she needed help.

He snorted quietly. As her husband he had every right to make a few decisions for her good, whether or not she liked it.

So he had stopped and signaled the reverend to join him.

"She needs your wife," Luke said. Mrs. Shepton would soon assess the situation and decide what needed to be done.

Mrs. Shepton poked her head out of the wagon. "Your wife is in labor. You won't be able to go on until she delivers."

Donna Grace called out. "I can travel." Her words ended in a groan.

Mrs. Shepton shook her head to indicate to Luke that travel was out of the question, then ducked back inside.

Luke had no intention of going on. The trail was rough. No woman in Donna Grace's condition should be subjected to the bouncing and jerking.

Buck rode up and inquired as to the reason for the delay. He listened as Luke explained.

Buck looked at the line of wagons passing them. "I need to get to the next stopping place where there will be water for the animals. You catch up as soon as you're able."

Luke nodded at the wisdom of Buck's words.

Warren offered to stay, but Luke said someone needed to see to their wagons. Mary Mae wanted to stay too, but Mrs. Shepton had said the less commotion around Donna Grace, the better, so she went on with Judith, her face wreathed in worry over her sister.

Luke wished he could offer Mary Mae encouragement, but after listening to Donna Grace's moans and cries for the past two hours, he was wrung out.

Her sounds of distress continued, but now with Mrs. Shepton offering encouragement.

The reverend took Luke by the arm. "Son, it could take quite a while. There's nothing you can do now except wait, and keep water hot. Maybe make some tea."

Luke built a fire and put water to boil, his actions so automatic he couldn't have told anyone what he did.

His mind was consumed with listening to Donna Grace.

She cried out.

He jerked upright and headed for the wagon.

The reverend caught his arm. "You can't go in there."

He shook off the man's grasp. "She's my wife."

"My wife knows what she's doing."

Luke faced him, frustration boiling within him. "Can you tell me she's never lost a mother or child in birthing?"

The reverend shook his head. "I wish life was that simple."

"Then how am I supposed to stand by and not do anything?" He took a step toward the wagon and stopped. What could he do? Besides stand by and wait helplessly, wanting nothing more than to make the cries stop.

The reverend removed his hat. "There is one thing you can and should do. Pray." He waited expectantly until Luke removed his hat and bowed his head. Luke could not have repeated a single word the man spoke apart from the Amen, but remembering that God was present calmed his agitation.

He paced the length of the wagon and back. Over and over. The sounds of Donna Grace's distress making his ears want to bleed.

The reverend perched on a stool and watched him.

The shadows lengthened. "Night will soon be upon us. We best prepare."

The two wagons alone provided little protection. Making them as safe as possible was one thing he could do and he welcomed the task.

He had the reverend move his wagon against the Clark wagon. They unhitched the mules and took them to grass. He filled a bucket with water and carried it to the animals.

The reverend looked into their larder and pulled out biscuits and cold bacon and handed some to Luke. "Eat up."

He ate mindlessly. "How long does this take?" He nodded toward the wagon.

"As long as it takes." The darkness closed in upon them. The reverend lit a lamp and handed it to his wife.

Luke sat with his head in his hands. If he could take Donna Grace's place, take her pain, he would. Instead, he sat there like a bump on a log, unable to do more than keep a fire going.

Wolves howled in the distance. He could also guard her against wild animals and evil men. He threw more wood on the fire, thankful they'd had time to lay in a store of firewood. He got his rifle and held it across his knees.

Donna Grace screamed, raising the hair on the back of Luke's neck.

Mrs. Shepton murmured encouragement.

Donna Grace groaned.

He strained toward the wagon, trying to decipher the muted sounds.

A thin wail rent the air.

Luke came to his feet. "Is that a baby?" Not waiting for the reverend to reply, he dashed to the back of the wagon. "Is that a baby?"

Mrs. Shepton chuckled. "Congratulations, Papa. You have a little daughter."

"Can I see her? Can I see Donna Grace?"

"Soon. We aren't quite done. I'll call you when it's time."

A little girl? Luke couldn't stop grinning. His wife had given him a little girl. His wife? He went to the edge of the light from the campfire and stared into the darkness. How had he let his thoughts and feelings drift so far from what he and Donna Grace had agreed to?

The baby cried again and he turned to watch the flickering light against the canvas of the wagon. Donna Grace was his wife until such time as a judge said otherwise, and this little girl would have his name. It was all that mattered at the moment.

He remained there, watching and waiting, his heart beating hard against his chest as he listened to the sounds coming from the wagon. Donna Grace murmuring, perhaps to the baby who gave a thin wail.

Mrs. Shepton called to her husband for a basin of water. The reverend seemed to know what she needed, and took it and some towels to his wife.

Luke continued to wait, near to bursting with so many things—pride, relief and an overwhelming desire to see for himself that Donna Grace was okay.

Mrs. Shepton handed the basin back to her husband, and accepted his help down from the wagon. She smiled at Luke. "Your wife and daughter are ready to see you."

Wife and daughter. The words sang through his veins as he carefully climbed into the wagon. The lantern sat on a trunk throwing light across Donna Grace's features—all golden and bright, her smile wide. In her arms lay a tiny bundle.

He fell to his knees beside them. He touched Donna Grace's forehead, felt the coolness as if she'd recently washed. The edges of her hair were damp and he smoothed back the strands. "Are you okay?"

She chuckled and tipped the baby toward him. "Isn't she beautiful? Perfect?"

He studied her. Dark eyelashes like half-moons upon her cheeks. Her little rosebud mouth moved as if dreaming of milk. Fists curled at the side of her head. So tiny yet so complete. A lump formed in his throat and refused to dislodge. His heart threatened to explode from his chest. "She's beautiful. She looks like her mama." His gaze went to Donna Grace. "You are beautiful." Their gazes held, hers brimming with joy. He couldn't say what she saw in his, but if she saw half of what he was feeling, she would know just how special and perfect she was.

The baby smacked her lips and they looked at her and chuckled.

"Can you tell Mary Mae to come and meet her niece?"

"They went on ahead."

She grabbed his arm. "You stopped? You shouldn't have."

He smoothed her brow. "We'll catch up."

"You know I don't want to inconvenience anyone."

He studied her a moment. "I think you should stop saying that. Isn't our little daughter going to hear it, and think you mean she's an inconvenience?" He caught the tiny hand and stroked unimaginably small fingers, marveling at how perfect she was in such miniature proportions.

Donna Grace pulled the baby closer. "I will never say it again. My baby is not an inconvenience now or ever."

Her response triggered a protectiveness as fierce as it was unfamiliar, and he realized he meant to defend this little girl from any criticism or dangers. "Do you have a name picked out?"

"I think Elena Rose after my mama and my friend, Rosa."

Luke smiled. "I like it. How about you, little Elena Rose. Do you like it?"

The baby cracked open one eye to explore the sound of his voice.

Donna Grace and Luke shared a joyous laugh over the wee girl.

"Your wife needs to rest," Mrs. Shepton called.

"My wife," he whispered and leaning down, caught Donna Grace's lips in a tender kiss. Even knowing he shouldn't have done it, and didn't have the right, he regretted it not one tiny bit and escaped the wagon as Donna Grace fumbled for a protest.

Mrs. Shepton held a cup of tea and some biscuits. "Please take these while I get inside."

"I could take them to her," Luke said. In fact, he couldn't think of anything he'd rather do than share a few more moments with her.

"You could, but I need to check on the new mama and baby."

"Of course." His cheeks stung as he realized Donna Grace would be wanting a woman to assist her.

"You have the rest of your lives together. A few minutes apart won't hurt either of you." Mrs. Shepton climbed in and Luke handed her the food and drink. Little did she know how short their time together would be. But all he could think of at the moment was the thrill of seeing the baby and being able to give her his name. Elena Rose Russell had a very nice ring to it.

He sauntered back to the fire, unable to stop smiling.

"Proud papa," the reverend commented.

Let him think that was the case. But although Luke thought Elena Rose beautiful, it was the stolen kiss that had him smiling so widely. A kiss, that as her husband, he had every right to.

Mrs. Shepton left the wagon, carrying the lantern. "I think we should try and get some sleep."

"Donna Grace," he said. "If you need anything, don't be afraid to call out."

"Thanks. I'll be okay." She sounded drowsy so he settled close to the wagon in a place where he could keep the fire going, not only for their protection, but to make it possible for Donna Grace to see to tend the baby in the night.

He slept lightly, coming fully awake when he heard the baby fuss. He waited a moment and when the baby didn't settle, threw another log on the fire. Twice more he wakened to the sound of crying. And once to the howl of a wolf. Each time he threw more wood on the fire.

It would be a relief to catch up to the others and know the safety of numbers.

He was up before dawn, added more wood to the fire and set a pot of coffee to brewing.

Donna Grace called out. "Is Mrs. Shepton up?"

The older woman climbed from her wagon and went to see Donna Grace. Although Luke strained to hear the conversation, he couldn't make out the words.

Mrs. Shepton left Donna Grace. "She's hungry."

Luke chuckled. "That's good, right?"

"Very good. She has to eat for two now." The woman set about putting oatmeal to cook and frying bacon and potatoes. When it was ready, she took a plateful to the wagon.

Luke waited for her to return. "How long before she can travel?"

Donna Grace heard him. "As soon as breakfast is over."

Again, silently, Luke asked the question of Mrs. Shepton.

"As long as she rests in the wagon for a few days, she'll be okay. She's young and strong."

"And stubborn," Luke added.

"I prefer to think of it as determined," Donna Grace called.

Luke chuckled as he went to the back gate of the wagon. "I want to see for myself you are both well and able to travel. May I come in?"

"You may."

He climbed in. In the morning light, things looked different. He saw them more clearly, but if anything, they were both more beautiful than last night. He knelt by Donna Grace's side. "You sure you're up to travel? We can wait another day if you want."

She pressed her hand to his arm. "Thank you for suggesting it." She seemed to consider her next words. "Bearing in mind what you said, I'm trying not to think how I've inconvenienced you. But I know we need to catch up to the others so, yes, I am ready to travel and so is this little girl."

Luke studied the baby in Donna Grace's arms. "Ma loved paintings of the Madonna and child. They never meant much to me until now." His throat clogged with emotion. "Now I see the beauty of a mother and infant." He couldn't go on and hoped Donna Grace wouldn't guess the way he choked up.

Her gaze was on her baby. "I had not guessed how overwhelming my love could be." Tears leaked out. "I will do everything in my power to make sure she receives the love and care as she deserves."

Luke caught a teardrop from each eye between his thumb and forefinger. "I will help you."

Her gaze came to him.

He would believe he saw nothing but gratitude in her eyes. He would not admit a flicker of warning existed. For now, they were united in name and in the desire to care for and protect this child.

"Maybe you should hitch up the mules," she said, with a note of amusement.

"I'll get right to it." He paused long enough to brush his knuckles across her chin. "Take care of yourself and our baby." And before she could protest, he hurried from the wagon.

A short time later, they were back on the trail. Luke hoped they would catch the wagon train by noon. Aware of how vulnerable they were traveling alone, he looked back at the trail several times.

Of course, Donna Grace noticed. "You expecting company?"

"One can never be too cautious."

An hour later they saw the dust of the wagon train in the distance. They clattered across some ruts in the trail and the wagon jerked roughly. He looked back. "I hope that doesn't cause you undue discomfort."

She chuckled. "Compared to yesterday, this is like riding a rocking chair."

He understood what she didn't say—that she had been in labor long before she admitted it. Stubborn woman.

In half an hour, they would overtake the wagon train. He took one last look behind him and sat down hard. Two men followed. They were a goodly distance back, and might simply be travelers on the trail, but he would be relieved when they were safely with the others.

As he'd predicted, the train was nooning by the time they caught up. He drew up behind the Russell wagon.

Mary Mae and Judith rushed toward him. "Where is she? Is everything okay?"

Donna Grace poked her head out the back opening. "I have a little girl. Who wants to see her?"

The women crowded around, demanding to know everything.

Luke rocked back on his heels watching them. No one noticed him, nor saw how his chest swelled enough to strain the seams of his shirt.

Warren came to his side. "A baby girl?" His words were heavy with sorrow.

Luke clapped him on the back. "I hope our joy doesn't make your pain worse."

Warren shook his head, but his face revealed how much this reminded him of his own loss.

Mary Mae took the baby and admired her perfect

rosebud mouth, so much like Donna Grace's ruby mouth. "What's her name?"

When Donna Grace said, "Elena Rose," Mary Mae broke into tears.

Polly sidled up to her. "I thought you would be happy."

"I am. These are happy tears. Elena was my mama's name. Would you like to hold her?"

"Can I?"

"Sit down and I'll put her in your arms."

Polly sat on the ground and Mary Mae settled the baby on Polly's lap, holding her securely.

Polly stared at Elena, touched her fingers and her fluff of black hair.

"What do you think?" Donna Grace asked.

"I think babies are better than pets."

The remark brought a smile to all the adults clustered around and served to break Warren free of his sorrow. He moved toward Mary Mae and bent over to look more closely at the baby. "She's a beauty, isn't she?"

Several voices murmured agreement.

Luke lifted his gaze to Donna Grace's. He moved closer so he could whisper for her ears only. "I think this is it."

"What?"

"The happiest moment of my life."

She nodded, a warm smile in her eyes. "Me too."

He didn't point out that the moment would be taken away from both of them when they ended their marriage. They'd deal with that when the time came. In the meantime, he fully intended to enjoy what each day held.

Until Santa Fe. Then what?

He wouldn't answer himself.

## 11

Two days later, Donna Grace, at Mrs. Shepton's insistence, took part in the Sunday evening service from the confines of the wagon. She joined in the singing and listened to the short message Reverend Shepton delivered.

"It's like what Grandfather Ramos would do to me," she groused as she sat at the back of the wagon able to see only a fraction of the world—the circled wagons, the darkening sky and mile after mile of prairie, now gray and disappearing into the night.

Of course, she thought with some sharpness, Luke overheard her. "What would your grandfather do?"

"Confine me to my quarters because he deemed something I did as unacceptable." She was feeling sorry for herself, but the inside of the wagon *was* crowded. Every time she moved she bumped into something. Her legs begged to be free to walk.

"I hardly think this is the same. You've done something marvelous in bringing Elena Rose into the world. It was a big job and you need time to recover." Luke leaned over the tailgate and brushed a strand of hair off her cheek. "Better to rest now than to regret activity later."

Easy for him to say. She tried to remain disgruntled, but her thoughts followed the path of his fingers as they trailed along her face, down to her chin. His thumb rested on her lips. She remembered how he'd kissed her after Elena's birth when he was overcome with awe at the little life cradled to her side. She'd not spoken of it. But now her curiosity and something more—a deeper need, a longing she was loath to admit—urged her to lean forward. "Why did you kiss me?"

He thumb stilled. "Because you deserved it."

"Oh." She had no response for that. "Because I had a baby?"

"Partly, but mostly because you are so strong, so determined, so kissable." He leaned closer, his intent to kiss her again very clear. He moved slowly, giving her plenty of time to withdraw. She didn't. Instead, she lifted her face and met him halfway. His lips lingered, sweet and claiming.

She told herself to pull back. There was no place for kissing in their agreement, but instead, she wrapped an arm about his shoulders and pulled him closer.

Luke was the first to ease back. He chuckled softly.

"That, Mrs. Russell, signifies my appreciation of who you are."

He strode away, a cocky swagger to his steps.

Appreciation? Humph. She sat back. What else did she expect? Or want? She grabbed a damp towel and tossed it to the corner. How had life gotten so complicated? She laughed. When hadn't it been complicated? Certainly not since her mama had died.

Elena fussed and Donna Grace picked her up. "I think Mama would be very happy to know she has a little granddaughter named after her."

Or would she disapprove because of the circumstances of Elena's conception? Donna Grace sank back to her narrow bed on the floor of the wagon, the baby cradled in one arm. She pulled the quilt to her chin and closed her eyes, the shame and misery of the moment she realized she wasn't married to Melvin sweeping over her. Tears stung her eyes, but she would not let them escape.

"Little Elena Rose, if I have anything to say about it, you will never know a moment's shame because he didn't have the right to father a child with me." At least Luke had allowed Elena to have a father's name.

Donna Grace swiped away an errant tear. Luke had given her a lot—a name for Elena Rose, his support and even a kiss.

She flung an arm over her head. It was getting harder and harder to remember that their marriage was pretend and temporary. She'd have to tell him not to kiss her again. But then he'd surely think she put more store in it than she should. The best thing she could do was pretend it meant nothing.

*It meant nothing.* There she'd said it. That made it true.

She refused to admit her reasoning was askew.

The next day it rained but Buck insisted they must move on.

Donna Grace remained under the leaking canvas as the rain continued hour after hour. Was there anything more depressing than being cooped up inside, with nothing to look at but sodden canvas and grey skies? Her only alternative was to study sweet Elena's features or stare at Luke's back. Water dripped from his hat to the shoulders of his black slicker. She dug a dry towel from her meager stack and handed it to him. "Dry your face. It will make you feel better."

"Thanks." He scrubbed at his face then handed the now-damp towel to her. "The oxen do better in the cooler weather, but if the rain doesn't let up soon we'll be struggling through mud." Tension crackled in his voice.

Now was not the time to ask if he'd ever lost a wagon or had his goods ruined. She sought for something else to say. "I don't suppose this day will go down in the happy memory side of things."

Luke laughed. "Don't think so, but, on the other hand, it's not the worst day either."

She longed for something to say to comfort him. Could think of nothing, so she switched subjects.

"Where did you learn that hymn you sing? I don't recall hearing it before."

"Do you like it?"

"The words give me comfort."

"Remember how I told you about the naturalist who traveled with us?"

She murmured acknowledgement.

"He taught it to us. Said it was a fairly new hymn that he'd heard while he was back in Philadelphia. What he loved about it was all the references to nature."

"What do you like about it?"

"All the ways God is described—the King—full of power and love, our shield and defender. When I think of the words, and even more when I sing them, I know God is both powerful and loving, and I feel—" He stopped.

"Luke, what do you feel?" She spoke softly, feeling as if they were walking a sacred trail together.

"Safe," he whispered. "I feel safe."

"I like that." She choked out her reply from a tightened throat. "I will remember it when I'm taking care of Elena on my own."

Luke shifted to meet her eyes. His brimmed with determination. "You won't be on your own as long as we are married."

"I know." Perhaps it was best not to think of how she must cope once they reached Santa Fe. Yes, she'd have Mary Mae, but she had no intention of preventing her sister from following her own interests. She retreated to the middle of the wagon and let the words of that hymn fill her mind and smooth away her worries.

The rain continued that night… a wet misery that held everyone in its grip. They couldn't start a fire, and had nothing but cold biscuits and beans. What Donna Grace wouldn't have given for a hot drink, but those outside needed it far worse than she.

The freighters hunkered under their wagons muttering about the discomfort. The animals tramped through the grass, turning it into a quagmire.

That night, Mary Mae crowded in with Donna Grace, who fashioned a little nest atop one of the trunks for Elena, for fear one of them would roll on her in their sleep.

It was a most uncomfortable existence. They wakened to still more rain, and ate a cold breakfast of the last of the beans and biscuits.

The men hitched and unhitched oxen to double harness and pulled wagons through the mud. Buck rode by often, yelling at the men to get moving. She overheard Luke and Warren worrying about how long it was taking to go a few miles.

"Sooner or later the rain will let up," Warren said. "You know it always does. We just keep pushing ahead as best we can."

"We've never had women folk to worry about before."

Donna Grace could imagine the way Luke frowned as he said that and knew he meant, in a good part, her presence on this wagon train. She tried not to let the words sting. Somehow hearing them from Luke mattered more than it should.

Warren chuckled. "There's almost always a few women on our journey."

"I've never felt responsible for them before."

"Likely because they weren't your responsibility, nor did you feel a deep personal connection to them. Now you have a wife and daughter and that makes a big difference."

"More than I thought it would."

Warren laughed, but Donna Grace didn't hear his reply as the men moved away to help pull a wagon through a mud hole.

She spent a few minutes trying to push away the sting of the overheard words. It wasn't until Elena fussed for her next feeding that she achieved any degree of success. Why did she let it matter? She knew without a doubt that her presence had slowed Luke down, had complicated his life, but he would be free of her as soon as they reached Santa Fe.

A drop of moisture landed on Elena's cheek. Donna Grace wiped it away then realized a tear had fallen from her eyes and she dashed them away. She had no patience with feeling sorry for one's self.

The freight wagons were finally all on the move. Donna Grace knew there were more mud holes ahead. More harnessing and unharnessing animals in order to get through the bog, but for now, they inched forward. Mary Mae climbed into the wagon in preparation for their departure. She paused at the back of the wagon to take off her wet coat and shake the water from it.

"Oh for dry clothes and a hot drink," Mary Mae murmured, then settled in a corner of the wagon, pulling a quilt about her shoulders in an attempt to get warm.

Luke climbed to the seat of their wagon and flicked the reins to get the mules to move. They leaned into the harness and pulled.

Donna Grace watched over Luke's shoulders. "Those poor animals are straining so hard."

"We have to keep moving."

"I know."

She heard the weariness in Luke's voice. "Did you sleep last night?"

"Some."

"Where?"

"Under the wagon."

"I'm sorry."

He glanced sideways at her and gave her a glimpse of the fatigue dulling his eyes and lining his face. "What are you sorry for? Making it rain? Turning the ground into mire? Having loaded freight wagons to pull through bottomless mud? Tell me, Donna Grace, which of those are you going to blame yourself for?"

She sat back on her heels, stung by his harsh words. Then something arose in her and she leaned close so he alone would hear her words. "I was going to say I'm sorry you haven't been getting enough sleep and maybe even that the weather is so foul. But your mood is even worse." She turned her back to him and pulled Elena into her arms.

Mary Mae looked ready to cry or demand Donna Grace apologize.

She would do no such thing. He had no right to speak to her that way even if he was tired and worn out from fighting mud for almost two days. He made her sound petty, self-pitying. That's what came of telling him how her grandfather's treatment had hurt her, how Melvin's actions made her feel as if she had no value. And then Papa abandoned them. She buried her face against Elena's blanket. No one would see the hot tears slipping from her eyes.

Late that afternoon, the sun finally came out. The canvas steamed. The inside of the wagon was hot and muggy. Mary Mae escaped the sweltering heat.

The ground was still saturated, making hard work for the animals.

"I hope we don't get bogged down again," Luke muttered.

He seemed to be talking to himself, so Donna Grace didn't answer. His curt comments had cut deeply.

She couldn't resist the sunshine though, so sat near the front of the wagon, enjoying the freshness of the world beyond the muddy tracks.

Luke shifted. "I'm sorry."

Donna Grace let the remark hang in the air. She would not ask for him to explain.

"I spoke out of turn."

"You only said what you thought." Somehow she managed to keep her voice steady.

"No, it isn't what I thought at all. I was tired and worried, and used that as an excuse to say hurtful things. I had no right. I know I failed you by acting in such a poor fashion. I won't ask you to forgive me, but I hope it won't make being together intolerable."

"I think I can learn to overlook it. In time. But don't expect it will happen automatically." She was being harsh, but couldn't stop herself.

"I understand." His gaze came to hers. His brown eyes clouded and filled with pain.

She knew something he didn't say. Likely didn't even realize. "I think—" She spoke softly, slowly, forming her words with care, not wanting to bring more hurt and pain into their troubled relationship. "I think you seek ways to prove you failed, just as you suggest I look for things I can blame myself for." She ducked her head, unable to meet his eyes, fearing he would take offense. "I am trying to stop doing that. I hope you will do the same." She sat back in the wagon, not wanting to see pain in his eyes if her words had struck deep.

They rode on in silence for some time. She drowsed in the heat.

"Donna Grace?"

Luke's voice jerked her to attention.

"What is it?" *Please, let's not fight any longer.*

"You're right. I never realized it before. I can't say I

will change right away, but I will try my best to be more mindful of how I choose to view things." His voice deepened. "It's hard to forget that I had some responsibility in Ellen's death, if only by neglecting to protect her."

Donna Grace would not point out that he could only do so much. "There comes a time when a person has to trust God to do His share."

Luke laughed. "Put that way it seems downright foolish to think otherwise."

Relieved the tension between them had eased, Donna Grace edged forward to look out the front.

The freight wagons were ahead of them, and slowly they came to a halt. "Not again," Luke muttered.

Buck rode up. "A couple of wagons are stuck. Come and give us a hand."

Luke jumped down as did Warren and they trotted to the front of the line.

Gil rode to Buck. "Let's take the others to the left. I think they can get around that hole."

Donna Grace climbed to the seat. If need be, she could drive the wagon. Papa had taught her. She waited as the heavy wagons slowly crept across the little draw and up the other side. Two teams were taken back to help with the stuck wagons.

Luke helped get the animals into place. Donna Grace could see he struggled with weary animals that knew what they would have to do, and had decided they didn't want to. The teamsters snapped their whip, yelled and cursed. Luke pulled and shoved.

No wonder the poor man was tired. He'd been doing this for two days now.

Donna Grace called out to Judith. "Can you drive your wagon?"

"Warren has been teaching me."

"I don't see any point in sitting here waiting and doing nothing while your brothers work so hard."

Judith nodded. "I agree. You lead the way."

Donna Grace took up the reins, sorted them in her hand the way Papa had taught her, and praying she was as good as she remembered, she flicked the reins. The mules startled. She chuckled. "Guess you didn't expect to have to move with Luke up there, did you?"

The mules twitched their ears then moved forward. Donna Grace glanced over her shoulder to make sure Elena was safe before she drove the animals across the draw, following in the tracks of the larger wagons. Her wagon hit a hole and jarred forward. For a moment, it stalled. "Giddup," she yelled.

The mules pulled and the wagon righted and moved forward. They reached drier ground and climbed to the hill. The freight wagons, except for the two without oxen, were lined up, waiting.

Donna Grace drew to a halt and looked back to watch Luke and the others trying to free the stuck wagons from the mud. One oozed from the mud and pulled up beside the Russell and Clark wagons.

Luke jogged over. "How did you get over here?"

"I drove."

"There was no need for that."

She met his angry glare with a triumphant little smile. "I saw no need to wait for you."

He looked ready to spit nails.

A groan from the teamster nearest them drew their attention and they followed his look back to the second wagon.

"That axle broke." Luke paused long enough to say, "We'll talk about this later." He jogged back to the second wagon. He, Warren, and the teamster examined the broken axle.

Buck joined them. There was much waving of arms, then Buck rode back, Luke jogging at his heels.

Luke climbed up beside Donna Grace. "We have no option but to stop here while repairs are made." Following Buck's hand signals, he pulled the wagon into place. Warren followed in his wagon, and then the reverend. Even before the other wagons were in place, Luke hopped down and unhitched the mules leading them to grass. At least there was water nearby for the animals. Luke and Warren went to the disabled wagon and began removing the freight. One of the pieces of lumber they had cut at Council Grove provided the spare axle.

Donna Grace picked up Elena then climbed down to join the others in preparing supper.

～

"If it isn't one thing, it's six others," Luke groused as he worked at unloading the wagon.

"I'll venture you aren't talking about the broken axle," Warren answered, his voice mild.

"That's not the only thing. Have you forgotten the last two days of rain? The endless mud?"

"Nope, haven't forgotten, but it isn't the first time we've dealt with all of it. It's not our first time on this trail."

His brother's calm voice did nothing to ease the burning sensation in the pit of Luke's stomach. "Can't even have a cup of hot coffee."

Warren continued. "Seems to me you're overreacting to things."

"Huh. I don't think so."

"T'wasn't too long ago you were grinning from ear to ear about that baby girl. What happened? You and Donna Grace have a spat?"

"What makes you say that?" He added a box to the growing stack of goods on the ground. "Sure hope it don't rain and ruin this stuff."

"I'm familiar with the signs of an argument between a man and his wife."

"I suppose you are." Luke's voice carried far more vinegar than his brother deserved. He straightened and faced Warren. "Sorry, didn't mean to take my frustration out on you."

"Then don't. What's going on?"

"She's so stubborn. Wouldn't even wait for me to drive the wagon across."

Warren's laugh scratched Luke's nerves in a place

they didn't itch. "Seems that's something you should be proud of."

"Proud of? What if the wagon had tipped? And who was looking after the baby?"

Warren brought out another box and set it down without taking a pause. "The wagon didn't tip and she took care of the baby, didn't she?"

"I suppose so." They walked back together.

"Well, little brother, it seems you're upset because she's competent and can take care of herself. Maybe you're afraid she doesn't need you."

"Humph. That's not it at all."

Neither of them spoke as they each grabbed another crate.

They crossed to the stack of goods. It irked Luke to no end that Warren had pinpointed Luke's irritability. Donna Grace didn't need him, didn't even want him, and he was learning more and more how much that hurt. What would Warren say if Luke told him that his marriage to Donna Grace was pretend and temporary?

It might precipitate one of those few occasions when Warren felt a good whopping was in order. Not that he could likely provide it, but he might try.

Luke came at his frustration from a different angle. "You'd think she'd have a little more sense seeing as she just had a baby."

"Do you mean you wish she wanted you to take care of her instead of her taking care of herself? You need to think that one through, my brother."

"What's to think about?" Seemed pretty obvious to him that Donna Grace should allow someone to help her once in a while.

"You can't always be available. She needs to be able to take care of herself and that baby, even when you're not around."

"Are you referring to Ellen? She didn't have a chance, and I should have been there to protect her."

"Maybe someday you will stop carrying all the blame for what happened to her. No one could have guessed those men would come back."

"Humph." They continued to empty the wagon as they talked.

Warren paused to wipe his brow. "Guess I don't have to tell you that there are no guarantees of forever. All I can say, little brother, is make the most of every moment you have." And he strode away.

Luke stared after him. *Make the most of every moment.* For Luke that was the space of a few weeks. Hardly counted.

He and Warren and the teamsters stopped when Judith called out for supper.

Luke could hardly wait to partake of a hot meal. But as he joined the others, his appetite fled.

Donna Grace had some kind of sling around her body that cradled the baby against her and she held the coffee pot, ready to fill their cups.

"What do you think you're doing?" His voice left no doubt as to what he thought of her being up and about.

"Unless I am mistaken, I am offering you coffee. Yes or no?"

"No. And I don't mean coffee. You have a newborn baby. Shouldn't she come first?"

Donna Grace filled his cup. She hovered with the hot liquid about ready to spill over to his hand.

He would not back away, not from the coffee, and not from his intent to make her realize she should be reasonable.

She slowly stopped pouring, but the look she gave him had the power to peel back skin.

His cup full to the point of overflowing, he turned away, and saw that every pair of eyes watched him. Everyone lowered their gaze as he looked at them.

All except Judith and Warren. In each of their eyes he saw shock and warning.

They simply didn't understand how stubborn this woman was being.

Why did he care what they thought? All that mattered was making Donna Grace see that she couldn't—

What was it he didn't want her to do?

He didn't have an answer to his own question, which did nothing to ease the tangled web of his thoughts.

Knowing he acted ungraciously, yet powerless to stop the churn of his emotions, he ate his meal in sullen silence then stalked back to the wagon awaiting repairs. He built a fire to provide light.

Warren and several of their teamsters trotted over

to join them.

The dog sat on its haunches watching and perhaps guarding them. No wolves or other wild animals could sneak up without the dog warning them.

With a grunt, Luke helped ease off the wheel.

The dog growled. The fur along his spine stood at prickly attention.

Luke looked the direction the dog indicated just in time to see the tall stranger slip away. The man and his traveling companion had joined the wagon train the day after the baby was born. Luke knew they were the same pair that had followed him at a distance as he rejoined the wagon train. The tall man was the same one who had come to the river at Council Grove when he and Donna Grace were there. A few too many chance encounters for Luke's peace of mind, and yet, apart from the man's skulking around, Luke had no real reason to object to the pair joining them. They'd paid the passage money, and unless they broke one of the rules, they were entitled to the protection the wagon train offered.

The man disappeared into the darkness and Luke turned his attention back to the task, hoping they would finish in time for them all to grab an hour or two of sleep.

He couldn't remember the last time he'd had a good night's sleep and the lack was making him short-tempered.

Was it the only reason for his current attitude?

It was the only one he was prepared to admit to.

## 12

Donna Grace lay awake listening to the muted sounds of men grunting, the pounding of hammer on wood, and the occasional shout as the men worked on the broken wagon. The light of their campfire threw shifting shadows against the canvas. The oxen shuffled about and the mules stomped. She should be sleeping, but the strain between herself and Luke made it impossible.

All she wanted was to do her share so he would have no reason to consider her presence an inconvenience, or worse, a problem. And yet every time she did anything, he objected. She understood he fought his own memories, dealt with guilt at Ellen's horrible death and the unfair remarks of Ellen's father.

But understanding did not make it any easier. The thought of several weeks of being at cross purposes with Luke did not sit well with her.

Sleep held her in its arms for a short time and then Elena wakened to be fed. Not wanting the baby's fussing to disturb the others, Donna Grace quickly pulled Elena to her breast where she suckled hungrily, her contented little sounds making Donna Grace smile.

The baby had eaten and gone back to sleep when she heard Luke and Warren return to the camp. Luke groaned as he stretched out beneath the wagon. Soon his snores indicated he slept.

Donna Grace smiled, glad he would get a few hours of sleep. The poor man was exhausted.

Elena wakened her in the dark and nursed again. Before the baby finished, someone lit the fire and Luke grunted as he pulled on his boots. Donna Grace quickly slipped from the wagon, leaving Elena to sleep. Warren and Luke had left. A fire flared at the wagon they'd worked on into the night, and then the men led the oxen into place. Donna Grace released her pent-up breath as she realized the wagon was repaired and ready to go.

Several of the freighters had trouble with their oxen and the yelling grew loud, the cursing colorful.

Mrs. Shepton rolled her eyes. "Someone should tell them there's a little girl hearing everything they say."

"I heard it all before," Polly said, with an air of dismissal. "But Uncle says if he ever hears one single word like that from my mouth he'll wash it out with soap." She shuddered. "I tasted some soap to see how bad it was and it's really bad. Besides, like Uncle says, my mama and papa would be very sad if I talked like that."

Chuckling to herself at the child's sweet wisdom, Donna Grace helped prepare a big breakfast. They'd made stacks of biscuits last night and had put more beans to cook. Mrs. Shepton cooked a huge pot of potatoes. Donna Grace made a large amount of dried apple cobbler—enough for them to enjoy it hot for breakfast and cold for the noon meal. Mary Mae fried up enough bacon to do them a couple of meals and Judith made corn dodgers. The men were going to eat well today, and they deserved it. Perhaps between a few hours' sleep, having the wagon repaired and a filling meal, Luke would be in a better mood today.

"Is breakfast ready?" Polly asked. "Can I call the men?"

"You sure can." Mary Mae smiled as the eager child ran toward her uncle calling, "Breakfast. Come and get it before it goes to the pigs."

Donna Grace laughed. "I don't recall us having any pigs."

Polly returned in time to hear Donna Grace's remark. "That's what my mama always said."

"Then I'd say it's a perfect way to call the men in for breakfast," Mary Mae gave the little girl a hug to accompany her words.

The men rushed in, brushing dried mud off their pants before they reached the campfire. They paused for Reverend Shepton to offer a prayer of gratitude, both for warm food, and dry weather.

The men all held out coffee cups and took plates piled high with food. Donna Grace made certain she handed Luke his plate and gave him what she hoped was a conciliatory smile. She did not want the strain between them to continue.

His gaze lingered on hers for a heartbeat and he smiled though it didn't reach his eyes. It was a beginning. The food on his plate disappeared quickly. "Is there enough for seconds?"

Donna Grace refilled his plate. "We made lots knowing how hungry everyone would be."

"Where's the baby?" he asked.

"Asleep in the wagon. I'll hear her if she stirs."

He nodded but his attention was already back on the food. He cleaned his plate and pushed to his feet. "I'll get the mules as soon as I help with that team." He nodded toward a teamster who hadn't been able to get his oxen into place.

It didn't take long to put away the breakfast things. Donna Grace looked to where she'd last seen Luke. The oxen were yoked and ready to go. Her gaze went further afield. There was Luke herding in the mules. All except one. She'd noticed this one before, how it often balked at the harness and nipped at the others. Now it ran past the wagon and headed for a clump of grass and stood with its head down, munching away as if it hadn't had plenty of time to fill its belly.

"Listen for the baby," Donna Grace said to Mary Mae.

"Where are you going?"

"I'm going to bring in that stubborn mule while Luke brings in the others." She pointed to him, as he came toward the camp. One of the freighters walked with him, and they were in such a deep conversation she doubted he had noticed the missing mule.

"You're sure about this?" Mary Mae had always been far more cautious than Donna Grace, which probably explained why Grandfather didn't accuse her of being more trouble than she was worth.

"I can handle one animal." She grabbed a length of rope from the side of the wagon and marched toward the mule.

The crazy critter gave Donna Grace one look and returned to nibbling grass as unconcerned as if a mouse walked toward it.

"I am no mouse, as you will soon discover." She approached slowly, murmuring softly. "No point in you making things difficult for anyone. Luke has had quite enough to deal with the last few days."

She looped the rope as Papa had taught her and held it out ready to drop around the mule's head.

With a speed that would have served the animal well in a different circumstance, such as being chased by wolves, the mule turned about.

Donna Grace saw the intent. "You evil creature." She back-stepped to avoid the oncoming kick. Hooves flew past her face as the mule gave a mocking bray. Her heel caught on a clump of grass and she fell to her back with a bone-jarring thud.

Polly screamed.

Mary Mae yelled, "Donna Grace."

Donna Grace could neither answer nor move. Her air had been knocked clean out of her and she could not get it back.

The mule brayed again and trotted away.

Footsteps thudded toward Donna Grace.

Luke knelt beside her. He slipped his arm under her shoulders. "Are you okay?" He touched her face. "Where did he kick you?"

She pawed at his arm, frantic for air.

His eyes narrowed and then he nodded, understanding her problem. "Take a deep breath."

As if she could!

He sat her up, leaned her forward and rubbed her back. "Use your stomach muscles to fill your lungs."

Was he referring to the muscles that had recently stretched so far with the weight of a baby that they were now flabby, and totally useless? But thinking about it made her able to suck in air. She took several deep breaths before she felt normal again. "I'm fine now."

He sat beside her, their faces close enough that she saw the little white lines fanning out from his eyes and the dark streak through his brown irises.

"Where did you get kicked?"

"I didn't. I saw it coming and backed away. I simply fell hard."

"You're sure?"

"I think I'd know."

"I saw his hooves come up and—" The way he

sucked in air one would think he'd had *his* breath knocked out.

"Why?" he demanded in a voice full of fury. "Are you out here trying to corral the craziest, most dangerous mule in all of New Mexico, and maybe even further afield." He spat out each word.

Inside, she shivered at his anger, but outwardly, she faced him with complete calm. "I thought I'd help."

"Maybe you should stop trying to help."

"And do what? Sit around and be nothing but a nuisance." She scrambled to her feet. No way would she rub at the bruise on her bottom. Any more than she would let him know that his words had hurt her deeply. He made it obvious her help was a nuisance to him.

He was on his feet before she took a step and stood right before her so she couldn't move. "You'd be more help if you stayed at the campfire and took care of the baby."

"How dare you? I have not neglected Elena for one moment and I never will." She pushed past him and hurried to the camp. So much for easing things between them. Instead, she'd succeeded in making them worse.

Mary Mae grabbed her arms when she prepared to steam past. "Are you okay? I thought for sure you were going to be killed." Mary Mae choked back a sob.

Donna Grace hugged her sister. "I'm fine. Takes a lot to kill someone like me."

Mary Mae's laugh was without amusement.

Without meeting the looks of the others, not wanting to know if they judged her for being foolish, a nuisance, or whatever they might choose to think, she went to the back of the wagon and climbed in. Elena slept peacefully, but nevertheless, Donna Grace scooped her up and held her tight to her chest.

She faced out the back as Luke harnessed the mules and climbed to the seat. He hesitated a moment before he flicked the reins, but she did not move, even though she was just a tiny bit curious to see if he looked toward her.

Elena thought she should be fed if she was awake, so Donna Grace nursed the baby. She tried to ignore her confused feelings, but they would not go away.

All she wanted to do was help and everything she did ended up causing problems. Just as Grandfather Ramos said. But to be told she neglected the baby, well, that was going too far.

"Donna Grace." Luke called her name softly.

Stubbornly, she stared out the back.

"I know you can hear me." A beat of waiting. She did not respond. "I wish we weren't always fighting."

She kept her response inside her. But the words did no good if she kept them to herself, so with a shaky voice she spoke them aloud wondering if he heard her. "Don't treat me like I'm useless or a nuisance, but most of all never suggest I would neglect Elena."

"I don't think you are a nuisance and I certainly don't think you are useless. Never have. Never will.

Any more than I think you would neglect the baby, but when—" His voice broke. "When I saw Old Achilles kicking and you go down... Donna Grace you have no idea how scared I was. I expected to see you all broken to pieces or worse."

Her heart melted as she realized what he expected to see—a scene similar to when he'd found Ellen. She edged forward and pressed her hand to his arm. "Luke, I am so sorry. I know now that it must have reminded you of Ellen. I never thought of it that way."

He nodded. "Truth is, I wasn't even thinking of Ellen." His gaze hit hers with a force it left her speechless. His look went on and on searching out and filling empty places that, until now, she'd been unaware of.

A teamster snapped a whip. The sound jerked her away from the long journey into her soul.

Her cheeks burned. What had just happened? She was at a loss to explain it and sought for a way to erase her uneasiness. She stared at the mules. "Old Achilles? Really?"

~

LUKE COULD HAVE LET Donna Grace believe he thought of Ellen when he saw the mule kick at her. But his first and only thought had been he would find her battered beyond recognition and hold her as she bled. Yes, it was much like what he'd gone through with Ellen. But this time it was different. And that left him fighting a war with himself. He couldn't grow too fond of Donna Grace, though he couldn't remember his reasons, apart from his promise to let her go when they reached Santa Fe. That was the fact of their relationship, but somehow knowing it and feeling it as he looked deep into her eyes were two distinctly different things.

He was grateful she'd looked away and asked about Old Achilles, and he chuckled a little though he wondered if it sounded as forced as it felt. "You remember the naturalist?"

"I think you've mentioned him a time or two."

Her wry sense of humor pleased him and his laugh was genuine. "I suppose I should call him by his name."

"Seems like, after all this time, a proper introduction would be in order."

His smile went clear to the pit of his stomach. "Mrs. Russell, allow me to introduce you to Mr. Dusty Leaf."

Her eyes widened. Her mouth opened and closed without a word coming out.

His laugh began deep in his chest and rumbled upwards.

"You are surely joshing me."

"Nope. He once told me his real name was Darwin Leaf but some classmates started calling him Dusty Leaf as a joke, and he liked it so much he went by that name ever after."

Her grin widened her mouth and sparkled from her eyes. "I like that. He sounds like a nice fellow."

"He was excellent company." Almost as good as

Donna Grace, but he was wise enough not to say that aloud.

"So he named the mule?"

"Yup. He said it referred to a weak spot on the body that gave a person grief." He touched the back of his heel. "He told a little story about a Greek hero called Achilles who was dipped into a special river to make him be strong." He'd forgotten most of the details Dusty had told him and struggled to complete the story. "His mother held him by the heels, so they never touched the water and so that became his weakness."

"So that mule is a weakness? I don't understand."

"Let's just say the animal tends to bring out the worst in me."

As soon as she understood his meaning, she had a good laugh. Her amusement ended abruptly. "Am I also an Achilles heel to you?"

He understood her need for reassurance, but he wasn't sure how to provide it. "Donna Grace, if I worry about some of the things you do, it isn't because you're a nuisance, it's because I don't want you hurt."

She studied her hands in her lap. "I'll try to remember that."

Elena fussed and Donna Grace went back to tend her.

Luke wished he could find a way to convince her she wasn't a bother. But perhaps he would always fall short of what she needed.

She had told him to stop seeing himself as a failure.

Was that even possible? He shifted his thoughts to how she'd laughed at his confession that the mule brought out the worst in him.

And Donna Grace? So far she hadn't brought out the best, but she made him wish it would happen.

They journeyed onward. Luke hunkered down in his thoughts as Donna Grace fed the baby. Elena fussed a little and Donna Grace hummed.

He recognized the tune as the hymn he'd taught her and softly sang along until Donna Grace whispered, "She's asleep." She settled the baby on a pad in the hollow of a trunk tray then eased forward to rest her forearms on the back of the bench. She was close enough he could admire the smoothness of her skin and see her dark and thick eyelashes. Not that he hadn't noticed before, nor had he failed to note that Elena had inherited those eyelashes.

"Clever way to keep her safe."

"Thanks. But that's my job, isn't it? To keep her safe."

"And mine as long as we're together."

They both fell silent. It would be difficult to relinquish his protectiveness when they reached Santa Fe.

～

ONE THING STAYED in Donna Grace's mind. He hadn't thought of Ellen as he rushed to her side when he thought the mule had kicked her.

She told herself it meant nothing, but her heart

refused to listen. The trouble was, she wasn't sure what to think. Finally, she gave up trying to reason it out. Better to continue as they had started, as they had agreed things would be.

Their noon break was short, as Buck wanted to make up for lost time. The animals grazed and the men rested and then they were on their way.

Donna Grace opted to sit beside Luke, the baby in her arms as they continued throughout the afternoon. When feeding time came, she wasn't sure what to do. She did not want to nurse the baby in front of a man. Yes, he was her husband, but in name only. She solved the problem by covering up with a thin blanket. The blanket slipped. She grabbed it. "If you stop, I can climb in back."

"I am your husband. I think it's acceptable to nurse the baby with me at your side."

What was she supposed to say to that? Point out that he wasn't really her husband? Confess that this whole business made her uncomfortable?

Elena wailed her distress at the delay and flailed her hands about.

"Feed the poor little mite," Luke said.

Seems she had no other choice and she struggled to keep the blanket in place while getting Elena to her breast. Finally it all came together. Donna Grace's cheeks burned at the suckling sounds from the baby. "She's rather a noisy eater."

Luke chuckled. "I think she's enjoying herself." He squeezed her shoulder. "Relax, Donna Grace; we'll soon learn to be comfortable with this whole process."

"I hope so." She wanted to explain she didn't know how to view Luke.

Before she could find the right words, Buck rode up. "There's buffalo off to the north. We're going to take a hunting party out to get fresh meat. Make camp early so the meat can be dealt with." He rode away, four men riding in his trail.

Luke's gaze followed them out of sight.

"Are you wanting to go with them?" Donna Grace asked. "If so, I can drive the wagon. You know I can."

"I'm sure they don't need my help."

*And I do*, she silently added, but found she didn't mind the thought as much as she likely should.

By the time they stopped for supper, Buck and his crew had returned with meat and distributed some to each camp. The women set to work cutting much of it into strips to hang by the fire to dry. Several hunks were put to roast. A large stew simmered for the evening meal, filling the air with delicious scents.

It would be a treat to have something besides salt-cured meat.

Donna Grace heard Elena fussing in the wagon and went to nurse her. The baby finished and smacked her lips contentedly just as the men came in for their meal. Donna Grace needed to help with last minute things, and she knew exactly what she wanted to do with Elena.

She marched up to Luke. "Sit down."

Too startled to argue, he did so.

"It's time for you to hold the baby." She placed Elena in Luke's arms.

Luke opened his mouth to protest, but Donna Grace moved away. The baby snuffled, drawing Luke's attention. Elena opened her eyes and looked up at Luke. Luke smiled and touched the little fingers.

"How can anything so tiny, be so complete?"

Elena pursed her lips as if considering his question. Luke chuckled.

Donna Grace knew Elena had won Luke's heart. It would be well to have a loyal, protective father figure for the rest of the journey.

She turned away. And then she would have to be both father and mother to Elena. Against her better judgment, she again watched them. Could she replace the adoration in Luke's face? Could she teach Elena how to measure a man by judging him against Luke?

She sank to the ground as if exhausted and Judith rushed over with a cup of tea. But it wasn't fatigue that weakened her knees. It was the glimpse of a future without Luke in it.

Pulling her determination into place, she reminded herself of the folly of expecting a man to want to stay with her forever.

Even a man like Luke? She had to tell herself yes, even a man like Luke.

The meal was ready and their little group gathered around to enjoy the succulent stew.

Eating with the others and listening to their news,

went a long way toward making Donna Grace feel like things were back to normal. Except for one big change —Elena Rose's presence. Donna Grace had taken the baby so Luke could eat.

Mary Mae had eaten her meal in a rush. "I'll hold her now."

Donna Grace handed over her little daughter. She sat beside Luke and ate. She had finished, and was about to take the baby back, when Judith set her plate aside.

"As another aunt, I'd like a chance to get to know little Elena."

Mary Mae kissed Elena goodbye and handed her to Judith.

"Hello, wee one. I am your Auntie Judith. It's a pleasure to hold you and tell you how special you are."

An extra-large dose of sweetness filled Donna Grace's heart at the love being heaped upon Elena.

After a bit, Mrs. Shepton begged for a chance to hold the baby she'd helped bring into the world. Polly hovered nearby until Mary Mae asked if she wanted to hold the baby.

"Oh yes, more than anything." So Polly held her under Mary Mae's care.

Donna Grace smiled. One thing she didn't have to worry about was having someone to take the baby when she needed help. In fact, Elena might become quite spoiled, but Donna Grace was okay with that. She didn't think a baby could get too much love.

Luke sat beside Donna Grace. "Do you think I

might be allowed to hold Elena again? After all, I am her father."

Mary Mae lifted the baby into Luke's arms. He cradled her on his drawn-up knees so they looked at each other.

"Elena Rose, you are a very special little girl. I know everyone else has already told you that, but now it's my turn. You will always have a spot all your own in my heart and I will do everything in my power to make sure you have a good life." Luke's voice grew husky.

Donna Grace's throat tightened. He made it sound like he meant to have a permanent part in her daughter's life. Would he be wanting to visit on occasion? Be involved in decisions regarding the child? Donna Grace wished she knew. Or did she? Perhaps it was best to accept his sweet regard for little Elena for the duration of the trip.

A harmonica played from the freighters camp. A familiar tune that stirred memories.

"Mary Mae, do you recall that tune? Papa taught us the song when we were on this trail with him." She listened for the note and then began to sing, "Buffalo Gals, won't you come out tonight?"

Mary Mae joined her in perfect harmony. The mouth organ accompanied them.

When the song ended, both camps clapped.

"Mighty fine singing," the man with the mouth organ called. "I could play you some more tunes."

"More," called the freighters. "Give us more."

"Please do," Luke murmured. "That was lovely."

"Very well." She called out the name of a song, and the harmonica notes carried into the air. She and Mary Mae sang three songs together. Then Donna Grace turned to the others. "Join us."

Song after song they sang, the freighters booming voices a drumbeat to the melodious harmony in the smaller camp. Luke's deep voice echoed inside Donna Grace's heart and found a home there.

The mouth organ changed and the notes of "Amazing Grace," drifted heavenward.

The two groups sang the stirring song. When it ended, silence followed, such as Donna Grace had never before heard in the camp.

"It's almost like being in church," she whispered.

"'Thou art holy, O thou that inhabitest the praises of Israel,' Psalm twenty-two, verse three," the reverend murmured. He edged closer to the fire. "How many of you know the story behind that hymn?" He went on as if someone had answered him. "John Newton spent many years as a slave trader. He had a reputation as one of the most obscene of men. His own captain once chained him up for his behavior. From what I've learned, a violent storm threatened to drown them at sea and he called out for the Lord to have mercy. The ship eventually reached shore and Newton began a journey to God. The knowledge that God would forgive a man such as him moved him to write this song."

Donna Grace realized she gripped Luke's hand and

wondered when she'd reached for him. Slowly she began to withdraw. She did not want him to think she wanted more than they had agreed to. Then she remembered he promised to be her protector and provider on this journey and she stilled her hand.

At that moment, Elena fussed.

"It's time to feed her." Donna Grace went to the wagon.

Luke followed, carrying the baby. He cradled Elena in one arm and reached out to assist Donna Grace into the wagon. She unbuttoned her dress to feed the baby.

Luke remained at the back. Shrouded in the darkness of the interior of the wagon, Donna Grace felt at ease with his presence.

"That was a good evening." Made better, she confessed to herself, because she and Luke had arrived at some sort of peace in their odd relationship.

"It was, wasn't it? I think I'll have to add it to my store of good memories." His soft chuckle warmed her insides.

Right then and there, she decided that sound would be one of *her* good memories. "I just realized how many of my pleasant memories were made on the Santa Fe Trail."

"Tell me what you mean."

"Well, traveling with Papa was a good memory. He let me help him, treated me like I mattered. It was such a contrast to the few weeks we spent with Grandfather. Of course, Grandfather Ramos had made his disapproval of me clear long before Mama died."

"Your mother must have been a very strong woman to stand up to her father and be loyal to your papa. I can understand where you get your strength."

"Thank you. I couldn't ask for a better compliment."

"It's more of a fact than a compliment." She heard the amusement in his voice.

"On the trail was where I shot my first deer." She laughed at his startled gasp. "Where I learned to drive the wagon and hitch up the mules. Where I encountered my first rattle snake, though I wouldn't say that was a good memory."

"I'm guessing you weren't bitten or you wouldn't be here."

"Papa shot the thing." She shuddered. "I hate snakes."

"Let's hope you don't encounter any on this trip."

"Amen to that." She shook aside the thought. "The best thing that happened on the Santa Fe Trail this time, is the birth of little Elena. I wanted her to wait until Santa Fe, but now that she's here, I couldn't be happier."

Luke touched the baby's head as she lay against Donna Grace's breast. "Yes, she is the best thing that ever happened on the trail."

"You must have lots of good memories of the trail, too. Tell me about them." She wouldn't come right out and admit it, but she wasn't anxious for him to leave.

He didn't answer for a moment and when he did, his voice had deepened as if he knew only regret. "I joined Warren in freighting simply to forget. So I mostly didn't take note of anything except the next task ahead of me. The only thing that mattered was getting the wagons to Santa Fe, and then getting back and doing it again."

She edged forward so she could reach out and touch him.

He continued, his voice growing stronger. "Then I began to notice things. Like the way the sunsets painted the entire sky red, or pink or orange, or a whole cast of colors. I began to admire the buffalo and the deer." He chuckled softly. "I think our friend, the naturalist, helped me to see nature and wildlife in a new way. I'd have to say spending a trip with Dusty Leaf was a very good memory."

"I'm glad."

Elena snuffled with contentment, asleep in the crook of Donna Grace's arm.

Luke pressed his hand over Donna Grace's. "This trip is the best I've ever had."

She would not ask why. She wanted him to say it was because of her, yet feared it would be some other reason. Likely Elena. Not that she didn't want him to think the baby was as precious as Donna Grace did.

"Aren't you going to ask why?" His low voice tugged at her resistance.

She tugged right back. "I don't think so."

He laughed low in his throat. "I know why."

She rocked her head back and forth, not caring

whether or not he could see her in the duskiness of the wagon interior.

He continued. "You want to be the reason, but you don't think you deserve to be." .

She would not indicate whether or not she agreed.

"Donna Grace, having you here as my wife has made this the very best trip."

Her throat closed off so she couldn't answer for a second. Then she said the first thing that sprang to her mind. "You might change your mind before the trip is over."

"Or I might not."

More than half-expecting he would be annoyed, she was surprised to hear the amusement in his voice.

Mary Mae called, "Good night, Donna Grace."

Donna Grace hadn't realized how late it had grown and withdrew into the wagon. "Good night, Mary Mae. Good night, Luke."

"Goodnight Donna Grace and Elena Rose." Amusement and pleasure filled his words.

Elena slept after her feeding and remained asleep as everyone went to bed. Donna Grace had opted to sleep in the wagon where she wouldn't disturb Mary Mae, and the baby could rest safely in the little nest she had fashioned for her.

Sleep had claimed her in its gentle embrace when crying jerked her awake. "Hush, baby. Hush." She pulled Elena to her breast and fed her. Again the baby slept. This being a mother wasn't so bad.

Elena wakened again before morning.

"You're a hungry little one tonight." Elena ate readily enough, but instead of going back to sleep, continued to fuss. "You'll have the whole camp awake." Donna Grace rocked as best she could in the narrow space, but Elena would not settle.

Luke whispered from the doorway. "Has she eaten?"

"Yes."

"Hang on a minute." There came the sound of wood being placed cautiously on the fire and then small flames made it possible to see. Luke returned. "Give her to me and I'll walk her."

"But you need your sleep." The men had put in long hours getting the wagons through the mud.

"So do you, and as the father I am responsible to help care for her."

She couldn't remind him he was only pretending to be Elena's father for fear someone would overhear her. "Very well." She swaddled the baby and handed her to Luke.

His footsteps thudded away and he could be heard making soothing sounds. The baby quieted.

Donna Grace lay back. Luke wanted to help, and she reluctantly admitted she didn't mind having someone take a turn with the baby. But she wasn't going to let herself get used to it. If she needed help, she would waken Mary Mae. She smiled at the thought. Her sister slept soundly enough to make waking her a bit of a challenge.

Later, as Luke hitched up the mules, Donna Grace

stood by watching. "Well, Old Achilles," she muttered to the mule. "You thought to do me harm, but you missed."

The animal lifted his nose and brayed.

Luke finished with the animals, then came to help Donna Grace up to the seat.

She'd had quite enough of being in the back of the wagon alone and much preferred Luke's company.

She waited for him to climb up beside her and head down the trail to ask a question that burned her tongue since she'd spoken to the mule. "Did you sell this team of mules to my papa?"

"I did."

"Why would you sell him Old Achilles when you know what sort of animal he is?" Selling a cranky, hard to handle animal didn't match the picture that steadily developed in her mind of Luke. An honest, thoughtful, caring man.

"Your father knew exactly what the mule is like, but he wanted him for the very same reason I keep him. Old Achilles can out-pull any other mule, and he'll do it once he's in harness. He just likes to exert a little independence once in a while."

"I see." She smiled at the backend of the mule in question. "Can't help but admire an attitude like that."

Luke gave his low-throated chuckle. "Kind of thought you might feel that way."

She slanted him a look meant to be scolding, but at the way his eyes danced, she couldn't help but laugh.

Elena wakened and shuffled. "Time for her to eat."

Donna Grace had grown more adept at feeding the baby with a cotton blanket to provide modesty.

The baby slept again. "She's such a good little thing," Donna Grace said.

"Let's hope she remains that way, and doesn't grow into a head-strong young lady."

Donna Grace decided to ignore how he talked like he would be there when Elena grew older, and instead, concentrated on the other part of what Luke said. "I hope she grows up to be strong and independent."

"Like her mother. I guess that would be okay."

"Oh, thanks for such high praise." She drew herself up and tried to look huffy.

All he did was chuckle softly. Little did he know how that sound affected her. Making her want to forget her own plans and follow him blindly.

She looked away, pretending an interest in the passing scenery, even though there was nothing to see but yellowed grass and blue sky.

Somehow—and really soon—she must learn to steel herself against the way her heart tipped toward him when he chuckled.

Thankfully, they soon stopped for the noon break, and Luke was busy with the animals and checking on the freight wagons. While the men rested, Donna Grace and the others checked the drying meat that had been hung on the sides of the wagons. Because of the recent rain and the fact they were among the first wagons on the trail, the meat hadn't gathered more than a sprinkling of dust.

They resumed their travels. The sun beat down upon them. For the most part, Elena slept.

But after the noon break, she cried and refused to settle even after she'd nursed. Donna Grace put her to her shoulder and patted her back. Still she fussed.

"Maybe it's something I ate."

"Could that be the problem?"

"I don't know. I've never had a baby before." Frustration made her words sharp.

"I'll take her."

"You're driving the wagon. What if Old Achilles decides to have a temper tantrum?"

"Like I told you, he's fine in harness." Luke shifted the reins to one hand and held out his arm for the baby.

What harm would it do? Donna Grace shifted the baby to him.

"There you go, little one." As he talked to her, Elena focused on his face, her mouth a perfect little rose. "You're snug and safe in your papa's arms. Isn't that a good place to be?"

Donna Grace leaned against Luke's arm, wanting to enjoy this moment and maybe even be a part of it.

Elena seemed mesmerized by the sound of his voice.

"That's a girl. You sit back and enjoy the trip."

Elena wrinkled up her face, ready to cry again.

Luke sang and Elena calmed.

The sound of Luke's voice soothed Elena's mother as well.

He was making it extremely difficult to imagine a future without him.

Buck must have been satisfied with the progress they'd made, or else he liked the spot he'd chosen for their camp, as he called for them to stop before dark.

Donna Grace and the other ladies set about making good use of the time to prepare more food. Not only for the cold meal they would consume at noon the next day. They had all learned to have a little ahead in case rain kept them from cooking.

Donna Grace straightened from tending the pot of beans intended to last them several meals. A movement past the wagon caught her attention. She hurried around in time to see a man duck out of sight. Had he been watching her? Perhaps he was one of the freighters looking for Warren or Luke and seeing they weren't there, had left without making himself known to the women.

She thought she would recognize each of the teamsters, but maybe not. Buck had gone out of his way to keep the women and the freighters away from each other. She hadn't asked why, but assumed Buck might consider the behavior and language of the teamsters to be unsuitable for mixed company. Donna Grace had heard enough of the language ringing through the air to agree with him.

She returned to her task, but twice more that evening she thought she saw the same man lurking about. After her encounter with the ruffians at the beginning of their journey, she had no desire to run into a stranger while on her own, and so she stayed close to the camp. Afraid her baby might be in danger, she kept a close eye on her, too.

Her nervousness had grown obvious enough for Luke to take her aside. "You don't need to constantly guard Elena. Anyone in our camp will watch her if you want to go for a walk."

"I know."

"Then come with me. I want to show you something."

For several seconds she hesitated. But she needed to learn to trust Elena was safe even when she was out of sight, so she asked Mary Mae to take care of the baby, and reluctantly went with Luke. It wasn't that she didn't enjoy his company, but her nerves were on edge after seeing that man skulking about.

Luke pulled Donna Grace's arm around his as they left the circle of the wagons and walked in the lengthening shadows. She pulled him to a halt as they passed the cluster of teamsters. One played a mouth organ and two did a little jig, but it was the man lounging against the wheel of a nearby wagon that she studied.

"I don't recall seeing that man here before." She pointed to the one she meant. "And the one beside him. Isn't the tall one the man we saw at Council Grove? Why is he here?" What was it about him that seemed so familiar?

## 13

L uke knew who she meant. The two men who had joined the wagon train after Elena's birth. "They were with the trappers, but had some sort of disagreement so they decided to go to Santa Fe instead." The pair made his nerves twitch. He'd seen them looking into wagons that were no business of theirs, and had watched the taller one wander past the smaller camp. Luke did not care for the way the man eyed the women. He'd alerted Buck and Gil who both promised to keep an eye on the pair.

"Let's move on." He guided Donna Grace away from the wagons to the crest of a little hill. "Look." He pointed to the north.

She squinted. "Buffalo! It's the first time I've seen them on this trip." With a happy laugh she sank to the ground and watched them. "When we came up the trail with Papa, we saw thousands of them run by us. The pots and pans rattled as the ground shook."

He sat beside her. It was pleasant to have her alone for a little time. Without anyone else around to over-hear their conversation, he'd be able to speak more freely. He patted his breast pocket where the piece of paper lay, then turned his attention back to the buffalo.

"They are fascinating creatures. Did you know a buffalo's hump is composed of muscle, supported by long vertebrae? It allows the animal to use its head to plow through snow."

"More information from your naturalist friend?" Teasing flashed in her eyes.

He laughed. "I enjoyed learning things from the man."

"I gathered that." Her gaze returned to the herd. At some unseen signal, or perhaps a threat of danger, the herd thundered away.

They watched until the animals disappeared from sight, but Donna Grace showed no indication she wanted to return to the camp and Luke was content to enjoy a few quiet moments in her company. He again patted his breast pocket where he had put the letter from his friend in California. What would Donna Grace say if he told her he was considering going there and starting a ranch?

Since the birth of Elena Rose, the appeal of a home and family had grown steadily. Before he could mention it, Donna Grace spoke.

"There's only one thing about my so-called marriage to Melvin I don't regret."

"Elena Rose?"

Her gaze stayed in the distant horizon. "That's right. I've been trying to understand why he would pretend to marry me when he was not in a position to do so."

Luke's fists bunched at his sides. Bad enough to do that to Donna Grace, but then to turn his back on his own flesh and blood. It made Luke's insides boil. And why Mr. Clark had not defended his daughter's honor truly baffled Luke.

"How could he so carelessly leave me with child, but without a husband?" She rocked her head back and forth.

Luke wanted to comfort her, but he also wanted her to say more about this Melvin character. He wanted to understand why she had married him.

"I think I am beginning to realize why. Melvin often talked about Papa's success on the trail. He'd heard somewhere that men could make thousands of dollars carrying freight back and forth."

He nodded. "There's good money to be made if everything goes well. Just as much to be lost if a wagon has to be abandoned, or a load is lost in a river crossing."

Her attention returned to the distance as if she saw her past. "I think Melvin thought Papa was rich and he hoped he could wrangle his way into Papa's good graces and become a partner." Her attempt at a laugh sounded more like a wail. "Not that I can see him ever actually coming on this trip. He liked his comfort too well for that."

Luke waited, wanting Donna Grace to answer the question that pressed at his thoughts. When it seemed she wouldn't, he asked it. "Why did you marry him?"

"I cannot, for the life of me, think why I did."

"You must have loved him at one time."

"I suppose I fancied myself in love with him. Or maybe I simply liked the idea of love and home and family. He never talked about his family, so I assumed he was alone in the world. I fear I thought that would make him look at me as totally necessary for his happiness." Her hands twisted together until her knuckles turned into tight little marbles.

He unfisted his hands and reached for hers, cradling them between his palms.

She leaned into his shoulder. "In hindsight, I see that I was foolish and desperately seeking approval, which he readily gave me, but it was only words. I meant nothing to him."

Luke rested his cheek to her hair. "Donna Grace, why would you want approval that badly? You are a strong, independent woman who—" He wanted to say she needed no one but he didn't want her to think that. No, wait, it wasn't needing someone he wanted her to believe, it was wanting someone. "You are capable of taking care of yourself, if that is what you want."

She sat up. "Melvin has left me little choice. All that matters now is taking care of Elena."

He wished he heard more conviction in her voice.

She rose to her feet. "I don't like to be away from her too long."

"Of course." The opportunity to tell her about the letter in his pocket had passed. Perhaps it was for the best.

They walked slowly back to the camp.

Again, she paused to watch the teamsters. The tall man she'd mentioned still stood by the wagon.

"There's something about him that seems familiar," she murmured. "But I can't place him." With a shake of her head, she moved on. "Surely, as I said, he simply reminds me of the kind of man I saw often back in Santa Fe."

Luke resisted the urge to say if that was the sort of man she encountered, it was no wonder that her grandfather didn't want her playing in the plaza.

Elena slept peacefully in Mary Mae's arms when they returned. Little Polly hung over Mary Mae's shoulder admiring the baby. Donna Grace hurried to her sister's side.

"Did she fuss?"

"She's been as good as gold."

Luke leaned back on his heels watching the cluster of people around the baby. He chuckled low in his throat, bringing Donna Grace's inquiring gaze to him.

Still grinning he answered her silent question. "I

find myself amazed and amused at how much attention one tiny baby garners."

"It's 'cause she's so sweet and little and everything,"
Polly said.

"I agree." His enthusiasm earned him an approving
smile from Donna Grace.

"I need to check on the freighters." He hurried
away, his thoughts haunting him. How was he to let
Donna Grace and the baby go when the time came?

But he couldn't go back on his word.

The next day brought no rain. Buck insisted they
travel long hours in an attempt to make up for lost
time. He insisted they would reach Cottonwood
Crossing before nightfall. And they did so by pushing
on until dark.

They circled the wagons and took care of the
animals, taking them down the steep bank to the river
for water while the women made a fire and prepared a
meal.

Luke returned to hear Donna Grace laughing and
paused to enjoy the pleasure that coursed through his
veins at the sound of her merriment. Having her on
this trip had changed everything about it. No longer
was getting wagons across the plains and the prairie
all that mattered. He looked forward to the evening
meal with far more anticipation than he ever had
when sharing it with the teamsters.

A man could get used to a woman to share his life.

His feet jerked to a halt.

He'd planned on sharing his life with Ellen and

learned how badly he could fail, and how painful his failure could be. It was foolhardy to contemplate repeating that lesson.

Rather than go to the campfire where the others gathered, he sidetracked toward the river again. A rustling in the nearby bushes brought him up short.

He put his hand on his sidearm and waited.

A tall figure eased from the bushes and strode toward the wagons without noticing Luke in the shadows. It was the man who had joined them. The one Donna Grace thought looked familiar. The man stopped by the Russell wagon. He appeared to be watching Donna Grace and the others.

Luke waited, watching. The man wandered back toward the teamsters. Only when he stepped over the wagon tongue and joined the others did Luke move. He would keep an eye on that man but doing so proved nigh unto impossible as they spent the next day getting wagons down the steep slope and across the creek. The women opted to stay on the near side searching the bushes for late gooseberries and raspberries. The men hurried back and forth, double teaming the animals to pull the wagons through the muddy creek. The tall man, whose name he'd learned was Manuel Garcia, made himself useful helping with the work. So long as Luke could see him he didn't worry.

∽

THE HOPE of finding berries this late in the season drew the women like the promise of ice cream at a summer picnic. Donna Grace fashioned a sling so Elena rode safely in front of her.

"I don't expect there will be enough to make a cobbler," she said with the authority of one who had been over the trail before. "When we were here last time, the bushes were loaded with gooseberries, raspberries and prairie plums, but that was July."

"I'm taking a pot just in case," Judith said. "The men would surely appreciate any sort of fresh fruit."

Mary Mae steadied Donna Grace as they made their way down the steep slope. Cottonwood trees held out arms with fingers of gold and yellow leaves. Bushes crowded to the edge of the stream. The women spread out and pushed their way into the prickly raspberry bushes with the occasional red berry clinging to the branches.

Donna Grace picked half a dozen and popped them into her mouth, pressing the fruit against the roof of her mouth to squish out the sweet burst of flavor. She almost moaned with delight. She moved on, drawn forward by the enticement of more, and was not disappointed.

A thicket of gooseberry bushes with its cruel thorns were no match for a woman set on enjoying their fruit. But she had to be careful not to let the thorns poke Elena, so she left the gooseberries.

Donna Grace moved on, now intent on finding enough fruit to take back for Luke—for the men, she amended quickly. She heard Mary Mae and Judith to one side. Polly was with them and her childish voice carried clearly in the air.

A soft voice informed her Mrs. Shepton was close enough to speak to the others.

The sound of one of the women thrashing through the bushes brought a smile to her lips. Seems they were all determined to find as many berries as possible.

She stumbled on a root and caught herself. Her heart kicked her ribs at the realization she might have fallen on Elena. She must be more careful. The bushes gave way to a small clearing and she stepped into it. That's when she saw the tall man from the wagon train, astride a horse.

What was he doing here? Fear turned her stomach sour.

She slowly retreated.

The rider rode around her, blocking her escape. Exactly the way Grandfather had herded her from the plaza. Anger replaced her fear, and she stood still and faced the man.

"Who are you and what do you want?"

He leaned over, resting his arms on the pommel of his saddle. "You don't remember me?"

She shook her head as she tried to place his familiar face.

"Well, I remember you, Miss Clark."

"It's Mrs. Russell." Hopefully the name would cause him to reconsider whatever evil intent he had.

"Señor Ramos is your grandfather."

She stared at him without acknowledging his statement. "Who are you?"

"I'm not surprised the high and mighty little girl who used to play with my Rosa would not remember a mere peasant."

She didn't remember him as a peasant. He'd had a tiny, but successful little trading post. "You're Mr. Garcia? Rosa's father? Where is Rosa? I have missed her so much."

"Little you care about Rosa."

"I named my baby after her. Her name is Elena Rose." She pressed a protective hand to her daughter as her mind raced. She had to convince this man that they should be friends. "I would love to contact Rosa. Do you have her address?"

"You'll never hear from her." He edged his horse closer.

Donna Grace backed away never taking her eyes off the man. The look in his eyes frightened her, but she would not let him guess it.

"What do you want?"

He laughed, a sound that sent a shiver across her shoulders. "Your grandfather put me out of business. He threatened my family."

"I didn't know. I'm sorry."

"Now he will pay." Mr. Garcia swung down from his horse and strode toward Donna Grace.

She glanced to the right and the left.

He gave another of those frightening laughs.

"There is no place to run." He took another step. "I wonder how much he will pay to see his grand-daughter and great-granddaughter safe?"

Knowing his intent fueled a burst of desperate energy and she feinted to the right and as he lunged after her, she ran to the left.

"Mary Mae. Help! Someone. Help!" Fear made her voice thinner than usual. How far would that weak cry go?

She made it to the edge of the woods before he clamped a cruel hand around her arm and jerked her to a halt. He pressed a smelly hand over her mouth.

"Here now. Don't be foolish. You can't get away, so no point in trying. And if you holler again I might have to persuade you to be quiet." He patted Elena and she understood his threat.

She bit her tongue to keep from spitting out the words burning in her brain. She would never stop trying to escape this man, but she would not put Elena at risk doing so. *God in heaven protect us and guide us.*

He forced her back to the horse. "You can get on or I can throw you on. Might hurt the baby if I do that."

She guessed he wouldn't hesitate to hurt Elena. "I'll get on." The horse was tall and the baby in front of her made it awkward, but she managed to pull herself to the saddle and sat astride. One of the many things her grandfather had objected to.

What would he say if he saw her now?

Mr. Garcia led the horse away. Donna Grace

ducked to keep from having her brow battered by the low branches of the trees as they entered the woods.

At least they wouldn't go fast with him walking.

Then she saw a second horse ahead, saddled and waiting and she pressed back a groan. "Where are you taking me?"

"Don't see that it matters to you." He swung into the saddle, holding her horse's reins firmly, leaving her no choice but to follow at his side.

Señor Garcia led them through thick bushes that tore at Donna Grace's skirts. Her legs would be a mess of scratches, but there existed no room for pain amidst her fear and anger.

Her knee pressed to the man's as the thin trail narrowed.

He leered at her. "You're not a kid any longer. You turned out to be a nice-looking woman."

Donna Grace stared straight ahead, praying her shock at his comments didn't show. Perhaps talking about his daughter would divert her attention from staring at her with that hungry look. "I expect Rosa is all grown up now, too. Is she married?"

He jerked his attention to the trail. "You never mind Rosa, you hear?"

Elena stirred. Donna Grace patted her. *Please, my sweet baby, don't need to eat right now.* The thought of having to feed her before Señor Garcia brought a bitter taste to her mouth.

The man turned away from the river and climbed the bank. With one hand, Donna Grace clung to the saddle horn to hold herself in place. With the other, she cradled the baby.

They left the bushes which allowed her to put a few more inches between the two horses.

Señor Garcia noticed her vain efforts. "Still too good for a Garcia."

It stung that her grandfather had judged her for befriending Rosa, and Rosa's father judged her for the opposite reason. "Rosa was my best friend."

At the man's cruel laughter, she wished she had kept her thoughts to herself.

They angled away from the river. Donna Grace looked about. She must take note of any landmarks because if... no, when... she escaped she'd have to know how to get back to the wagon.

Señor Garcia saw how she looked around and he laughed again, sending shivers up and down her spine. "You think you might be coming back this way? Forget it. You will stay with me until your grandfather pays."

"Are you taking me to Santa Fe?"

He snorted. "In Santa Fe your grandfather can buy loyalty. That'd be the last place I'd take you."

So what would be the first place? She could not imagine. They were miles from any settlement. What did he have in mind? Her jaw ached from clenching her teeth and she managed to unpry the muscles. How long had they been traveling? She looked to the sky. Still several hours of daylight. Where would darkness find them?

*Luke,* she silently called. *Will you come looking for me?*

She smiled despite her situation. One thing she knew for sure about the man she had married. He took his responsibilities—whether real or pretend—seriously. He would track her until he found her.

But it would mean losing time. Buck would insist on going on. Oh, she did not want to be the cause of so much trouble.

No, far better to find her own way out, with God's help.

Never before had she felt the need to trust God so completely.

# 14

The last wagon crossed safely and Luke rushed back to bring over the Clark wagon.

"Donna Grace, we're ready to cross," he called. Not getting an answer, he went to the back of the Clark wagon to see if she rested inside. She did not.

He went to the Russell wagon. Judith was busy sorting the berries they'd picked. "Where's Donna Grace?"

Judith looked about. "I don't know. We just got back."

Mary Mae came around from the back of the wagon. "Maybe she stopped to feed the baby. She should be along any minute."

They all stared toward the bushes, waiting for her to appear. A hundred different reasons for her delay raced through his mind. The baby might be demanding attention. She might be struggling to climb the hill with the baby in her arms. Or she might have fallen and hurt herself. Each thought made her situation worse in his imagination.

His heart thudded. "I'll get her." He skidded down the slope to the cottonwood trees and the tangle of bushes. Birds stopped singing as he paused beneath the trees. In the quiet stillness, he strained to hear any sound to indicate where he'd find Donna Grace and Elena. A crow cawed. A chickadee scolded. Somewhere, a seed pod snapped. Nothing that sounded the least bit human. No sound of movement. No baby cry or mama's crooning.

"Donna Grace, where are you?" he shouted.

Birds flapped from the trees at his noisy intrusion, but no answering call came from Donna Grace. Had she fallen asleep? He pushed through the bushes, easily following the trail the women made earlier by the broken twigs and branches picked clean of berries. A bit of material clung to a thorny branch. He recognized it as fabric from the dark blue dress Donna Grace wore this morning. She had been here, but where was she now?

Again, he stopped, listened, and called her name. Still nothing. He pushed onward.

Perhaps she'd gone too far and got turned around in her directions.

He came to a small clearing and bent down to examine the ground. Tracks of a horse. The grass had been disturbed as if a man had stood there. He thought he saw smaller boot tracks perhaps made by a woman, but they were trampled by the horse tracks.

Luke straightened. His skin twitched. What was going on? Slowly he turned full circle studying every inch of the woods circling the clearing.

A narrow trail led from the opening, away from camp. Should he follow it, or search the nearby bushes to see if Donna Grace lay hurt somewhere?

He considered his options, could think of no reason she would be riding a horse down a trail through the woods. Thinking he must have missed her, he searched the bushes more thoroughly. Nothing. "Donna Grace," he called several times, each time his feeling of frustration mounting. It was impossible for a woman and baby to vanish.

There had been one sign and he returned to the clearing and examined the ground more closely but the only tracks he could make out with any certainty were those of a man and a horse. Desperate to understand what had happened to Donna Grace, he followed the narrow trail studying the ground for clues.

A boot track. Was the man leading the horse? Why? He examined the horse tracks more closely and could see no sign of the animal favoring one foot.

Not knowing what else to do, he continued to follow the trail. It widened and he made out a second set of horse tracks, this one a heavier, bigger horse. Two horses for one man? Or was there a second mounted man?

And where, in all this, was Donna Grace and the baby?

Desperate for answers or clues, he continued to follow the trail. The bushes thinned slightly as the river valley widened.

He jerked to a halt. The tracks led to the right, away from the river. He scrambled up the bank. The tracks continued at an angle. He cupped his hand over his eyes and stared into the prairie.

But he saw nothing even though he stared long enough that the distance began to shimmer.

He squatted down to think. He could chase after a mirage while Donna Grace lay somewhere behind him, needing help.

But if she had ridden away—why would she do that?

He went back to where the horses had turned away from the river, hoping and praying for something to guide him. There was nothing but tracks that told him only that two riders had passed this way. No indication of who those riders might be. He stayed hunkered down studying the ground as if he waited long enough, the earth itself would rise up and provide the answers he needed.

"Oh God," he groaned. "Show me where she is."

He waited. Had he expected an audible voice to answer him? Of course not. With a sigh that came from deep inside, he pushed upright, prepared to hurry away. Instead, he stared. A few threads of material clung to the thorny gooseberry bush in front of him. He plucked them free. Blue. He pulled out the bit of fabric he had earlier taken from the bushes near the camp and held them side by side. An exact match. She had been this way. Was perhaps mounted on one of those horses.

Why? Or where she meant to go were questions he would ask her as soon as he caught up to her.

He'd need a horse and he headed back to the camp, trotting through the bushes, paying no attention to the thorns that caught at his clothes or the low branches that slapped at his head. By the time he reached the camp, air wheezed in and out of his lungs.

"Is she here?" he squeaked.

Mary Mae looked ready to cry. "I thought you went to get her."

"I couldn't find her."

Buck rode up. "Why aren't these wagons moving?"

The women all spoke at once.

Luke held up a hand to silence them. "Donna Grace is missing."

Buck blinked and looked around the circle of people. "Missing? Did you look in the wagons?"

"We looked everywhere. I tracked her through the bushes. It looks like she might had ridden away on a horse."

"A horse?" Mary Mae could barely choke out the words and Judith grabbed Luke's arm.

"Are you sure?"

"I need a horse to follow her." He reached into the

back of the Russell wagon and took his gunbelt. He strapped it on and strode toward the river.

Buck turned to the reverend and Warren. "You two see about getting these wagons across." Then he rode after Luke. "Why would she ride away?"

"I don't know, but I intend to find out."

"Get on and I'll take you over."

Luke swung up behind the other man and they splashed across the river.

The freighters stood in a knot, yelling and waving their arms. Luke dropped to the ground and followed Buck to the group.

"What's going on here?" Buck demanded.

"My horse is missing. Someone has stolen her."

Luke recognized the speaker as one of the men who had joined the wagon train. The shorter, swarthier one.

"Where's your friend?" Luke demanded.

"I not know." The man's words were heavily accented.

"Did he take the missing horse?" Each word came out harsh and deep. He had not liked that second man from the beginning, and if he were somehow connected with Donna Grace's disappearance...

He pressed his hand to the sidearm.

The man nodded. "I tell him not good idea. He not listen."

"What was he planning to do?" Buck's sharp tone informed the man of his anger.

The man hung his head.

Buck leaned from his saddle and grabbed the man by his collar. "If you know something you better tell us."

"He say he want justice." The man's voice grew high and thin.

"What do you mean by that?

"Señor Garcia—"

"Garcia! I know that name." He tried to remember where he'd heard it.

"Sí. He know Miss Clark too."

Luke and Buck looked at each other to see if either of them understood. Seems they didn't.

Luke turned back to the quivering man. "Miss Clark or Mrs. Russell?"

"My apologies. I mean Señora Russell."

Luke's insides turned to steel and he leaned close to the man to give him a hard look, full of threat and promise. "It's time you started making sense."

"Sí. I try. He say he know her from Santa Fe. Say he hate her grandfather."

Luke sat upright. Things were beginning to add up. "Donna Grace's best friend was a girl named Rosa Garcia."

"Sí. That what he say."

"Her grandfather did not approve of the friendship."

"Sí. He say that too."

Luke leaned forward again. "My wife is missing. Two horses are missing. And Señor Garcia is missing.

If you know what's going on, you better tell us real quick."

The man jerked off his wide brimmed hat and nodded vigorously. "I tell you all I know. He say the grandfather be willing to pay money to see his granddaughter safe."

"Are you saying he kidnapped my wife and child for ransom?"

"He not say so, but, sí, I think that what he be doing."

"I'm going after them." He needed a horse. Gil led forward one that was saddled and handed Luke the reins. Without another word, Luke swung into the saddle and galloped back to the river. Buck yelled at him to wait, but he had no intention of wasting one more minute.

He crossed the river, unmindful of how much water his horse kicked up and skidded to the camp. "She's been kidnapped," he hollered as he jumped from the horse. "I'll need some supplies." The sun already dipped low in the sky and Señor Garcia and Donna Grace had several hours head start.

Buck and Gil rode up.

"What do you plan to do?" Buck demanded.

"Find them. No need for you to delay on our account." He threw food into a saddle bag as he talked. "We'll catch up."

"You might be riding into a trap," Buck warned.

"I'll be careful." He looked about for anything else he might need. "Baby things."

"I'll get them." Mary Mae jumped into the back of the wagon and seconds later, re-emerged with a little bundle.

"I'm going with you," Gil said. "Can I get supplies here?"

Judith filled his saddle bag with food.

Luke mounted up. "Daylight is wasting."

Mary Mae grabbed his knee. "Bring her back safely."

"I will." He kicked his horse into a gallop.

"We will," Gil said, following on his heels.

They kept up the pace until they reached the spot where Garcia had angled away from the river then had to slow to follow the trail. It should have been easy but Garcia obviously thought he might be followed and left a trail that crisscrossed itself and disappeared on hard ground. Luke and Gil had to watch carefully to know which way to go.

As the light faded, they both slipped from their horses in order to see the ground better.

After several minutes of straining to find the trail, Gil stood up. "It's too dark to see. We'll have to wait until morning."

"And leave her alone with that man?" He could barely push the words past the tightness in his throat.

"If you keep going you could head in the wrong direction and miss her completely. Don't think you want that."

Gil's calm voice did nothing to ease the tension that held Luke in a vise-like grip.

Luke squinted into the distance. "I don't see any evidence of a campfire."

"Garcia is too smart to light one."

"Gets cold at night." Luke knew it was useless to think of striding across the prairie hoping to run into them, but that's exactly what he wanted to do.

"Your wife is strong and independent. She will do well."

"I expect you mean to be encouraging, but I'm sorry to say, you failed."

Gil chuckled quietly. "I suggest we also forego a fire tonight. Let's have some of those victuals the women sent and get a good sleep so we're fresh in the morning. A tired man tends to make mistakes. We need the horses ready too." They unsaddled in the thin light of the moon and led the horses to a puddle of water. Then hobbled them so they could graze.

Gil chose a spot on a slight rise that allowed them to see some distance and they tossed their saddles to the ground. Luke stood and stared, turned and stared some more until he had gone full circle. No sign of a fire to indicate where Garcia might be. He forced his legs to fold and lowered himself to the ground. He pulled some food from his saddle bag but couldn't have said what he ate.

Gil spread his bedroll and stretched out.

Luke did the same but he couldn't close his eyes. Every few minutes, he sat up with a jolt and stared into the distance. *Where are you, Donna Grace?* His insides twisted cruelly to think of her alone with Garcia and what the man might do.

"Settle down, man," Gil murmured.

Luke tried but every muscle in his body twitched and his nerves strummed like over-tight guitar strings. The night would be long, lonely and filled with worry about Donna Grace and the baby.

The ground stuck mocking knuckles into his body in several places and he sat up. "This is too much like last time." He blurted out the words.

"Last time?" Gil sounded mildly interested.

"Three and a half years ago the girl I meant to marry was murdered. I didn't trust the men who did it, and yet I did nothing to protect Ellen."

Gil sat up and looked at Luke. The moon allowed Luke to see his movements, but not his features as he spoke. "If Garcia hopes to get money from Donna Grace's grandfather, he isn't going to harm her."

"Depends what sort of harm you are thinking of. But that's not what I mean. There was something about Garcia I didn't like. I noticed him watching the women and snooping around wagons. I should have run him off before he could do something evil."

"Can't go running off every shifty-eyed man you run into, especially along the Santa Fe Trail. I've seen more than my fair share of them." He lay back down. "First time one of them has kidnapped a woman. Now get some rest."

Luke lay back prepared for an uncomfortable night both physically and mentally. His brain played every sort of possibility for what Donna Grace might be enduring. And at the same time, left Luke struggling to save her. His frustration mounted until he could hardly breathe.

The words of the hymn he sang so often for Donna Grace and Elena filled his mind. *Frail children of dust, and feeble as frail, in thee do we trust, nor find thee to fail.*

He hadn't asked God for much of anything since Ellen's murder. It seemed kind of pointless when God hadn't stopped those wicked men. In the last few weeks he had thought of God more and more as he and Donna Grace discussed their pasts and their families. He had no doubt that his ma and pa would have prayed faithfully for him since he left. But they weren't here nor were they aware of Donna Grace's dire need. That left Luke to pray for her. Did he have the faith to trust God to help him find them and keep her safe until he did?

Bible verses his ma had him memorize came to him. Ma had insisted he always know where each verse was found in the Bible. A smile flickered over his face at the memory. Deuteronomy 31, verse 6: *And the LORD, he it is that doth go before thee; he will be with thee, he will not fail thee, neither forsake thee: fear not, neither be dismayed.* He repeated the words over and over in his head.

Now was a good time to choose to trust God. Luke's breathing eased as he acknowledged that God was far more powerful than himself, and right this very moment was with Donna Grace and the baby. *Lord God, keep them safe and guide us to them.*

~

DONNA GRACE JOSTLED UNCOMFORTABLY in the saddle. She wasn't used to riding, and her muscles had begun to protest. At that moment, Elena refused to be patted into silence any longer and let out a wail.

"Shut that brat up," Garcia growled.

Donna Grace choked back a protest at having her sweet daughter spoken of in such a fashion. To feed the baby with that cruel man riding so close filled her with dread. But she'd grown adept at nursing without exposing herself. She pulled the fabric of the sling up to her neck before she unbuttoned a few buttons and put the baby to her breast.

"No need to be modest on my account." Garcia leaned toward Donna Grace with a leer on his face.

She pulled the sling tighter about her and stared straight ahead.

Garcia gave a mocking laugh that grated across Donna Grace's already-tense nerves.

He crossed a rocky stretch of ground then turned back toward the south. She'd long since lost track of the many twists and turns he'd taken. She'd stopped asking where he was taking them. But she tried to pinpoint their location, trying always to keep centered to the river. But even that had grown futile as he criss-crossed streams. She had no way of knowing if it was the same one over and over or different ones and wondered if he was lost as well.

The baby finished nursing and slept. In an attempt to forget her present discomfort and fear, Donna Grace thought of her mama who had been such a strong woman to face grandfather's disapproval of her marriage to a white trader, and yet remain polite and kind to the old man. Donna Grace had once asked her why she didn't simply stop seeing grandfather. Mama had said, "Because I choose to obey God. He says we should honor our parents and so I do."

"Why? Grandfather isn't nice to you."

"He loves me and feels I have disappointed him. But that isn't what truly matters. I believe that God is faithful. He says, them that honor Him, He will honor. I long for His honor and approval."

Donna Grace's throat clogged with tears. Mama would be so disappointed in Donna Grace who had not had the same level of faith. She'd found it hard to trust when Grandfather was so critical.

Her spine straightened. God had not changed. She had. God's promises were faithful and true. Donna Grace simply had to choose to trust in them just as her mama had. *He shall call upon me, and I will answer him: I will be with him in trouble; I will deliver him, and honor him.* The words were a Bible verse that Mama often quoted.

Donna Grace took in a deep breath. The first that truly filled her lungs since Garcia had made his presence known. *God, I trust you to be with us and protect us and deliver us.* Luke would be looking for her by now. *Guide him to us.* She shuddered to think what Garcia would do if he saw Luke. It took a few moments before she got to the place where she chose to trust God to protect him. *Be his shield and defender.* The words of the hymn comforted her and she sang it over and over inside her head.

The sky went from blue to grey. Pink streaks colored it on one side. At least she was now certain what direction was west. She hoped Garcia planned to ride through the night otherwise she would be forced to make camp with him. A thought that made her insides brittle. No amount of trusting God would make the prospect pleasant or safe.

The ground was black, the sky gunmetal grey when Garcia stopped. "We're here." He swung from the saddle. "Get down."

She struggled to dismount with the baby in her arms and her legs sore, but if Garcia noticed, he paid her no mind. Not that she wanted his help. The thought of him touching her made her skin crawl.

Her legs balked at holding her weight, but she steadied herself as Garcia led away the horses.

A slight hill faced her, blocking out the quickly darkening sky.

Garcia grunted as he removed the saddles and led away the horses. They must be near a stream of some sort as she could hear the animals drinking.

Slowly, she turned about, hoping, praying for a place to hide. If she moved silently he wouldn't be able to see her. He had gone left, so her opportunity lay to the right. She slipped one foot forward and then another and another. She'd made perhaps ten feet when he grabbed her by the neck.

"There's no point in you trying to get away. You got no place to go. Nope, Miss Clark, you belong right here with me until your grandfather pays to get you back."

"My grandfather will exact justice." She said it with absolute authority. Grandfather was not a forgiving man.

"He'll never catch up to me."

She kept her opinion to herself because a bigger problem faced her. If he meant to get to Santa Fe, that required several days of hard riding. Did he think to make her ride with him or did he have in mind to leave her somewhere?

Neither prospect offered comfort.

He pushed her forward until they were right against the hill she'd faced a few minutes ago and reached around her to push on something. The darkness before her deepened, accompanied with a musty smell.

It was a house. Or something with a door.

He shoved her inside. "Make yourself comfortable." The door slammed shut.

She spun about, one arm protectively around the baby. With the other hand she pawed at the door but found no handle. A hole indicated where one might have been. She poked a finger into it, but found nothing but rough wood. After a few minutes, she gave up and felt her way cautiously to her left, running her hands along the rough walls. Sod. This was some sort of soddie. She reached a corner and searched for any chink in the walls. Nothing. She moved onward, sliding a foot ahead of her to check for furniture or holes. Again she came to a corner. How far had she gone? She tried to estimate and guessed no more than six feet, eight at the most. She continued, coming to a third corner, and then a fourth and back to the door. It was a hovel of very small dimensions. She did not venture across the middle, fearful of what might be there. The interior was black as pitch. Even the roof offered no hint of light. She sank to the floor, her back to the earthen walls. How was she to take care of Elena in such darkness?

She strained for any sound beyond the walls of this place. Even sound did not penetrate.

Elena fussed and Donna Grace managed to feed her. The poor mite was soaked and couldn't be left in such a state. She removed the wet diaper and tossed it aside. Fumbling in the dark, she found the edge of her petticoat and caught it between her teeth to tear at the fabric. Going by feel alone, she ripped out a section and tucked it between the baby's legs.

"Poor little girl."

At least she had the place to herself. Her heart rattled against her chest. Had Garcia left her here until he could contact Grandfather? She had a little canteen of water, but there was only a mouthful or two left, and she had no food. How long would they survive? Tears streamed from her eyes and she dashed them away.

In an attempt to soothe both herself and the baby, she softly sang the words to the hymn Luke had taught her. Then she prayed aloud. "God, I am finding it hard to trust You, but I can do nothing to help myself. I can't even see my hand in front of my face. But You say the darkness and light are the same to You." From the depths of her past came the Psalm in which that verse was found. Mama had taught Donna Grace and Mary Mae to learn it by heart.

"You will someday find the verses exactly what you need."

Mama would not have been able to know the circumstance Donna Grace would be in but the Psalm was indeed exactly what she needed, and she repeated it over and over.

*Thou hast beset me behind and before, and laid thine hand upon me.* Where could she go from His loving presence? He was with her and Elena, and would surely send rescue.

And if He didn't?

Then He would be with her to the end.

She tipped her head back against the earthen wall and slept, though her slumber was disturbed by the ache in her legs, and frightful thoughts that jerked her awake, out of breath and with her heart racing.

*Thy right hand shall hold me.* She murmured the

words over and over until her heartbeat and breathing returned to normal.

Elena demanded to be fed. If Donna Grace didn't eat and drink soon, her milk would vanish. *I will trust and not fear.*

The door rattled and a wedge of light stung her eyes.

"You wanting some food?"

Donna Grace squinted against the glare, but she didn't turn toward Garcia. She scanned the inside of her prison. Nothing but four earthen walls, an earthen ceiling held in place by thin poles, a solid earthen floor and not a stick of furniture.

"What is this place?"

"Shelter for some trapper. I 'spect he mostly slept outside, though. Or maybe he used this to store his furs in. You want food or not?"

He didn't need to ask again. She scrambled to her feet, catching herself against the wall as pins and needles shot up her legs. Somehow she made her way to the door. The sky was pink. She'd expected a fire, but saw no evidence of one. He knew there would be people out looking for her and hadn't wanted to alert them as to her whereabouts.

"Help yourself." He jerked his thumb toward the canteen and a handful of biscuits.

She took her time crossing the few yards to the place he indicated, partly because she wanted to be in the sunshine as long as possible and feared he would send her back to the darkness of that place, but also because her legs hurt from yesterday's ride.

Hungry to the point of weakness, she slowly ate six biscuits, washing them down with a large amount of water.

"You eat like that all the time and we'll soon run out of rations."

"I was hungry." She studied her surroundings. The soddie was more of a dugout, built into a low bank which explained why the interior walls on three sides were so smooth and the fourth lumpy and layered. A copse of trees crowded up to the edge of the hill, providing a barrier to hide them from any passersby. On the other side, scrub trees and bushes ran down a small coulee. She guessed a stream of some sort lay on the other side of the trees.

"Where are the horses?"

"Can't see them?"

She peered into the trees. There might have been two horses there, or she might have been imagining it. Either way, they were invisible, she guessed, unless a person knew where to look.

A perfect place to hide.

An impossible place for anyone to discover unless they stumbled upon it by accident.

"How long do you plan to stay here?"

He tipped back on his heels, his evil smile revealing stained teeth. "Until your friends give up looking for you."

She turned away. Her insides might be as weak as

butter left too long in the sun, but she would not reveal her fear to him. She would trust God. No matter what the outcome.

How long would anyone look for her before they gave up?

## 15

Luke was up as soon as the sky went from indigo to dark grey. A fire would have been nice. Coffee even better, but he saw no point in informing Garcia of their whereabouts. He could be nearby. Luke strained to pick up any sound of them. Perhaps if Elena cried. In the distance some coyotes sang a lonely morning song. The horses rustled. But no baby wailed.

Gil grabbed his saddle and went to his horse. Luke did the same. They ate cold bacon and biscuits as they sat astride their horses.

"What do you suggest we do?" Luke willingly would follow Gil's lead. The man was a good scout and knew his way back and forth along the Santa Fe Trail, and likely most of the area surrounding it.

"There's a creek to the west of here. Let's ride over and give our horses a good drink. It would be the easiest place for them to camp, so we can have a look for signs of them. If we find nothing, we'll come back to this spot and pick up where we left off."

"Fine by me," Luke said. They needed to fill their canteens and a splash of water on his face might help him think more clearly. "I feel so helpless. My wife and child are in the hands of a kidnapper and I can't even find them."

"You a believing man?" Gil asked.

"Somewhat. Sort of let it go for a while."

"Seems to be now might be a good time to seek some help from a God who sees everything."

"I've been trying. Last night I realized I could do nothing but ask for His help. I'm trying to trust Him, but it would be a whole lot easier if I could do something to help Him."

Gil chuckled. "Did God need your help when He made the world or hung the stars or, for that matter, made that little baby of yours?"

Only the Russell and Clark family knew the details of Luke and Donna Grace's marriage, and the circumstances of Elena's creation. But he understood Gil's point. "Nope. He seemed to manage quite well without me."

"And He will continue to do so." They rode as they talked and reached the creek. It was a narrow, gurgling little stream, though Luke knew it would run fast and deep following a heavy rain.

They dismounted and before they allowed the horses to go to water, they squatted down and examined the rocky shore.

"A rock has been disturbed here," Gil said. "Looks like a horseshoe print." He straightened. "He went into the water. He could have gone either direction and left the creek on either side."

"There's only one way to find out. You ride up one side, I'll do the other. If we find nothing in one direction, we'll return and go the other way."

"Right." They watered the horses, filled their canteens and mounted up, riding slowly, bent over in their saddles, as they looked for any sign of Garcia and Donna Grace leaving the water.

They rode for the better part of an hour. Then Luke pulled up. "How far would he ride in the water?"

"That, I cannot say. He's half loco. Makes it impossible to judge what he'd do. But let's try the other direction."

They reined about, but afraid he might have missed some clue, Luke rode back slowly, studying the ground before him.

They passed the spot where they had watered the horses and Luke dismounted. "I'm afraid I might miss something if I ride."

Gil dismounted too. An hour later the sun was warm upon their shoulders, but they still had not found anything to indicate what direction Garcia had taken.

Luke straightened and looked about. "He can't have vanished into thin air." Frustration grated through his insides. "We must be missing something. I can only think of one thing to do." He fell to one knee, pressed his hat to his chest and bowed his head. "God, You see everything. You know where Donna Grace and the baby are. We're lost and hopeless. Please show us where to go and keep them safe. Amen." He kept his head bowed a moment. When he looked up, Gil stood across the stream, his hat to his chest and his head bowed.

The moment seemed blessed and holy. Gil looked up. "It's Sunday today."

"God's day."

They both stood silent, waiting. For what, Luke could not say but neither moved.

"Let's go on," Gil said. "I can't help but think he would want to get as far from the wagon train and his pursuers as possible. Besides, if memory serves me correctly, the stream veers to the southeast ahead." He planted his hat on his head and took up his horse's reins. "Something is tickling at the back of my brain. Something I should remember, but can't quite seem to."

"That's helpful. Should certainly guide us in the right direction."

Gil chuckled. "Have faith. It will come."

They continued on, eyes to the rocky, unrevealing ground.

They reached the curve in the creek that Gil remembered. "Wait. I know what it is."

"Mind sharing the information with me?"

Gil led his horse across the stream. "There's a tale about a crazy old trapper who had a cabin of sorts around here. I thought it was a made-up story, so one day I went looking and found this cave cut into the side of a dirt bank. There was a door on it. And buried deep in the thicket of trees, was a little corral where he'd kept his mule."

"You think that's where Garcia had gone?"

"I can't think of a better place to hide. It took me a long time to find it. I probably rode past it two or three times before I spotted it. You have to come at it from the right angle to see it."

"Let's go."

Gil caught his arm. "It's also very hard to approach without being seen. I don't know how Garcia is going to react if we come riding in. Like you, I never did trust that man. Shouldn't have let him join us, but Buck said he paid the fare and hadn't done anything to justify saying no to his riding with us."

"I don't intend to stand by and not do anything." Luke slipped his foot into the stirrup.

"We need a plan." Gil tapped his chin. "We need to surprise him. Catch him off guard."

"How?"

"Let's think this through. Come on. I'll show you the lay of the land." He went to a spot of bare ground and picked up a stick. "The stream runs like this." He drew in the dirt.

Luke squatted beside him as Gil sketched out every detail of the place.

"We aren't even sure he's there." If he wasn't, they were wasting precious time.

"Luke, we prayed. That's when I remembered something I'd plum forgotten. I, for one, am thinking that was an answer to our prayers."

Luke wasn't quite so willing to throw all his marbles into one game, but he didn't have a better idea. "Fine. The sooner we find out, the sooner we will have an answer one way or the other." He carefully studied the diagram Gil had produced. He could see why surprise might be a challenge. But—

"What if we do this?" He grabbed a stick and showed Gil the details of his plan.

"That just might work." Gil clapped Luke on the shoulder. "He won't suspect a thing until it's too late."

They mounted up and rode along the river making as much noise as possible, yelling and laughing as if they'd imbibed freely on their ride.

They neared the spot where the trapper had built his secure place a short distance from the stream. Luke slipped from the horse and made his way round the hill, falling to his stomach to wriggle closer.

Gil stopped by the edge of the water, still laughing and carrying on.

Luke smiled as he listened to the racket. He reached the top of the hill and looked down. His heart stopped. Donna Grace sat on the ground, baby Elena at her breast. Her skirts were torn and dirty. Her hair falling in strands from her usual tidy bun or braid. He saw one side of her face, enough to see dirt smudges.

He tore his gaze from the pair to locate Garcia. The man faced the stream and the noise Gil made.

Donna Grace finished feeding the baby and eased to her feet. With her attention on Garcia's back, she began to inch toward the creek.

He couldn't say if she recognized Gil's voice, or simply figured her chances were better with anyone else but Garcia.

Garcia glanced back and saw her intent. "Sit down," he ordered, sending an angry chill through Luke.

Donna Grace hesitated.

*Please don't challenge him. He's not a reasonable man.*

She sat down. Smart woman that she was, she made sure to sit directly behind him so he had to turn to watch her.

Satisfied at her cooperation, he turned back to the racket Gil made. He pulled a gun from his waistband. "That rowdy bunch needs to move on."

Indeed Gil made it sound like at least half a dozen men caroused.

Gil was ready for the man, so Luke forced himself to remain motionless until Garcia ducked into the trees, intent on surprising what he thought were a bunch of noisy cowboys.

Luke slipped silently down the hill and made it to Donna Grace's side without alerting her to his presence. He covered her mouth with his hand.

She jerked and fought him.

"Donna Grace, it's me. Don't make a sound." He removed his hand slowly.

Tears puddled in her eyes, but there wasn't time to comfort and reassure her.

"Come on." He helped her to her feet and cupped his hand to the bundle cradled to her chest. "Is the little one okay?"

Donna Grace nodded.

He led her up the hill, half dragging her. He didn't slow until he reached his horse and safety in a thicket.

"You're safe." He pulled her into his arms, the baby sheltered between them.

She sobbed into his shirt front. "How did you find me?"

Before he could answer, a shot rang out.

And then another.

*Gil. He was supposed to be ready.*

Luke's instinct was to race toward the stream to help his friend, but Garcia would be after Donna Grace as soon as he discovered her gone. Luke couldn't leave her, nor would he risk taking her toward that man.

Donna Grace clutched at his arm, her eyes wide. "Who is down there?" she whispered.

"Gil."

"Who else?"

He spared a quick smile. "He was trying to sound like a bunch of wild cowboys."

The fleeting movement of her mouth suggested she had tried for a smile and failed. "He succeeded." She pressed her hand to her mouth. "Did Garcia shoot him?"

"I don't know."

"Shouldn't we check?" She took two steps that direction before he pulled her up short.

"We might walk right back into Garcia's arms." His jaw creaked so he could hardly speak. "I have no intention of doing that. I need to plan our next move carefully."

Donna Grace sank to the ground with a suddenness that said her legs had given out.

He squatted beside her, brushing the hair from her face. "Are you hurt? Did that man—?" He could not finish.

## 16

Donna Grace trembled inside and out. Her stomach rolled and she swallowed hard to force it to settle. He had come. Luke had rescued her, but it wasn't over. Luke seemed to think that shots meant Gil had been—she closed her eyes. Garcia would not let her go so easily.

"Donna Grace?"

The worry in Luke's voice made her realize she must answer his questions. "I'm not hurt. Just scared. He didn't harm me."

He plunked to the ground as if his legs were as weak as hers. "Did he say anything about his plans?"

"Just that he meant to make Grandfather to pay for my freedom." She groaned. "I don't even know if Grandfather would."

"I would never give up looking for you." Each word came out as a firm promise.

"I know." She touched his cheek. "I know."

He looked deep into her eyes, his gaze probing secret places. At any other time she might have hidden her heart, guarded her feelings, but today her fear and relief mingled to undo any caution she normally exerted.

He caught her hand and turned to plant a kiss in her palm before he turned away. "I have to see to Gil."

She tapped his shoulder. "*We* have to see to him."

"I can't ride into danger with you."

"I am most certainly not staying behind with any chance Garcia might be after me." Bile rose in her throat and she coughed.

He got to his feet, pulled her up. They faced each other. She could not miss the worry in his eyes. Likely he would see the same in hers plus a healthy dose of stubbornness. She would not be left behind with the possibility that Garcia could again capture her.

"Very well. We'll have to be quiet. Is Elena going to wake up and cry?"

"I just fed her. She will be okay for a couple of hours." *Please, baby, sleep through this.*

Luke caught her hand. "First, we will pray." He grabbed his hat, held it to his chest and bowed his head. "Father in heaven, You have promised to guide and protect us. I'm confessing we need that in a mighty big way. Please help us." He slapped his hat back on his head and took Donna Grace's hand. "I know a way that will provide some cover until we are almost there."

They hurried down the side of the hill and reached a stand of trees. "Stay behind me and mind where you put your feet."

She reluctantly let go of his hand, cradled the baby close and eased between the trees, careful to avoid twigs on the path. Wildlife likely used the trail, but whatever sort of animal they were, they were skinny, which meant Donna Grace had to wriggle between branches in many places.

Luke stopped moving. She placed her hand on his back needing the strength the touch provided. He held up his hand with one finger extended, signaling he wanted her to either wait or be quiet.

What was he looking at? She tried to see around him. The stream ran by. The rocky shore was visible. She leaned a little more to the right. Did she see a boot? One that seemed to have a leg attached?

She pulled upright, a hand to her mouth to keep back a squeak. Was it Gil? Where was Garcia? She feared the sound of her breath would alert the man to their position, so she kept her hand at her lips, allowing only the tiniest bit of air to enter and leave her lungs.

Luke eased forward, his gun in his hand.

She would gladly have stayed right where they were, motionless, silent, for as long as it took for Garcia to forget all about her. Fear had rendered her motionless.

Luke squatted by a still form, looked over his shoulder. "It's safe. Garcia is dead."

The air left her lungs in such a rush that she clung to the nearest tree for support. Dead. He could no longer threaten her. As soon as her legs would cooperate, she inched forward.

Luke had moved, allowing her to see the still form of Garcia. She hovered at the tree line, watching and waiting, fearing it was a trick intended to draw them into a trap.

A dark stain covered the left side of his shirt and soaked into the ground beside him. Still, she kept her eyes on his chest to see if it rose even a little.

It did not move. Slowly, still half fearful, she pulled her gaze from the still form.

Luke bent over another figure. Gil. She rushed forward. "Is he—?"

"I'm alive." His voice cracked. "He nicked my shoulder." Gil sat up. "It's just a flesh wound. I wanted to let him think it was more until I was sure he wasn't going to shoot me again. How are you, ma'am?"

"Glad to be free. Thank you for your part." She untied the baby and handed her to Luke.

Elena wakened and found Luke's face. The baby was too young to smile, but Donna Grace fancied she relaxed when she saw Luke.

"I'll clean your wound." Donna Grace tore the shirt to reveal a gouge. She dampened a bit of material from her rapidly disappearing petticoat and sponged the blood from Gil's arm. "It's not serious unless it gets infection. I have some ointment at the wagon that will help it heal."

Finished with the task, she sat on the ground, pulled her knees up, pressed her face to her up-drawn knees and burst into tears. Sobs clawed up her throat despite her best efforts to still them.

"I'll get your horse." Gil hurried away. Either her crying bothered him, or he thought she and Luke needed a few minutes alone.

Luke shifted Elena to one arm, sat beside Donna Grace and pulled her to his chest.

She wrapped her fingers in the fabric of his shirt, and buried her face against him as fear and regret and a dozen other emotions washed from her.

He rubbed slow circles on her back and hummed.

Her tears were spent and she relaxed against him. "Rosa was my best friend," she said after a bit. "Grandfather made them leave. He destroyed Garcia's business."

"He made himself an enemy and it became a threat to you." Luke pressed his face to her hair. "I'm grateful you are safe and sound." His arm tightened about her. "I—"

Gil returned with Luke's horse. "Best we take care of this body and get back to the wagons."

"Let me take Donna Grace and the baby someplace where they don't have to watch." Luke pulled Donna Grace to her feet and led her around the corner of the stream. "Stay here until we are done. You can hear us. We can hear you if you call out."

She sank to a grassy spot and took Elena, burying her face against the sweet baby's neck.

"Phew." The sweet baby wasn't so sweet. "She needs clean dry clothes."

"We all need hot coffee and a wash." Luke soon had a fire going and a pot of water heating. He left to join Gil... or so she thought. Minutes later, he returned with a small bundle. "Mary Mae sent things for the baby."

Gratitude threatened to bring a fresh flood of tears.

Luke brushed his knuckles along Donna Grace's cheek. "You're safe now."

She nodded. So long as Luke was there.

After he left, she spread a baby blanket on the ground, and dampened a cloth with the warm water, and gave the baby a thorough washing before she put on the clean dry clothes. "There you go, little one. That has to feel better."

Donna Grace washed her own face and grimaced when she saw how dirty it made the cloth. She rinsed it in the stream and wiped it over her hair. What she truly longed for was to sink into a tub of warm, scented water and wash away every memory of the past twenty hours. Instead, she settled for finger combing her hair and braiding it.

She fed the baby then lay back beside her, staring into the sky. Now that the initial shock of her rescue had passed, she felt a strange peace, mingled with an unfamiliar restlessness as if an itch needed scratching, but she couldn't locate the spot.

The clatter of boots and horses made her sit up. Luke and Gil brought in the four horses.

Gil brought his saddle bag and set coffee to boil.

Luke sat beside her. "We took the liberty of going through Garcia's things. We found this." He handed Donna Grace an envelope. "You might want to read the letter."

She pulled out the single sheet of paper and unfolded it.

*Dear Papa,*

*I am writing to inform you that I am married. I had hoped you would come to the wedding. I hope it's because you didn't get my previous letter in time and not because you prefer to be angry. Please, let your anger go. I fear it is going to destroy you. You are welcome to visit any time. Papa, I long to see you.*

*Your loving daughter,*

*Rosa.*

There followed an address in Missouri.

"Rosa!" Donna Grace looked at the address. "She was not far from me. And now her papa is dead." She didn't realize she cried until Luke wrapped an arm about her and dabbed at her tears.

Donna Grace returned the sheet of paper to the envelope. "May I keep this? I'd like to write a letter to Rosa. I'll have to tell her about her father, but I can also tell her about Elena Rose."

"It's yours. There are a few things that Rosa might like to have." He indicated a bundle slightly larger than a water bucket. Not much to show for a man's life.

"I'll send them as well."

The coffee boiled and Gil poured them each a cup

and passed around biscuits, cold bacon and cookies. "Judith wanted us to eat well."

They ate in silence. Donna Grace couldn't say for the others, but she needed time to process all that had happened and try and come to grips with her wayward emotions.

Though she supposed it was natural, under the circumstances, she wanted to cling to Luke and make him vow to never leave her.

They had promised each other a pretend marriage, but right now she wanted more.

⁓

THEY WERE SOON RIDING toward the wagon train, hoping to catch up to it before nightfall.

Luke's heart fairly burst with things he wanted to say to Donna Grace, but he understood how fragile she was at the moment. She needed to be back in the safety of their company, surrounded by friends and family for a few days before he could say anything to her.

Best for him to wait until things settled down.

They stopped twice on the trip back. Donna Grace needed the break, and the baby needed to be fed.

Although Gil would never admit it, Luke suspected he didn't mind a break from having his arm jarred for a short time.

Late in the afternoon, they spied the wagons, drawn into a circle, fires burning.

"Buck must have called an early stop," Gil said.

"Because it's Sunday?" Donna Grace's voice suggested she hoped this was the case.

"Maybe. Or maybe to give us a chance to catch up."

"He wouldn't stop because of me, would he?" Luke didn't know if Gil would hear the note of regret in her voice, but he did.

"I expect he would. Of course, he might also be thinking of me and Luke." The droll tone of Gil's voice made Donna Grace blink and then she laughed.

"I suppose he might not want to lose his scout."

"It's nice to be thought of as important."

Donna Grace didn't answer.

Luke wished he could say something that would make her see she was as important as Gil. Especially to him.

He reached over and caught her hand. "Gil's a good man and I surely do appreciate all the things he does, but I hope no one asks me to choose between him and you."

Gil laughed uproariously and rode his horse a little faster, leaving Luke and Donna Grace alone.

Luke saw the heightened color in her cheeks and smiled, pleased that his words had touched her.

She glanced at him from beneath her thick lashes and her cheeks grew rosier.

He would have spoken what was on his mind right then and there, but remembered the promise to himself to wait for her to recover from her ordeal.

The company had been watching for them and the women trotted toward them.

As soon as they were close enough, Donna Grace reined in and dropped to the ground. She was immediately engulfed by three pairs of arms. Mary Mae cried.

Warren, the reverend and Buck strode toward Gil and Luke and demanded details. Buck held the two horses Garcia had taken.

"I'll return these to Garcia's friend and tell him what happened."

The rest of them made their way to the campfire where they were supplied with food.

Luke kept a close eye on Donna Grace thinking she'd had about enough excitement and fear and other emotions to exhaust her. She ate little, as if food had lost its appeal, and instead of eating, stared into the distance.

Mary Mae glanced at Luke and they silently shared their concern. Then Mary Mae touched Donna Grace's hand, gaining her attention.

"You look tired. Would you like help getting ready for bed?"

Donna Grace rumbled her lips. "What I'd like more than anything else is a bath."

"We can surely do that. Unless—?" Mary Mae gave Luke a questioning look and he shook his head. If she meant did he want to be in charge, the answer was certainly no. Donna Grace would not be comfortable with that. Nor would he. What none of them realized was the temporary, half-truth of their marriage.

What would Donna Grace say if he said he regretted that agreement?

Judith pulled a tub off the side of the wagon.

Luke sprang to his feet, grabbed the buckets with ungraceful haste. He trotted to the stream, brought water and set it to heat.

Meanwhile the ladies fashioned a barrier with blankets and rope.

The tub was set in the privacy provided by the hastily erected walls and the women kept guard while Donna Grace went into the enclosure.

Warren grabbed Luke's arm. "I think you have time to come with me and check on our wagons."

Luke might have had the rest of his life, but the last thing he wanted to do was leave Donna Grace alone... well, except for three females guarding her and the reverend sitting nearby. Even Elena was taken care of, resting contentedly in Mrs. Shepton's arms.

His insides taut with so many things, he allowed Warren to lead him away.

He saw Garcia's friend. "I need to speak to the man." He shifted direction. "What's your name?"

"Manuel."

"Manuel, I'm sorry about your friend." He offered his hand and they shook.

"Sí. I tried to tell him."

They continued on their way, speaking to the drivers and checking their wagons. Everything seemed in order, but Luke knew he could have overlooked any number of problems. His thoughts were back with Donna Grace.

Would he still want to say the same things to her, once the emotions of the day had settled into the far corner of his heart?

Or would fear, at some point, remind him of the risks of caring for someone?

≈

DONNA GRACE LET the hot water soak away the dirt of the last two days. If only her mind could so easily be soothed. A thousand emotions marched through her head. None of them stopping long enough for her to examine and decide where it belonged. Remnants of fear, amazement that God had answered her prayer. Sorrow over Rosa's loss of her father. Hope that she could reconnect with Rosa. And bigger than all of that, the wonder of her changing feelings toward Luke. How was she to explain it? Even to herself?

Too weary to sort things out, she gave herself over to enjoying her bath.

"Do you want me to wash your hair?" Mary Mae called from beyond the fabric walls.

"That would be nice." She leaned forward and let her sister scrub the dirt from her hair.

A bit later, Donna Grace sat by the fire, in a loose gown, wrapped in a warm blanket as Mary Mae brushed her hair to dry it. Luke returned and sat nearby. She grew uncomfortably warm, and it wasn't because of the hot flames. No, she felt his eyes upon her. Although she knew he couldn't read her mind, she felt raw and exposed.

He watched her a moment then set up the tent.

"I'll sleep with Mary Mae tonight." She did not want to be alone in the back of the wagon.

They retired shortly after that, Donna Grace's hair in a long braid. She nursed the baby, then fell into a sleep filled with shadowy images that tried to capture her. She must have cried out and wakened herself.

From outside the tent where Luke lay under the wagon, his voice came to her. "You're safe now, Donna Grace. God is watching over you even in your sleep. There's a Bible verse that says, 'He that keepeth thee will not slumber.'" Softly, he repeated the Twenty-Third Psalm.

She closed her eyes and slept.

The next morning, her limbs reminded her how many hours she'd spent riding a horse. She gratefully accepted Luke's help up to the wagon seat.

He chuckled. "A little sore this morning, I expect."

She groaned. "That's a large under estimation."

He handed Elena to her, then took his place beside her. He squeezed her hand and kissed the top of Elena's head. "This is where you belong."

"Thank you for rescuing us." She'd earlier thanked Gil and asked about his arm. He assured her it was nothing.

Luke wrapped a hand about hers, his strength

steadying. "You know I would find you, no matter how far Garcia took you."

She turned her hand into his and their fingers twined together. "I hoped you would. I asked God to guide you, and I believe He did."

"I do, too." He told her how he and Gil had come to the end of their resources and prayed for guidance and had received it. "That night I chose to trust God. My faith wavered, but He proved faithful. I am determined to follow Him more closely from now on."

"It seems you and I have learned the same lesson." She told him of being shut into the dark dugout of a building. "I couldn't see anything. But things Mama had taught me came back. I remembered the verse that said the darkness and light were the same to Him. I decided I would trust Him no matter what." She let that sit for a moment, wondering if he realized she had been afraid she would not survive her ordeal.

He squeezed her hand. "I'm so grateful He chose to allow us to rescue you."

"Me too. Poor little Elena. I had wanted so much to bring her into a world of safety and security, and instead she was kidnapped. I'm so grateful she wasn't hurt in all of that and isn't old enough to remember it."

Luke pulled a piece of paper from his breast pocket and handed it to her. The page was worn on each fold and frayed on the edges. "Read it."

"Okay." She unfolded it carefully, mindful of its fragile condition and read aloud, "There is land here a plenty. Great for cattle. You couldn't find a better place to start ranching, if you're still interested." She refolded the letter and handed it back to Luke.

His gaze met hers, full of depth and openness. She felt herself being drawn into his thoughts.

"I've decided I want to follow my dream and get a ranch."

She tore from his gaze and looked straight ahead. "I'm glad for you." She would go to Santa Fe and start a new life. He would go to California and start his own new life. She expected no different. Their agreement came to an end. "Do you mind if I walk a bit? I think it will do my legs good."

"Donna Grace— Forget it." He pulled the wagon to a halt and helped her down.

Mary Mae joined her.

As Mary Mae talked about how worried she was when Donna Grace was missing, Donna Grace's thoughts circled like a crow over a morsel of food. She was happy for Luke. Of course she was.

Then why did his news sit like a sour drink in her stomach?

## 17

L uke banged his fist to his knee. He wasn't handling things well at all. He had so much he wanted to say to Donna Grace. Instead, he'd simply announced he meant to go ranching and she had scurried away.

She walked until they stopped for the noon meal.

"You look tired," he commented, as he returned from taking care of the animals, hoping she would choose to ride beside him. This time he would make certain to say what was on his heart.

"I guess I am. Perhaps I'll ride in the back of the wagon for a bit and rest."

He helped her into the back and she lay down, with the baby at her side. He watched her for a minute as she closed her eyes and let out a deep sigh. Perhaps it was for the best.

He spent the afternoon turning his thoughts over

and over. They had an agreement. Would she be willing to adjust it a bit? He'd never find out if he didn't ask.

He waited until after they stopped for the night and they'd had their meal. He waited until Mary Mae took Elena. "Donna Grace, would you walk with me?"

She looked about to refuse.

"Please."

"Very well. Mary Mae, do you mind keeping Elena?"

Mary Mae laughed. "You don't have to ask, do you?"

Donna Grace chuckled, but her smile left her eyes as she joined Luke. It didn't bode well for what he hoped to accomplish.

They walked around the outside of the circled wagons. Two of the freighters did a little jig to the music from the harmonica and Luke and Donna Grace paused a moment to watch and listen before they moved on.

Wanting a few quiet moments alone with her, Luke led them toward the stream. "Let's sit." He indicated a nearby fallen tree and they perched on it. Throughout the long afternoon, he'd rehearsed various ways of introducing this subject, but every one of them had fled.

"How are you feeling?" he asked. The question had not entered into his practiced speeches.

"Fine. How about you?"

"I'm fine thanks." He did not want to talk about

their good health. "I thought I didn't want to ranch any more after Ellen's death." Again, not what he wanted to say. Why couldn't he bring the words that really mattered to his mouth?

"I suppose that makes sense."

"It did for a while. But lately, it doesn't."

The water flashed by, catching the light of the distant fires in a rippling dance. Nearby an owl hooted, as if mocking Luke's foolish inability to say what he meant. "I think the reason it made sense is because I wanted more than land and cows and horses. I wanted a home. Guess I still do."

"It's what I want too. A home where Elena will always know safety and security."

"What about love? Won't she need that too?" He wanted to be the one to give it to her.

Donna Grace jerked about to face him. "She will know love no matter where we live. But I want her to have more than that."

"Donna Grace, you told me that you once dreamed of being part of a ranch. Come with me to California and you can have that."

Despite the darkness creeping in about them, he could see the surprise in her face. "It will be a safe, secure place for Elena."

"I don't understand what you are saying."

"We are legally married. We don't have to end our marriage. We can stay together and run a ranch."

She turned away.

He pressed his wishes. "It would be a good home for Elena. I'd make sure of that."

She rocked her head back and forth. "You aren't obligated to be her father. Really, I'm so grateful you have given her a name, so she will be spared the shame of being illegitimate. I ask nothing more of you." She pushed to her feet. "You don't need to look after us. I can do it."

He caught her arm before she escaped. "Donna Grace, what I'm trying to say is I want us to stay together. We can be a family. I won't ask you to be any different than we are right now."

She pulled away. "A pretend family?"

"I think we'd be a real family. Father, mother and baby."

"Then a pretend marriage?"

It was not what he wanted, but if that was all she'd agree to, he would accept it. "Just like we are now."

They walked toward the wagons.

He didn't want his offer to be ignored. "Won't you please think about it?"

"I will."

They rejoined the others and prepared for the night. She slept with Mary Mae in the tent, and he slept nearby, though sleep did not come easily.

The next morning, Donna Grace was understandably distant, which he feared indicated her answer.

He slumped on the wagon seat as she walked with the other ladies.

When would she tell him her decision? More

importantly, how would he endure several more weeks of appearing to be man and wife if she refused his offer? How could he hide the pain of knowing he would have to say goodbye?

He could do nothing, but pray that God would hear his heart and make her open hers to him.

An hour later, he pulled himself up. Had he not learned a lesson about trusting God when Donna Grace and Elena were missing? God had not changed. He was all powerful. He could change the heart of a woman. Luke had to remember to pray and trust.

Feeling lighter by several pounds, he glanced about for Donna Grace. Mary Mae and Polly skipped along together to the right. Beyond them, Judith and Mrs. Shepton walked more sedately. He looked ahead, behind, to the right and left. He did not see Donna Grace and his heart clawed up his throat.

"Judith," he called. "Where's Donna Grace?" Surely she had simply sought shelter in one of the wagons.

Mary Mae hurried closer. "We left her a little bit ago. She said she needed to be alone to think and would catch up soon." Worry creased her face. "We shouldn't have left her. What if something happens to her again?"

Buck rode up, drawn by the fact Luke had stopped the wagon and held up progress. "Something wrong?"

Luke shook his head. "I don't know, but Donna Grace isn't here. I intend to go find her. Can you tell Manuel to come and bring a horse?"

Buck rode back and Manuel came on his stocky

little horse. "Señor Buck say you wish to see me."

"Manuel, will you drive my wagon for a bit?"

"You trust me?"

"I don't hold you responsible for Garcia's actions."

"You are a fair man." He swung down and climbed to the seat. "You will not be disappointed in me."

"One more thing. Can I borrow your horse?"

"Mi caballo is your caballo," he said with an expansive wave of his arm.

"Gracias." Luke mounted and turned to the back trail.

He rode a couple of miles before he spotted her sitting on the ground by some bushes, the baby asleep on a blanket beside her. He trotted over.

She jumped up at his approach. "I didn't mean to worry you."

"The ladies said you had stopped. I thought… " He shrugged.

She sat down again and he sat beside her.

"Have you been thinking of what I said?"

~

"I HAVE." Donna Grace had thought of little else since he'd spoken. A real family for Elena held a lot of appeal. Not that Donna Grace couldn't give her love and security. But she couldn't give her a father without agreeing to this arrangement.

Was she being selfish to want more? To want more than a pretend marriage?

She'd argued back and forth with herself for much of last night and the better part of an hour as she sat alone with her thoughts.

One lesson she'd learned while in Garcia's clutches was that God heard her prayers. And she'd opened her heart to Him.

*God, is this what I should do. Is this the life I deserve?*

She would gladly spend the rest of her life with Luke. But as a pretend wife? But was she giving up what she really wanted by saying no?

Mama's words came to her. "God is with us in good times and bad. Nothing can ever take His love from us. If you ever wonder if it's enough, remember that God loved you enough to send His Son. There is no greater love known to man."

It was the answer she needed.

She faced Luke, taking in every detail—his brown eyes that held a mixture of hope and fear, the bronze of his skin from so many days lived outdoors, his dark brown hair that had grown noticeably since they left Independence. Her gaze lowered to his broad shoulders that had held her, his chest where she had shed tears, his hands that had comforted and encouraged her. She loved him. She wanted more than a pretend marriage.

It would be hard to give her answer, but she must.

"Luke, you are the most generous man. I don't know any other who would take in a woman carrying another man's baby and give her and the child his name. You will surely be rewarded for such a gift."

"I don't want a reward."

"Let me finish. Please." If he presented any defense, she would not be able to say what she must.

He nodded. "Go ahead. I'm listening." The caution in his words tightened her throat. How she hated to hurt this man.

"Over and over I've said words about how I'm a nuisance and a bother. I've repeated the things my grandfather said to me. I've found proof in the actions of Melvin and my father. Even, perhaps, in Garcia's actions."

Again, he interrupted. "You aren't to blame—"

She held up her hand. "I'm not done."

He sank back, though his expression made it clear he didn't like not being able to speak his mind.

"Things changed when I was locked in that dugout. I realized that God loved me. He didn't judge me for my humanness or the things people did to me. All He wanted was my trust and obedience." She paused as her throat constricted. "His love is enough for me." It would have to carry her through the lonely days of missing Luke.

She sat up straight and pushed her shoulders back. "Luke, it's true I'd love to be part of building a new ranch. But I want to be more than a pretend wife. I want to be more than good enough. I want it all. So I am saying no to your very generous offer." She couldn't go on and ducked her head so he wouldn't see the tears threatening to overflow.

He jerked to his feet and strode away to stare at the wagon train as it continued its journey.

She watched him from under the curtain of her tear-studded lashes.

He came about to look at her and she stared at the ground in front of her.

His boots appeared in her field of vision. "Donna Grace, let me get something straight. You don't want a pretend marriage?"

"That's right," she managed from her constricted throat.

"You want more?"

"Everything," she whispered. "I want everything."

"Why?"

She jerked her head up to look at him. Couldn't stand tipping her head back so far and got to her feet. The movement put her so close, she had only to lift her hand to touch him, but she squeezed both hands into tight fists to keep from doing so. "Because I think I deserve it."

"So if I said we would become man and wife in the truest sense, that would be enough?"

She rocked her head back and forth. "Not nearly enough."

His gaze caught hers and she could not look away as he searched her secret, hidden places looking for the meaning behind her words.

"What would be enough?" His voice had grown husky. He caught her chin between his thumb and finger, his touch warm and gentle and sending a burst of such longing through her, she thought she might have to grab his arms to keep from swaying.

He trailed a finger over her lips until it came to rest at a corner of her mouth. "Would me telling you that you are everything to me be enough?"

Her heartbeat picked up pace like a horse racing toward home, but she shook her head and kept her gaze on his chin. "Still not enough."

"What if I said without you I will continue to wander aimlessly back and forth across the plains?"

"You would?" Her gaze met his. Nothing short of a thunderclap would make her able to break free of his look. And even that might fail.

"I would have nothing but an empty, aching heart that needs you."

"Me?" Was it enough? Dare she hold out for more? Before she could come to a conclusion, his arms went around her.

"What I am trying to say, is that I love you, Donna Grace, and without you my life is empty."

He held her in the circle of his arms, waiting.

She touched her fingertip to his chin, then trailed it over his lips, much as he had done with her, and wondered if her touch made it as difficult for him to think rationally, as his had made thinking impossible for her.

"Is that enough?" he whispered, his voice deep with uncertainty.

Her arms went around his waist. "It is more than enough. Luke Russell, I love you. I am so pleased that you are my husband." Her voice thickened on the final word. Husband. *Her* husband.

He pulled her close. She lifted her face to receive his kiss. Neither of them seemed in any hurry to end it.

After a bit, he pressed her head to his shoulder. "Mrs. Russell. The title means so much to me now. No more pretending."

"No ending it when we get to Santa Fe."

He sat down and pulled her to his side. "Do you really want to go on to Santa Fe?"

"What do you mean?" Then she realized what he meant. "No, there's no need to go there. It was my plan because I was looking for happiness in the only place I'd ever known it. Now it is right here."

"We'll make plans to cross the mountains in the spring when it's safe to travel."

"To California and our own ranch."

For some time they stayed there, dreaming and planning.

Finally Luke pulled her to her feet. "Time to catch up to the wagon train." He caught up the reins of Manuel's horse and she picked up little Elena who gurgled happily.

"What are we going to say to the others?" she asked.

"About what?"

"Our marriage."

He chuckled. "What's to say? We're already married, so that's taken care of, and if they notice any difference in how we look at each other, I'm more than proud for them to see how much I love you."

"Me too."

He pulled her to his side. "Let's tell them of our plans to go to California."

Those words gave her a moment's pause. "What about Mary Mae?" She and her sister had planned to stay together.

He stopped to face her. "Your sister is welcome to accompany us. I would never say no to any of your family, or any of your needs."

"Thank you." Neither of them moved as they looked deep into each other's eyes.

He had given her the gift of assuring her she wasn't a bother. She wanted to do the same for him. He'd been told he wasn't good enough. She must make him see that he was. "Luke, you are a good good man. I am honored that you love me. Please take my love and use it to erase the unkind words that Ellen's father said to you."

He cupped his hand to the back of her head and pulled her close to rest his forehead on hers. "I know I must have done something good to have a wife like you." He paused. "That's not what I mean. I think God has shown how much He loves us by giving us each other and this little girl." He placed his hand on Elena's head as if blessing her then caught Donna Grace's lips in a kiss full of so many things—love, joy and a shared future.

## SNEAK PEEK OF WAGON TRAIN WEDDING

"What do you mean she's missing?" Gil Trapper, scout for the Santa Fe Trail wagon train looked at the worried faces around him. How could Judith Russell be missing? She'd been traveling with the train since they left Independence near on to a month ago. From the beginning she'd been a good traveler, doing her share, and helping others. His observations said she was not the sort to do something foolish. He tried to think what else he knew of her. Sister to seasoned traders on the trail, Luke and Warren. Younger than either of them. Seems he'd heard Luke say she was twenty. Not that her age had any bearing on this situation.

"She was out walking by the wagons. We didn't

think much at first when she wasn't here when we stopped. We thought maybe she'd fallen behind and would catch up. But she should have been here by now and she isn't. And we don't see her coming." As she talked, Luke's wife, Donna Grace, clutched her infant to her breast as if afraid the baby girl would up and disappear.

The others joined in, voicing their concerns.

Before Gil could reassure them that she had simply fallen behind, Luke and Warren rode up on horseback.

"We're going to find our sister," Warren said.

Gil nodded. "Let me inform Buck and I'll join you in searching." As the wagon master, Buck needed to know what was going on. "The rest of you stay here and take care of things."

Having noticed the worried knot of people, Buck rode up, demanded and received an explanation. He didn't offer any empty consolations. They were all aware of how many disasters could have befallen the woman.

"We'll ride along the back trail," Warren said.

Gil accompanied the brothers. After two miles with no sight of her, they reined up to consider what to do.

"You two stick to the trail," Gil said. "If she's simply fallen behind, she'll know enough to stay on it." Or if she'd been injured in a fall or—there were hundreds of reason she might not be able to catch up. "I'll ride toward the river and search there. Not that I expect to find anything."

They parted ways and Gil turned off the trail. Every nerve in his body twitched with tension. If she'd simply fallen behind, they should have come upon her by now. Unless she'd gotten turned around and lost her way. Or had been set upon by one or more of those preying upon the wagon trains.

He guided his mount toward the bushes and trees along the river, pausing often to listen for any sound. Crows squawked at his intrusion. Smaller birds rustled in the autumn dried leaves. Coyotes began their mournful cry. His skin prickled with the knowledge that wolves had been spotted a day ago.

He rode onward, looking for any sign, listening for any sound. It would soon be dark. *Lord, help us find her.*

He jerked forward and strained toward the faint sound of a... baby crying? Surely he was mistaken. It must be some wild animal, though he couldn't think what one made that sound.

Edging his horse toward the sound, he picked a path that allowed him to move quietly. He stuck his handgun into his belt and pulled his rifle from the scabbard.

A flash of movement caught his eye. He reined in and slowly dismounted, easing forward with the skill that four years on the trail had taught him until he had a clearer view.

"Judith," he murmured.

She turned. "Thank goodness. I am thoroughly lost and so is this little one." She tipped her head toward a girl child in her arms.

"Where did you find that?"

At his voice, the child looked at him with wide blue eyes. Her tousled hair was the color of liquid sunshine. She stuck two fingers in her mouth and sucked noisily.

He squatted down five feet from the pair, knowing he would be less scary to the girl if he wasn't towering over her.

"I heard her crying, though at the time I was simply curious as to what it was. I know she must have parents somewhere but I've looked and looked. That's how I became so disorientated and lost sight of the wagons." She glanced past him. "How far are we from them?"

"Five miles more or less." He pushed to his feet. "I best find her parents." But as he headed back to his horse, Judith hurried after him.

"I'm going with you."

He considered his options. If he took them with him it would slow him down but he would know they were safe and wouldn't have to back track. "Come along." Upon his return to the horse, he reached for the child.

Judith hesitated before she released her hold.

Gil took a good look at the little one who returned his study, her lips quivering. "She's just a baby."

"Old enough to walk. I think she must have wandered away. Her parents will be beside themselves with worry."

Gil helped Judith to the saddle with one hand then

lifted the little girl to her. Leading the horse, he slowly made his way through the bushes, looking for any sign of the parents.

"Where would she have come from?" Judith's voice revealed a good deal of worry and a hefty dose of fatigue. She must have wandered about for several hours, anxious to reunite the baby with the doubtlessly worried parents.

"There's a wagon train a few days ahead of us. They left a month before us." What sort of delays had caused them to lose so much time? "One of the wagons must had dropped out." He could think of no other explanation for a baby out in the wilds.

They continued for the better part of an hour, his attention on the ground. He often stopped and studied his surroundings. Something caught his attention and he bent low to the ground. "Wagon tracks." They were several days old but no mistaking them and they went straight toward a thicket of trees. "You better stay here while I have a look."

She looked ready to argue until she looked at the child in front of her. "I'll wait here." She'd correctly read his concern about what he might discover.

He led the horse to the protection of some trees against a rocky bank.

"If you hear gunshots, ride up the hill. You'll come to the dusty trail in about a mile. Turn right and keep going."

"And leave you? That doesn't seem correct."

"You can send back Buck or your brothers. But you must protect the child."

Judith's brown eyes held his, direct, challenging. He'd noted this about her already. A woman who wouldn't back away from a challenge and who made it clear she didn't expect to sit back and let others take care of her.

He waited for her cooperation.

Only after she nodded did he cradle his rifle in his arms and on silent feet, make his careful way toward the trees and whatever he might find there.

The bushes and branches were battered by people passing through. A few more feet and he saw a wagon tipped over, contents scattered wildly. He remained in the trees, watching for signs of danger. A groan drew his attention and he slipped through the trees to the other side of the clearing.

His heart gave a violent beat at the sight of a man and woman on the ground, their clothes blood soaked. A glance informed him the woman was dead. He passed her and fell to his knees by the man. The color had left his face. Gil knew he watched the life leaving him.

"What happened?" Gil asked.

"Left wagon train. Wife sick. Robbers came upon us. Baby?" He tried to sit up.

Gil eased him back. "We found your daughter. She's safe."

"Thank God." The man shuddered. "She's Anna Harris. Anna. Eighteen months old." He grabbed the front of Gil's shirt. "Take her. Raise her as your own. We have no family."

"She'll be well taken care of. I can assure you of that."

Mr. Harris's grip tightened, his strength surprising considering his condition. "Promise me *you* will raise her."

How could he? He wasn't even married. Had no intention of entering that state. Oh sure. Once he'd thought it was what he wanted. Before Lillian had made him think otherwise. Finding her in the arms of another man when she talked of love and marriage to Gil had left him disillusioned about the faithfulness of a woman. He certainly had no notion of repeating his mistake.

Mr. Harris clutched at Gil's shirt, a look of determination on his face. "I won't let you go until you give me your word to take Anna."

Gil unhooked the man's fingers and eased him to the ground. "You have to understand I am not married. I can't raise her." Gil's insides shriveled as the man sobbed. "But I promise I will find a good family for her."

"Thank you." Mr. Harris closed his eyes and struggled for breath. "We've been robbed but if there is anything you can use…"

"I'll take care of everything. You sure there's no one I should notify?"

"Tell Anna how much we loved her." A inhalation shuddered in and out.

Gil watched Mr. Harris's chest. But he'd taken his last breath. "Good bye. I'll make sure Anna knows she is loved."

He pushed to his feet and looked about. Torn clothing tossed about. Flour scattered recklessly. A trunk with the top torn asunder. Two bodies to take care of.

An hour later, with darkness closing in about him, he returned to Judith. Little Anna slept in her arms. He carried with him a bundle of clothing for the girl and a few items that had not been destroyed.

"What did you find?" Judith asked.

Gil could not say if it was fear or fatigue or even hunger that made her voice quiver. The darkness had deepened so he couldn't make out her features well enough to read her expression.

"You might as well get down while I tell you." He reached up for the sleeping Anna, holding her in one arm while he assisted Judith to the ground.

He led her to shelter by the trees. They sank to the grass and he told her what he had discovered. "I promised him I would see that the baby had a home."

"I'll keep her."

Now available.

## BONUS SNEAK PEEK OF RENEWED LOVE

Faith White needs to get safely to California. She's desperate for a fresh start after being jilted by the man she'd planned to marry. There's nothing left for her but memories and disappointments and a lost love.

For years Gideon Holder slaved away in a coal mine to save his father from going to jail. He earned his father's freedom but lost everything else that mattered--including the woman he loved. Now Gideon plans to make up for lost time by searching for gold.

Gideon and Faith are shocked and dismayed to discover they're both on the same wagon train to California. Gideon doesn't want Faith to know about his father's secret shame. Faith only wants to avoid the man who broke her heart. They vow to stay far away from each other, but that turns out to be impossible when they are assigned to travel as part of the same unit.

Can the adventures and challenges of the journey make them realize that their love is still alive?

Coming early 2021. Preorder now.

Crane's Bride

Hannah's Dream

Chastity's Angel

Cowboy Bodyguard

Made in the USA
Monee, IL
03 May 2023

32910383R00184